ISLAND REVEAL

ALSO BY R.T. WOLFE

ISLAND REVEAL

ISLAND ESCAPE SERIES, BOOK 3

R. T. WOLFE

 ePublishingWorks!
love what you read.

Book and cover design by eBook Prep
www.ebookprep.com

May 2022
ISBN: 978-1-64457-122-4

ePublishing Works!
644 Shrewsbury Commons Ave
Ste 249
Shrewsbury PA 17361
United States of America
www.epublishingworks.com
Phone: 866-846-5123

Thank you to my dear friend and AMI PPH, Suzi Fox, for all you do. You are appreciated.

ONE

The toasts, the ogling newlyweds, the dancing guests. This was more happy than Raine Clearwater knew what to do with. It was early enough that the scent of cologne and flowers filled the pub more so than the sweat or liquor. Leaning on one of the tall wooden tables, she sipped an MGD with one hand as her bridesmaid sandals dangled from the other.

One of the newer busboys paused at her table. Empty bottles covered the surface of the giant wooden spool. He glanced at her, dipped his head, then rotated on the balls of his feet and moved to the next table.

"They're not all mine," she yelled at his back over the music and loud conversation.

Her baby sister glowed. Raine supposed that was what newlyweds did. The floor shook under her bare feet as Zoe danced to a place called Kokomo in the crowd of friends and family. What she and Dane were doing looked more like mating than dancing.

Her middle sister was much the same, minus the gyrating. Willow circled her fiancé like a flower child dancing around a Clearwater family fire. Like most restaurants and pubs on an island in Florida, two sides of the dance floor in Luciana's were open,

1

allowing the crisp scent of beach and salt water to add to the ambiance. Willow hadn't been this happy since before her first husband died at war. It was about time.

Her parents even sashayed to getting somewhere faster if they took it slow.

"Great party," a deep voice yelled from over Raine's shoulder.

Tilting her chin, she noted the voice was directed at her and that it was male. One of the few men in the place she didn't recognize. His light brown hair was cut short around the back with a fluff of some left over his forehead.

The man inched his gaze down to her bare toes and up again. "You part of the wedding party?"

Raine's hair twisted high on her head with curled pieces dangling between clusters of some kind of small, white flower. The straps of her dress were solid lace and her sandals a matching powder blue. "You must be a detective."

Tapping his temple, he winked. "Just observant."

She tilted her head back as she took a swig. "You, uh, one of the guests?"

"Me? No. Just came to check out the new place." He looked around as if he'd forgotten to before.

"Renovated," Raine corrected but assumed he didn't hear her over the noise. She had to admit that Willow did a knock up job with all of it. Luciana's. Named after the historic Luciana Bezan. The sitting area dripped with thick ropes. Porthole windows lined the booths. The new dance floor looked as if it could have come from the original deck of the legendary Luciana's lover's sunken ship.

Over the bar hung the poem her dead brother had penned. To think his obsession with the legendary Luciana Bezan dowry was legit. A warm breeze of sisterly pride filled her soul.

Her Legacy
The wet uncharted
The cornerstone that is Home
The under under

Willow had it framed. The treasure her sisters had found in 'the under under' opened the wave of tourist activity to the island and the pub. Their brother died for the booty he'd hidden in the wet uncharted, and everyone seemed to be looking for the cornerstone that is Home.

"What'd you say?" the guy's mouth was much too close to her ear.

Pulling away, she answered. "The place isn't new. It was reno—" Thankfully, her phone buzzed in the lacey crossbody purse Zoe gave her for the occasion. She pulled it out and waved it in front of the man. "Sorry, duty calls." The guy wouldn't need to know what kind of duty. Raine was the Primary Permit Holder and head of Ibis Island Turtle Watch. The distraction was a life saver.

She held the phone to her ear, even though there was no way to hear the message with the noise.

The guy shrugged but didn't budge.

Taking a deep breath, she gave up and read the voicemail transcription.

"Is this Ibis Island Turtle Watch? It looks like a turtle is bobbing in the water near the old wooden abandoned pier."

A tidal wave of tension clenched her shoulders. Her instinct was to bolt, but this was her sister's wedding reception. She had eighty-seven Turtle Watch volunteers. She could call one of them. Darting her eyes around the room, she noted that most, if not all, were in the pub.

"Damn." She said it in two syllables, then slipped on the torturous shoes. She swung by the bar on her way out. "Paula," she yelled to Willow's head bartender over the voices and music.

Paula looked over the tapper as she filled a mug. "Sugar, you are not leavin' your sister's reception."

How did she know? "Only for a minute. Let them know if they ask?" Raine didn't give her a chance to answer. She jogged out the door, cursing the damned heels all the way to her truck.

———

Matt Osborne watched as she rushed out the door. Raine Clearwater. She didn't fit the mold of a Clearwater.

Resting his elbow on the new section of bar top, he sipped his whiskey on ice.

Raine wasn't peaceful, organic, or gentle. She was introverted and bitchy and might just be carrying.

Checking his phone one more time, as Ibis Island interim chief of police, he hoped he missed a page. Not that he wasn't honored to have been asked to stand up in Dane and Zoe's wedding. He was, yet still honestly pissed off that the family concocted the plan to dive the under under behind his back.

A woman might not be lying in a coma if the family had given him a heads up about their plan.

Which he wouldn't have allowed them to do.

Which might have allowed the perp to get his hands on the treasure instead of the Clearwaters.

Tipping back his last finger of whiskey, he reiterated his internal pledge. No dwelling while at Zoe's wedding reception. There would be plenty of time for that in the morning.

It was no wonder he hadn't had a single page in the last several hours. What could happen when nearly every local on the island was here at the pub?

Glen Oberweiss stepped to the spot next to him. As the new chief, Matt needed to pay close attention and remember faces and names. Oberweiss was easy. Not many male islanders had a long gray braid that lay down the middle of his back. So much for waiting until the morning.

Matt lifted his empty toward the bartender. First name Paula. Wild red hair, wound tall on her head. Tiny woman who was front heavy and slightly terrifying.

"Another round, Chief?" she asked.

Paula pulled a pencil from her hair. She scribbled something on a notepad with one hand as she flicked a draft pull to top off a pitcher with the other. He nodded to her before setting his empty glass on the bar mat. "Sure thing, Paula."

"Evening, Chief," Oberweiss offered first. That was helpful.

"Evening, Glen. What do you think?" Matt gestured around the room with the back of his hand.

"Of the pub or the party?"

Matt shrugged. "Either, I suppose." Oberweiss was one of the original six that dove with Seth Clearwater the day Seth was murdered. He may have been taken off the short list of Matt's suspects, but that didn't mean he was off the hook.

"Well, as owner of the town museum, I feel as if I have the right to say that the pub is an excellent replica. Willow knows her 16th century legends."

"We handed over several million in treasure to the state that says it wasn't legend."

Oberweiss nodded and gestured to the front wall. "See those?"

Matt had no idea which "those" Oberweiss referred to. The wall was covered in worn tools secured with nails and screws.

"The nautical chart and quadrant alone could be mistaken for authentic historical artifacts."

If he said so. Matt lifted the drink Paula set in front of him. "Cash me out and add a glass of ice water?"

She saluted as she scribbled down the next order from a couple Matt recognized as employees from the dive shop the bride and groom ran.

Matt asked Oberweiss, "How do you feel about the state taking all of it?" As a historian, Oberweiss would be the most disgruntled with the state confiscation.

"I feel like they did exactly what the law says."

"That's not a feeling." Matt looked into his glass as the ice melted into the brown liquid. "Angry, frustrated, and indifferent are feelings. The confiscation was procedure. I know I'm not all too happy about it."

"It takes a lot to get me the former as I tend to hover around the latter. Just ask my first wife."

Matt laughed. He barely put the glass to his lips when his phone buzzed. Finally.

"Is there a Mrs. Chief?" Oberweiss asked as Matt grabbed his cell from his belt.

Matt shook his head and read the text.

Possible body floating at Bay Street beach access.

"Gotta go, Glen," Matt said. "We'll continue another time."

Oberweiss waved as Matt bolted through the crowd to his black and white SUV parked out front.

Shifting into neutral, Raine pulled her truck to the Bay Street beach access and yanked the emergency brake. She jumped out and jogged through the narrow path toward the beach. Cloud cover was thick, but the color of the sand gave enough light to find the way until her eyes had a chance to adjust.

The only sound was the water rushing the sand. She spotted the silhouettes of a small handful of people who stood pointing out over the Gulf. Ditching the damned sandals at the access bench, she ran the rest of the way to where they stood.

"Did someone text Ibis Island Turtle Watch?" she called out, sucking air. She definitely had to start working out with Willow again.

The group turned to look at her. The woman in front opened her mouth, looked Raine over, then shut it again.

Raine gave her a break since the sight of a woman in a brides-maid's dress might not be what she had expected. "I'm Raine Clear-water of Turtle Watch," she said as she scanned the Gulf for signs of a distressed sea turtle. "Did someone call and leave a message?"

"I did," the woman admitted. "It was right out there." She turned on a flashlight and pointed it north of the dilapidated wooden posts jutting out from the water.

"No flashlights after dusk, please." Raine squinted in the direction the woman pointed. "Not good for the turtles." She couldn't see anything but a few white caps as the water tumbled in. High tide was coming.

The distinct sound of a police walkie talkie from behind made her left eye twitch. Purposely, she didn't turn, but instead continued to scan the water. Turtles naturally came up for air. It was an easy mistake.

"Did someone call in a possible body in the water?" the chief yelled from across the sand.

A body? Like a human body? She rolled her eyes. Without acknowledging him, she stepped away from the group and edged into the Gulf. Warm waves crashed over her feet and the crisp scent of salt water cleared her mind. It didn't suck.

"We're not sure," a younger male with the open-and-close-her-mouth woman answered.

She heard pages flipping and stepped farther into the water. Her dress was short enough to risk her ankles and calves. Tea length, Zoe had said.

"Raine?" the chief called.

Damn. Shit. Damn. She glanced over her shoulder. He still had on his shoes. The nice ones from the wedding. She took a step deeper into the water. "Present."

"What've we got?"

We? She shrugged. "I don't see anything." The current was strong and headed north. Raine scanned the water. She started at the wooden posts and traveled her gaze north.

A head popped up from the horizon. It was out there. Definitely a turtle.

The woman behind her yelled, "There!"

Holding out her arms to prevent any heroics, Raine waited and watched. "Hold on now. Turtles need air. She might just be coming up to get some." Or coming out to dig a nest. It was late in the season, but not unheard of.

The chief kept away from the water and asked, "How sure are you it's a turtle?"

"Pretty sure." Her answer was probably more sarcastic than it needed to be, but it was what it was.

There. It came up again. Her brows knit closer together. That wasn't right. "Shit," she said, looked down at her dress, sighed, then dove in.

TWO

Matt stood with his mouth open. It took a lot to shock him, even with someone as brassy as Raine Clearwater. She jumped into the Gulf wearing her bridesmaid's dress. On her sister's wedding day.

What was he supposed to do? Be chivalrous and go after her? He knew zero about aiding marine life.

He had no idea if the group was tourists or residents, and even with his walkie, they wouldn't know he was a cop. Still, they gawked at him as if they waited for him to do something.

He noted there were four of them. "I am Chief of Police Matt Osborne. We have this under control." Raine had earned his trust in this area.

Her arms broke through the waves. Damn, she was fast.

Toeing off his shoes, he called it in. "Looks like a turtle, over."

"Ten four." Matt recognized the voice. Officer Walt Pence, the officer who had taken the 9-1-1. Walt was old as the hills and one of the few on the force Matt trusted so far.

He stuffed his socks in his shoes and rolled up his dress pants like an idiot. There wasn't any thrashing out there. When Raine began a single-armed backstroke, he hoped she was right that it was a turtle and not a human.

"Look." One of the men next to him pointed. "She's pulling it in. It's huge."

"Ohs," and "ahs," resounded among the small group as Raine swam a much slower descent inland.

When she stood, he caught his breath. Her back was to him. The light blue dress clung to her. It was only for a second, but he was frozen. Curves in all the right places. A package attached to an ice princess.

The male in the group waded in to help.

"Thanks," Raine panted. "Take that side?"

Matt splashed in as well.

"Don't need you, Chief," said the ice princess.

He held up his arms in surrender and stepped out of the way as they pulled the lifeless creature onto shore.

Raine collapsed to the sand. She sat on her heels and clenched her thighs. Her lungs heaved and her chin dug into her chest. The white flowers were gone and dark hair stuck to her face.

He wasn't distracted by the wet dress anymore or the smartass dismissal. An orange fishing line wrapped around a front flipper and the head. Strangled? Drowned? A gust of anger blew through him, and he wasn't the one who was part of sea turtle conservation.

Stepping in front of her, he helped the dude pull the remains the rest of the way out of the water. It was all senseless. "Thank you, sir," he said to the male without introductions.

The guy nodded and stepped out of the way. The solemn silence by all was deafening, broken by a steady crash of waves as they rushed in, sinking Raine's knees into the sand.

She set the back of her forearm over her nose, sniffed loudly, then pulled her shoulders back. One foot, then the other, she stood and cracked her neck before she marched with purpose to a cinch sac he hadn't noticed before. Some detective.

Pulling it open, she dug her arm in and came out holding a large tape measure. She seemed to try and attach it into her belt loop before noting she didn't have one and, instead, stuck it under an arm.

As she gathered the rest of whatever it was she was gathering, he forced himself to look over the creature. The flippers were bigger than he imagined they could be, especially the ones in front. Its head cocked unnaturally from the taut fishing line. He didn't care if it was stupid, it bothered him. He took out the Swiss Army knife he kept in his pocket and started at the net.

"Why are you still here?" Raine growled as she pecked away at a tablet she'd retrieved from the sack.

She didn't get a patent on being angry with this. "My job," he said as he sliced through the line.

"This," she said as she measured the length of the shell, "is my job. Finding out who killed my brother is yours."

Personal jab. No eye contact. She went back to pecking on the tablet, then measured from head to tail.

He didn't respond and instead asked, "What now?"

"I measure, record, and report. Walter will come by and scoop him up."

He would find out who Walter was later. For now, he asked the more pertinent question. "Him?"

"Big tail."

It was enormous. Gross, really. "Scoop him up and put him where?" He was the size of a Volkswagen.

Raine shrugged. "New construction hole, probably. It's nature," she said matter-of-factly, no sign of the distressed Raine he'd seen moments before.

There was nothing natural about the fishing line. He kept cutting as he asked, "Don't you have to do an autopsy or something?"

"Laparoscopy, and no," she said as she did the same measuring for the width. "That will just piss me off."

"Excuse me?"

She measured the width as she said, "Eighty-five percent of sea turtles have plastic in their digestive tracts. Plastic bags look like jellyfish. I hate plastic. This one died from that damned fishing line, which is the number one cause of death for adult sea turtles."

Matt screamed like a girl and fell backward into the sand. "It blinked! It blinked!"

"What?" Raine barked. "You're drunk. No it … shit, he's alive."

And just like that, she sprinted away.

"I, uh," he said to the small group as he scrambled to the tangled flipper. Working furiously to free the beast, he stuttered, "We, um, have this under control." He trusted Raine on this, even though she'd left him with an injured Volkswagen.

As he freed the flipper, it, or he, moved it over the sand, landing on Matt's leg. The backs of Matt's eyes burned. How long had it suffered like this? The head. He had to get the rest of the line from around the head.

The sound of a vehicle came from a block south. He recognized Raine's truck as it neared. She passed the group as he freed the last piece of damned fishing line and set it aside.

Raine backed her truck up to them and jumped out. She picked up the discarded line, then looked at him and squinted. "Thank you."

She meant it. Go figure.

The turtle seemed to know he was free and started moving forward.

"What now?" Matt yelled.

"You," she said to the male beachgoer, "get that side. Grab the shell here." She touched a spot by the front flipper, "And, here," she instructed, tapping a spot near the back.

"Chief, you'll get the other side."

Matt nodded. "Into the bed? It's moving. Shouldn't we just—"

"He's injured, dumbass. Hurry up."

He and the man reached down. "On three," Matt said. "One, two, three." They lifted as far as the top of Matt's thigh. The beast thrashed his flippers in the air, making it near impossible to raise it up any farther. "Ready for the rest of the way?" he yelled. The man nodded and they heaved. Matt's head nearly exploded. Not at all gently, they made it to the end of the bed.

Raine appeared through the tiny back window of her truck and, as they pushed, began pulling beach towels that were beneath him. With another towel in hand, she jogged to the water, dipped it in, then covered the animal with it.

Matt's walkie buzzed. "Reported water main break at Bay and 6th, over." Officer Pence again.

That was three blocks away. "This is Chief Osborne," he said to Pence. Much better than a possible body bobbing in the Gulf. "On my way, over."

He turned to see her head bowed in the front seat. Texting or dwelling? Ice princesses were hard to read.

When Raine's tires cleared the sand, she pulled over to text the marine animal hospital as well as her baby sister. Looking down at the lacy wet dress, she remembered this was Zoe's day. How had she forgotten?

It was all getting to her, that was it. Finding her missing brother's skull in the Gulf cavern, discovering he had been murdered. She wiped her face with both hands and shook her head clear. Or, at least less fuzzy.

Five locals who resided on this island longer than she'd been alive dove with her brother the day he died. All suspects. All of them except Chief Roberts, who was murdered while awaiting trial for trying to kill his wife and Zoe along with her.

The porch awning at The Beachfront had been vandalized. Willow almost lost her life, and Chief Osborne was spotted out sandbagging? He should have people for that. He should have people to answer calls for possible drownings while he worked on catching the one who murdered her brother.

The fact that Seth had found Luciana Bezan's treasure, that it was even real, was just icing on a wedding cake from hell. Looking up, she spoke to the roof of her truck. "Sorry, Seth. I am so proud of you. You did it. You really did it. You found that ancient treasure, but now a third of what you found is missing, another third is in the hands of the state of Florida, and everyone from everywhere is here on the island looking for the cornerstone that is Home for the rest."

The sound of a giant flipper scraping the bed of the truck brought her back to the now.

this is ibis island pph raine clearwater
have a severely injured male loggerhead
around 300 pounds
be there in 40.

She chickened out and texted Willow instead of Zoe.

Severely injured full-grown loggerhead.
On my way to Mote.

Slamming the gear into first, she spun the tires of her truck and took off south.

Her eyes opened wide as she approached the chief.

The sand bagging, coming to the hospital after the roof awning collapse on Willow. Now this? She could count on one hand how many times Matt's predecessor was seen out in public during his entire career as Ibis chief.

It could be a distraction from having to work on her brother's murder case. More likely it was his way to impress the board and get them to vote him in permanently.

Water gushed over the pavement. Matt parked just out of the way and popped his trunk. As he set out orange pylon cones, Raine passed. She craned her head, eyes wide open, staring at him all the way as she drove by. Damned confusing ice princess.

With the noise of the rushing water, he nearly missed the next call from headquarters. Luckily, the rookie had activated the flashing call light on his phone and Matt was able to spot it in his peripheral.

"Chief Osborne."

"Disturbance called in at Yancy's Bar, 1063 Palm Tree Lane. I'll meet you there, over." Definitely Officer Pence, but meet there? Cryptic small island stuff.

"Water main break confirmed and area secured. Call it in to twenty-four-hour emergency. I'll be at Palm Tree in five, over."

He jumped in his black and white SUV deciding 'disturbance' warranted lights but no siren. He hadn't made it out to Yancy's Bar yet. Two birds.

At this hour, the custom drizzle of the occasional closing time staggering tourist caused Matt to drive slower than cop speed.

Most of Yancy's patrons were locals. Or, so he was told. An enclosed establishment, which he learned was rare for island life. No dancing.

As he rounded the last corner, he noted that there must be a lot of locals who preferred an enclosed establishment. The lot was packed. No visual disturbance noted, so he turned off his lights.

The walls were brown stucco. The front door could use a paint job. Neon beer signs glowed in front of closed window blinds. The parking lot held aged cars, motorcycles, and a handful of bicycles.

Pence was already there, leaning his butt against his cruiser. Since he must have raced over, Matt's internal red flag waved. Glancing up at the single light in the lot, he made a mental note that it was amber and turtle friendly. He was learning.

Matt's window was down. Pence started in before Matt had a chance to come to a complete stop. "Now, Chief, I wonder if you want to pick your battles, here."

Walt's neck was wrinkled with his years of living in the sun and sometimes folded over his shirt collar when he was riled. Like that moment.

Matt shifted into park and lifted his brows. "Please go on."

"I know rules are important to you."

"Me being chief of police and all." Matt waited for the rest he expected was coming.

"You've got your seat belt project."

"Yes," Matt said slowly.

"On an island," Pence continued. "That's the size of a postage stamp."

Matt smiled. He couldn't help it. "What's the disturbance, Officer?"

"Owen Branch is drunk and breaking shit."

Matt didn't know any Owen Branch, but regardless hurried from his SUV and headed for the door. "And, we're out here talking about seat belts?"

THREE

"This here's a smoking and dancing bar," Walt called from behind him.

Matt's feet stopped. He turned, making the soaked bottom part of his pants stick to his legs. "As in inside smoking? They don't have a dance permit. Let's take a look." As he headed for the front door, he asked, "Is this Yancy's like Luciana's?"

"Owen doesn't usually hurt anyone," Pence veered. "And no, Yancy isn't any legend. He's just the guy who owns the place."

"Usually doesn't hurt anyone," Matt mumbled as he opened the door. Inside smoking was an understatement. The place was a cloud. Weathered floor and weathered tables were pushed together to make room for the line dancing.

Two men who could have been twins, if not for the twenty plus years between them, stood behind the bar. It went the entire length of the place with a broken mirror above the bar back.

One by one, feet stopped stomping, the patrons quieted, and heads turned to stare at the new visitors until all Matt could hear was the juke box and one Mr. Owen Branch. Branch had a face that said he was a hundred-fifty years old, but the rest of him said strong and healthy, albeit drunk.

"We got a code in here," Branch slurred as he staggered unafraid toward the two police officers. Even if one was in a wedding suit, the other wore his full uniform.

Even minus the gear, Branch had no trouble recognizing Matt as chief. "Who called the cop?" he yelled and jabbed his finger near Matt's chest.

Cop singular? Matt guessed Pence didn't count. Or maybe it was Matt who didn't count. Matt was still analyzing the scene and picking his battles.

A cigarette dangled between the fingers in one of Branch's hands and a spilling glass of what looked like a few shots of vodka in the other.

It seemed Branch's was a question of interest as most everyone looked around for the guilty party.

The younger version of the twins behind the bar stepped forward. "I heard this chief does stuff, and you keep breaking our stuff, Mr. Branch."

Matt held out both hands, palms down. "I'm not here to break up island customs that—"

Mister Branch threw back the rest of his shot, wiped his mouth with the back of his hand, and chucked the empty directly at the younger Yancy. "I don't gotta listen to you," he bellowed as the boy ducked, and Branch's empty glass shattered the mirror above the bar back.

"What the hell?" In one swift motion, Matt took Branch's free hand and tucked it around and up his back. He wasn't sure if Branch was referring to the younger Yancy or to him. Regardless, he said, "Yeah, you do," and made sure to say it loud enough that everyone could hear.

Branch must have had this move executed on him once or twice before because he backed up so that Matt was sandwiched against the front door. Since Matt had this counter move executed on him once or twice before, he slithered his other hand over drunk Branch's shoulder and locked both behind his head.

"You okay?" Matt yelled to the younger Yancy as Branch thrashed and yelled obscenities.

Yancy Jr. nodded fast as he looked to the floor.

Pick his battles be damned. "You wanna press charges?"

The older Yancy pulled his chin back, looked at his son, then to the broken mirror and back to Matt who suspected Branch was the cause of the first break as well.

The older Yancy answered with a non-answer. "I've never been asked that before."

Matt spoke loud as if he didn't have a thrashing man in a head lock. "You take some time to think about it while Mr. Branch, here, takes some time as well in the county jail."

"You can't lock me up," Branch shouted and shook hard enough so that Matt lifted the arm behind Branch's back until he stilled in pain.

"I can and I will. You might not like outsiders. I don't like attempted assault."

It was Willow's idea, and since it was before visiting hours, Raine and her sisters used the ER entrance.

The three of them approached the hospital admitting counter. "I want the next section coordinator position that comes available," said Raine's youngest sister, Zoe.

Without turning her head, Raine glanced over at her. "Random."

Zoe shrugged. "I dodged death by fire. I'm training divers again and am a newlywed."

"In that order," Willow added and waved to the single hospital admit receptionist as they passed.

"I'm getting my life together," Zoe explained. "I want to serve as an Ibis Island Turtle Watch beach section coordinator."

Raine shrugged. Zoe wore her Sun Trips Touring t-shirt and had a scuba group later that morning. As they veered toward the elevators, Raine answered. "I'll get you in, but that's a lot of new, and I'm adding rebuilding Dane's house to your list."

Willow amended, "Dane and Zoe's house."

"Potato, potah-do. Why are we here again?" Raine asked.

Zoe pressed the elevator button. "I second that question. The woman put a knife to my throat."

"To your air hose," Willow corrected, before her eyes grew wide. "I'm only making that distinction, because Miriam didn't hurt you on that dive, and she did try to save your life from said death by fire."

"Dane's air hose was the one that was sliced," Willow continued. "Miriam is the one in a coma."

The elevator doors opened, but Raine didn't move other than to place her hand over the sensor that kept the doors from closing. "Still in the coma? I repeat, why are we here again?"

Willow took her hand and pulled her along. "Because Seth loved her. Enough that he was going to run away with her."

Raine started to argue but decided not to. She hated hospitals. It was a Clearwater genetic thing. Her nostrils filled with rubbing alcohol, bleach, and the smell of latex. Everything was too white, too plastic, and too quiet. Taking a deep breath, she followed her sisters onto the third floor.

Willow headed toward Room 319. The door was propped open. Raine took caboose. Before she entered fully into the room, she heard Willow greet someone. "Oh, hello. We are friends of Miriam's."

Raine reversed her feet and began to creep out.

"I'm Willow and these are my sisters Zoe and Raine."

Clenching her fists, Raine forced her feet to take the last steps into the room.

It was a thin woman with jet black hair. She was well dressed and didn't get up.

"My name is Harriet. I am Miriam's mother. While it's nice of you to stop by, visiting hours begin at 8 a.m."

Raine could say the same to her.

"We hope this is okay." Willow took a baby step forward. "Each of us serves on Ibis Island's Turtle Conservation Watch. We just finished our morning beach duties and came by to support Miriam. We are so sorry this happened."

Raine held back a snort. *This* would not have happened if

Miriam hadn't joined an unknown diver in trying to steal the treasure their dead brother had found and hidden.

Raine glanced toward the hospital bed. Miriam lay gray and unmoving. She didn't respond as Willow wrapped her hand around her fingers.

Harriet's lungs expanded fully. "I will make sure to contact you if there is any change of status. Thank you for coming."

The woman would need a phone number to actually contact anyone.

Willow didn't move. In fact, from behind, Raine could see her cheeks were raised from a slight smile. Willow's Zen master smile. Good luck, scary Harriet woman.

Willow didn't let go of the fingers on the ghostly hand. A blood pressure cuff circled Miriam's upper arm and a tube emanated from the back of her hand that led to a maze of more tubes and bags hanging next to her head. Machines flashed and beeped. The noise must not matter much to someone in a coma.

"You are the Clearwaters?" Harriet said as if she just had an epiphany. "What happens to Miriam's portion of the treasure?"

Zoe's shoulders pulled back, and Raine swore Zoe was about to scrape a foot against the tile floor like a rhino ready to charge. Raine stepped to her, circling fingers around Zoe's upper arm.

"The treasure found from the Luciana Bezan shipwreck," Raine said loudly before Zoe had a chance to, "belongs to the state of Florida. The government decides what to do with it."

Harriet straightened her already stiff back. "The finders are not allotted any of the artifacts?"

Raine tightened her grip on Zoe's arm.

"No, ma'am," Zoe said as she craned her chin far to the side and scratched the back of her head with her free hand. "Not even one piece. It's the law."

"I see," the woman said without moving anything but her lips. "Well then, thank you for coming," she said for time number two. "I'm sure the doctors will be here soon."

The double dismissal worked as Willow stepped away from Coma Miriam.

Since she wasn't confident with releasing Zoe's arm, Raine held on and tugged her out of the room.

Willow, of course, had a few more words to share. Raine could hear her from the hallway but didn't know what she said.

"What in the living hell?" Zoe screeched.

Raine moved her hand to Zoe's shoulder. "You showed a lot of restraint in there. Kudos. That woman is certifiable. Did you get a load of the pearls? Who gets all prim and proper to sit in a hospital room? Apples and trees."

"Willow's right, though," Zoe said and leaned her backside next to the numbers on the wall that read 319. "Seth loved her. She didn't hurt me under the water in the Gulf, and she could have."

"Well, you two keep the sunshine going," Raine said. "I've got work to do."

Raine left her sisters, not quite sure if she'd done a good thing or not.

CJ's was quickly becoming one of Matt's favorite spots. A little bit of everything without sixteen varieties of any one thing. Bag of donuts in hand, the wooden floor squeaked as he walked toward the coffee station. The place was a symbol of everything that was this island. Weathered, solid, and welcoming, even if not counting Raine Clearwater. As he added what he liked to think of as wimp creamer to the extra cup of java, he spotted some Cubans that wouldn't break his wallet.

Clarence Jenkins leaned against a bookcase behind the register, reading the Ibis Island Sun Times. "Morning, Chief." Setting his paper aside, he poked a few buttons and rang him up. "Donuts, two coffees, one that smells like ice cream, and two cigars. Are you bringing breakfast to my friend, Walt, or bribing a witness?"

Clarence owned the place and was likely most of the reason Matt favored it. Hands of leather, a head full of white hair, and a peaceful nature that might not be moved by even a hurricane.

"Now, you know I can't choose favorites, even if Walt is a friend of yours. You might not be too far off on the latter hypothesis, however." Matt couldn't help but grin. "How are things up here on the north end this morning?"

Craning his head around Matt so he could get a glimpse out his front window, Clarence answered, "All is well 'cept the overnighter sleepin' on the beach up there. Been rolling over fine, so she's not hurt."

"She?" Matt asked and craned his head out the glass of the front door. That was a first.

Clarence put the coffees in a drink carrier and the donuts and cigars in a small paper bag. "That's what bothers me."

"I'll check on her as I head out," Matt said.

"See, now?" Clarence put a fist on one hip and shook his finger with his free hand. "That's what's got people confused around here. I know you hear 'em talkin'."

It would be rude to look like he was in a hurry, but Matt hoped to clear off the pile of work on his desk, then get to Owen Branch before Booking and Release arrived for the morning. Since people had to come before paperwork, he left the bag and the coffees on the counter and asked, "Confused?"

"You're visible. Ya know, doin' stuff."

"Stuff?" There was that word the younger Yancy had used the night before. Two grins in one morning. Yep, Clarence was a favorite.

"Police chief stuff."

Matt rubbed the back of his neck. "Not to sound dense, but I am the police chief. At least for now."

Clarence brushed the side of his nose with his thumb. "We had that Chief Roberts for a lot of years, God rest his murderous soul. Never saw him out and about unless it was leading a parade. You are gonna lead the fall parade, aren't you?"

Parade? "Well, thank you for the compliment." Maybe. "The parade is one of those things I'll need to look into. I better be checking on our overnight beach guest. You have a good day now, sir."

"You too, Chief. You have my vote to stay on Ibis. Remind Walt we have poker tonight, will you?"

Matt juggled the coffee and the bag in one hand as he waved with the other and opened the door. He alternated his gaze from the beach access point to dodging potholes in the gravel lot. As he approached his island issue SUV, he spotted her. She lay in the shade sprawled out in front of the beach access bench. If he were going to use the beach to squat, he would lay *on* the bench. To each his own, or her own in this case.

He discarded the coffee and bag on the seat of the SUV, then headed toward her. Streets of Ibis were mostly empty at this hour, but a single golf cart made him wait before crossing the road. Two females. One held a toddler in her arms in the passenger seat.

The woman had masses of hair, one of those part blonde, part brunette, part redhead dye jobs the girls did these days. The air was thick. He was sure sand was in his shoes, and even under the shade of growth over the beach access, it was already hot enough that sweat dripped down his back in a steady stream.

As he got closer, he realized the hands and feet were actually paws.

FOUR

Like everyone else on the island, Matt learned that if you can't beat 'em, join 'em and had put Raine Clearwater on speed dial. He called as he got closer, ducking beneath the overgrowth.

She answered after a single ring. "Raine, here. What've you got, Chief?"

Apparently, she had him in her phone as well. "Good morning, Miss Clearwater. What I have is a dog on the beach."

There was a distinct pause before she responded. "Let me answer again. Hello, this is Raine Clearwater with Ibis Island Turtle Watch," emphasizing the word 'turtle.'

"Seriously," he said. "What do I do?"

There was a longer stretch of silence as he reached the...dog? This was more like a small Holstein. Its tail wagged but the rest of him stayed put on its side. This did not look like a Florida dog to him. He had to be sweltering, but since Matt knew nothing about dogs and not much more about Florida, he decided not to judge and, instead, find the owner.

Clarence said he'd been out here a while, but as Matt waited for the princess to answer, he looked up and down the beach for ... for what? Someone walking up and down with a giant leash looking for a dog?

"Dogs are not allowed on the beach," Raine finally said. "Anything else about your job you need me to tell you?"

Matt pulled the phone away from his ear, took a deep breath, then placed it back. "This one seems to be a stray." Slowly, he reached down and scratched its side. The ribs were awfully close to the skin. One paw at a time, it rolled over, exposing his entire underside. Apparently, he was a she, and Matt obediently rubbed her belly before trailing his hand up around her furry neck. "No collar. I got the no dogs on the beach part, but what do you do when you find a stray?"

"We don't have animal control on the island and the one inland doesn't open until 9 a.m. I'll text you the number."

And, just like that, she hung up. Before he had a chance to put his phone in its holster, she texted the number. The beast rolled over and used her front paws, inch by inch, laboring to a sitting position. She moved her butt over, sat on his feet, and lay her head in Matt's lap. A breeze of calm blew over him, even with the added distraction of his already late morning.

Stray dog. He had more jobs with this job than he could count. A little food and water until 9 a.m. What could go wrong?

Her giant nose started to squirm as if it wasn't attached to its face. Like a divining rod that just found water, it moved faster and faster as it traveled toward Matt's left hand. "That would be my donut hand," he said to the beast. "Should we call you Detective Beast?"

Getting her in the car could be a challenge. He stood. She did a circle and sat back on his shoes. He tried to coax her with the donut hand. He tried calling her, patting his leg, walking away. She lifted her drooping eye lids to watch him but didn't budge.

Time to man up. Squatting down next to her, he scooped his arms around her legs, and picked her up. She was heavy all right, but his eyes didn't nearly burst from his head like they did with the injured turtle.

The clean, white button-down was good and sweat-soaked by

that time. How long would a giant dog with thick fur have lasted in this heat?

Matt had found a plastic bowl in a breakroom cupboard. He expected the beast to be thirsty, but this was something beyond that. Water drizzled in a steady stream from the sides of her mouth, soaking the carpet in the corner of his office. Squinting, he couldn't quite look away. Drink. Look up and around. Drizzle rivers of water on the carpet. Repeat until a small pond formed.

Cummings opened the door just enough to put his head through. He was thin, a rookie, and Matt doubted the boy grew facial hair.

Matt lifted his brows. "You're a cop. Come all the way in like a man."

Cummings nodded, stepped in, but stayed close to the door. "You called?"

"I'm headed back to county. I need you to go out and get her a collar. A big collar." The beast licked the bottom of the bowl. "And fill that back up again." Matt eyed his pile of untouched paperwork as he pushed away from his chair.

"Okay, Chief. You need a leash, too?" The beast walked over to Cummings, turned around so her back was to him, and sat on the rookie's feet.

Huh. That wasn't just for Matt. "Leash. Yes, and some food. A small bag of food." Matt set a hand on Cummings' shoulder as he headed out the door. "She's friendly, you know."

The rookie crossed his arms high on his chest. "Sure. Yes, sir. I'll be all right. I'm just more of a cat person."

"Keep the door shut. I'll be back in thirty."

He could hear the beast whine as Cummings shut the door. Hoping the girl didn't eat his office, Matt hurried down the short hallway toward the common area with the coffee, the Cubans, and what was left of the donuts.

Most of the day shift was cruising the island, leaving the metal desks pushed together in twos in the common area empty. Passing the code enforcement officer, Matt headed to the back of the building. Officer Rodney Sheridan had to be one of the busiest people in the place, yet Matt knew little of what he did. He was next in line for a sit down so Matt could learn exactly what codes needed enforcing on an island.

Ibis Island City Hall doubled as the county jail. It was just after 7:30 a.m. Lucy Green was in charge of booking, release, and general check in and check out. Her hours were 8 a.m. to 5 p.m.

If anyone needed to be booked or released before or after, one of the officers did it themselves. Matt bet Owen Branch didn't know that.

Before reaching the door to the cell wing, Matt stopped at Lucy's check-in counter. Reaching through the small sliding window, he grabbed the clipboard with the waivers. He checked himself in, filled out all the appropriate paperwork, grabbed the key card, and made his way through the two sets of locked doors.

The place was dated but clean, and for an island this size, just about right. Other than the officer on guard duty, Owen Branch was the only occupant.

"Morning, Mr. Branch. I thought you could use some breakfast." The man looked ten years older than the hundred-fifty years Matt had surmised the night before and like he could use another night's sleep. He sat on the side of his cot with his forearms on his thighs. Dark rings circled his eyes and his skin was gray.

Matt held out the to-go cup. Branch curled his lips but seemed to soften when he inhaled the smell of wimp coffee. "I don't like you," Branch qualified before reaching through the bars for the java.

Grabbing the closest folding chair, Matt pulled it up near the cell door. "You don't have to like me, but you do have to follow the law." He took out a long john, then held the bag out to Branch. "Miss Green comes in at eight. She does the paperwork and will release you at that time."

"Did I make bail?"

An involuntary grin spread over Matt's face. "Not exactly. Mr.

Yancy agreed not to press charges if you pay for what you broke. I'm okay with that if you promise to stop breaking stuff."

"I didn't hurt nobody."

Branch opened his coffee, then sniffed before taking a drink. "You can't just walk onto our island and change things," he said and added, "We got rights."

Keeping a straight face was a significant challenge since Branch spoke tough around a chocolate sprinkle donut.

Smoking and dancing where both are prohibited? Matt took out the Cubans. "I'm new here. A city guy. You know that. I don't know much about island life, but I do know about the law. It's what they hired me for, and I intend to do my job. You think breaking people's stuff doesn't hurt nobody?"

Choosing his battles.

Matt leaned back in the chair and put one of the cigars between his teeth, rolling the other between his fingers. Talking around the one, he said, "I'm not here to bust heads of islanders not hurting nobody."

He took the cigar out of his mouth and looked down at it. "Illegal to smoke inside public buildings," he said, even if it was passive aggressive. "What do you say we go sit on the back porch and give these a try while we wait for Miss Green to arrive?"

———

Beyond the parking lot, a large green area the size of a small baseball field boarded the property. He and Branch leaned back in their chairs and lit the Cubans. White birds on stilts poked their long orange beaks in and out of the grass. A chorus of bugs cheered in sync from somewhere Matt couldn't tell.

The light blue Jaguar wasn't exactly inconspicuous. It was one of the classic models with a figurine sticking up at the end of the hood. Mayor Green drove with his daughter that day. The mayor eyeballed him and Branch as he exited the vehicle. His signature suit jacket and matching bow tie were navy blue today. The receding salt and pepper hair was all in place. Matt and Branch sat in the chairs, smoking cigars, and drinking coffee. Matt would come up with a convincing explanation later.

"Morning, Mayor," Matt said as they passed. "Lucy."

The mayor nodded, but his expression said he wasn't in any kind of agreement.

"Morning, Chief." Lucy smiled. Her red waves bounced as she pushed them away from her face.

To top off the scene, Officer Cummings opened the back door before the mayor had a chance to. He led the detective beast out of the building. More like the dog led Cummings.

"She was sniffing," Cummings explained. "Walt said it means she needs to, you know."

Matt closed his eyes in hopes he might disappear.

While the mayor and his daughter went into the building and the dog did her business, Matt tried to get back to being chief. "Let's say you get it fixed and paid back by the end of the month."

"All right, all right," Branch said as he chewed on his cigar. "I didn't hurt nobody."

As he'd said. "Say, Owen." Matt took a puff on his cigar and let it billow around his face. "Have you noticed anyone around town with a limp?"

"A what?"

"A limp. One that was recently acquired."

"Ah, the underwater treasure thief. Nope, and I'd tell you if I did, that mother fucker. I had a Saint Bernard as a kid," Branch said.

Matt had to shake his head to keep up. Is that what the dog was?

The dog pulled Cummings in a straight line to Matt, turned around, sat on his feet, and put his head in Matt's lap.

Branch added, "That's what they do when they want to protect you."

Or because he fed her donuts. "The dog's a stray. I'm taking her to the shelter inland when it opens at 9 a.m. An apology might be in order as well."

"For what?" Branch pulled in his chin. The muscles in his face softened. "Oh, that. I guess I could do that. Keep treats in your pocket."

That actually made sense. "Will do." Matt stood. "Lucy's ready. She'll get your personal belongings for you."

Matt made a point to block the door as he put out the cigar on the sidewalk.

Branch took the bait and did so as well.

They walked inside, and Cummings followed with the dog.

"End of the month?" Matt held out a hand.

Branch nodded. It was slight, but it was there. He took Matt's hand, and they shook on it.

"Get the dog back to my office, Cummings. You get her fed?"

Cummings eyes grew large, and he nodded slowly.

FIVE

M ayor Green had an office at the opposite end of the small hallway leading to Matt's office and across from the conference room. The door was cracked, but Matt knocked anyway.

The mayor opened the door with one hand, holding his cell to his ear with the other. He waved Matt in, and Matt sat down in front of his desk. "Oh, yes, yes, yes. I have it on my calendar right here," the mayor said in the phone. "Let's hope for good weather this year."

Yellowing framed newspaper clippings hung on the wall behind the mayor's desk. Titles read Ibis' First Beach Restoration, New Ibis Mayor Elected, and Volunteer Firefighter Coalition Formed.

The mayor hung up and held out a hand. "Good day, Chief. Did we acquire a police dog for Ibis?"

Matt let out a laugh, relieved he hadn't asked why he was smoking cigars and drinking coffee with an inmate. Giving the mayor a firm shake, he answered, "No, sir. That's a stray I found on the beach."

"Ah, yes, yes, yes." The mayor thumbed through paper phone messages sitting in the middle of his desk. "The inland animal control facility doesn't open for another hour. What in the world is a Saint Bernard doing on an island in Florida?"

Did everyone know the breed except Matt? "I wondered the same. I wanted to let you know that with the recent turn of events, I'll be re-interviewing the original six."

Since the mayor was one of them, he would know Matt referred to the original six divers who dove with Seth Clearwater the day he went missing. The day he was murdered. The mayor stopped what he was doing and looked up over his reading glasses.

"You are referring to the recent discovery of Luciana Bezan's missing treasure." The mayor sighed.

Matt nodded. "I like how you say missing rather than legendary."

The mayor moved his head and shoulders in a combined nod shrug. "I suppose it's both."

Matt copied the mayor's straight face and added, "And, the stabbing of Chief Roberts right here in our county jail."

"And, if we know anything about the attack on Liam Morrison, Dane Corbin and Zoe Clearwater in the Gulf."

Matt looked him in the eye. "Now, wouldn't that be helpful?"

"No one has checked into a hospital with a stab wound to the leg?"

No one visibly limping around town, and since the mayor was one of the six, not him either. And, yes, Matt had checked. "You know I'm not allowed to discuss an open case. Miriam Roberts is still in a coma." At least that part was public knowledge.

The mayor looked to the side, set his chin in his hand, and let his lungs expand and release.

Matt waited patiently. The mayor finally nodded and turned back to him. "Is Owen Branch once more overindulging and breaking items at Yancy's?"

The turn of conversation was appreciated. "Sure was. Yes. I think we may have reached an agreement."

"Good." The mayor nodded again. "He rarely hurts anyone, but good. Thank you."

It was the first compliment from anyone on the Ibis Island Board Matt had received since he arrived on the island. It might turn out to be a good day yet.

Twelve loggerhead nest hatches, a small turf battle between section coordinators, one visit to the hospital, and a public nest evacuation. Raine sat alone in her truck, tapping the side of her thumb on the steering wheel.

Tourists trickled in over Pelican Bridge. They came from as close as just the other side of the bridge to as far as the other side of the world.

Like clockwork, a pair of manatees lounged around the southeast corner of the island. Hopefully, the visitors would take advantage of the experience without taking too much advantage. It was against the law to touch or even approach the protected species.

"Oh, what the hell," she said to herself, released the emergency brake, and shifted into first.

Miriam was in the hospital. It was semi-safe to assume Miriam's apartment was unoccupied. Easing out of the lot, she turned onto the bridge. She was one of the only cars in the outbound lane.

A boat approached that was tall enough to initiate the raising of the bridge. Lights flashed as she shifted into neutral behind the painted line. In slow motion, the road split like giant clasped fingers pulling apart. The sailboat made its approach as the giant fingers spread and lifted high in the cloudless sky.

It wasn't like she was going to break in. Raine honestly didn't know what she planned to do. Maybe talk to the landlord. See if Miriam had any guests. Any male guests. Any male guests who had been stabbed in the right leg while trying to steal treasure from Raine's sister and brother-in-law.

Incoming traffic backed up several blocks inland as the top of the sailboat mast traveled between the east and west section of the road.

It was an idea. A hunch. Her phone would probably ring any minute and she'd be called back to the island. It wasn't like Chief Osborne was doing anything about her brother's death. Or at least, sharing about it with her family.

The bridge sealed, and she moved forward over the spot that, if she had traveled moments before, would have dropped her into the waves.

Assist with shoveling some sandbags and answer a call about water main breaks and the guy was hailed hero of the island. Raine wasn't fooled. He was out for a promotion, out to pad his resume. She knew the type. The cop type.

As she drove, she listened to a few messages she'd been avoiding. The first was Realtor Richard Beckett's daughter, Lou. "This message is for Miss Raine Clearwater."

As if anyone else ever answered this number?

"Beckett Realty and Rentals will not be paying any fine for leaving rental furniture on the beach overnight."

As if Raine sent the fine? She pressed delete and played the next.

It was the Primary Permit Holder of the island due south of Ibis. "Raine, we need you. Sunnydale Island and the wildlife need you." His board had presented plans to rip up over a mile of mangroves and build a strip mall. Idiots. The PPH kept bothering Raine to present to his board regarding the importance of mangroves in the integrity of island and wildlife stability. She deleted that message, too.

She saw the vehicle as she turned into Miriam's lot. Ibis Island police SUV. "I'll be damned," she said to the wind. The chief was doing something about her brother's murder?

As long as she was there, she pulled into the spot next to him. It might not be the chief, she tried to tell herself until she admitted that was dumb.

Looking at his vehicle, she noted the windows had been slimed. The stray. She checked her phone and noted it was long past 9 a.m. He must have stopped by Miriam's after dropping the dog off at the shelter. She wondered if he knew his windows had been slimed and decided not to tell him.

It came out of the door before he did. Saint Bernard. The chief followed behind, running as the dog dragged him to the patch of grass between the building and parking lot. Rolling down her window, she covered her mouth with the back of her hand, stifling a smile until he noticed her.

His attention didn't last. The dog spotted her, too, and ran over to her truck, lifting its front feet onto the window well. Raine scratched the top of its head. "Change your mind?" she asked the chief.

"What brings you inland?" He answered the question with a question, then added, "To Miriam Brown's parking lot?"

The dog rubbed its face against her arm. She grabbed its cheeks and scratched its ears. "Aren't you a happy dog?" She looked up to the chief. His expression wasn't readable. Two could play that game. "Shelter closed?" she asked, ignoring his question.

He wrapped the leash around his hand twice more, then pulled the dog down. "I didn't change my mind," he said and maneuvered it to the back of his SUV.

She had to see this. She got out of her truck and followed. The dog stopped pulling, lifted its feet onto the back of the chief's bumper and looked over its shoulder.

Stuffing a file folder she hadn't noticed before under his arm, he lifted the dog's butt the rest of the way into the back. The chief turned and sat on the bumper. "There were other dogs," he said with a straight face.

A large snout appeared over his shoulder.

"At a dog shelter," she said as a statement and crossed her arms.

He didn't try to remove the dog's head from his shoulder and instead reached up and scratched its cheeks. "They jumped and barked. She didn't like it."

It was a her. Raine laughed. "So, you're keeping a Saint Bernard. As interim chief of police. On an island in Florida."

"Fostering. Well, not officially. Since I didn't drop her off, I don't have to apply or register, or whatever they call it. They said with a

Saint Bernard, it won't take long for her to be adopted. Are we having an actual conversation?"

Raine shook her head. "No." She stepped in and scratched the dog's ears. "What are you going to name her?"

"I'm just fostering," he repeated. "You want a dog?"

"Oh, no. When I have to care for another creature, it will be kids."

"Plural."

"Two." Raine shrugged, then put her forehead on the dog's. "Are you scared of those other dogs?"

She inhaled. The closeness filled her with a sexy scent of cologne. She sensed something with sandalwood. Eww. Scrambling away, she straightened her shirt. "Do you have stuff for her?"

He nodded. "I have food and water."

"What about chew toys?" she asked and paced as she considered. "She may be big, but she's obviously still young. She needs to chew."

The dog followed her as she paced. When she reached the opposite side of the SUV, Raine stepped to the dog and wrapped her arms all the way around her. "She needs a bath. You got dog shampoo?"

Rubbing a hand along the back of his head, the chief nodded. "I've got a rookie who can pick up the stuff."

Typical. "That's exploitation," she said. The dog pressed her snout against Raine's waist and pushed. "I can keep her for the day." She had no idea where that came from.

"That's nice of you to offer, but I can just keep exploiting Officer Cummings."

"What about a crate? Saint Bernards pee buckets of urine."

Matt's eyes grew as large as saucers. "Rather, I would appreciate the help."

Stepping back, she pulled in her chin and looked him in the eyes. They were light brown like her mother's, which meant they were nearly the same color as her own. "You choke on those words?"

"No." He turned his chin away and mumbled, "Maybe."

36

"You can have the exploited rookie drop off the stuff on my doorstep." She pointed to the file folder. "What's in there?"

He looked down at it as if he'd forgotten about it. Or else, thought he'd gotten away without her noticing it. "Evidence."

"In my brother's murder investigation?"

SIX

"You know I can't say." He sighed, closed his eyes, and shook his head. "The poem. The hike you. It appears to be the original."

"Seth's poem?" The one her sister, Willow, had found a copy taped to the back of one of Seth's dresser drawers. The one Willow framed and displayed over the bar back in Luciana's. "It's a haiku," she corrected. The one that led to the three places Seth used to hide the ancient treasure he had discovered. The treasure he died for.

"I knew it." She started to pace again. "Ugh," she said and grabbed the sides of her hair. "And to think I went to visit that bitch!"

"Bella," he said out of the blue.

"Excuse me?"

"I named her Bella."

Bella. A disconcerting warmth spread to her heart.

Her phone rang. She could go back to the hospital, wait until Miriam woke up, and make her talk.

"Raine Clearwater," she said into the phone. Her throat dropped to her stomach as she listened.

Matt didn't know what the call was about, but the expression on Raine's face was enough for him to shut the hatch and dig his keys out of his pocket.

"I'm on my way," she yelled as she ran to her car. "Keep them away."

On her way? The traffic was backed up for miles. Sprinting to his vehicle as well, he looked over to her as he started his engine.

She met his eyes as she rolled up her window. They were glossy and red.

He pointed toward Ibis and mouthed the words, 'follow me.'

She nodded. He ran both his lights and siren. As they reached the end of the line of traffic heading to the island, he changed lanes and led her on the wrong side of the road.

His phone rang. Caller ID said it was Raine. "Where are we headed?" he said as a greeting.

"Guard station four."

"Not sure where that is."

"South end," she explained. She sounded worse than she'd looked. "Cluster of pines behind the shower and changing station."

"Affirmative." He knew the spot. Sirens still blaring, he slowed down at the intersection, then went through the light with Raine on his tail.

Blankets of brown pine needles covered the ground from the pines that grew on this end of the island. They made the ground slick beneath his tires as he approached guard station four.

Three pedestrians wore the telltale t-shirts that read Ibis Island Turtle Patrol. One wearing an American flag bandana as a head-band stood with a broom jabbing at something like he was jousting. Thunderous barking came from the sunroof. "Whoa, girl. I didn't know you could make that noise."

He heard Raine pull her emergency brake before she came to a complete stop. She bolted from the car and ran toward the trio.

He didn't want to ditch Raine but also didn't want to upset an emergency with a crazy foster beast. So, he rolled down the windows letting the scent of pine and saltwater flow through his SUV. He left the car running with the air blasting. "You wait here," he said to the dog over her barking.

Sliding out, he jogged over to the group. The sand here was filled with bits of pine needles, making it look more like pepper than the almost white sand up north.

It was racoons? He counted four. They huddled on top of pine needles around a small metal cage. Each time the jousting volunteer approached the circle, the racoons snapped and snarled before ducking their heads back to the cage. They were eating something. "No," Matt said under his breath. They were eating sea turtle hatchlings.

The one female volunteer sucked air in quick gasps as tears flowed down her face. "Why are they out in the daylight? We've tried to chase them away." Her body shook with sobs. "We can't get them to stop."

Raine looked from side to side for something Matt couldn't tell what. "You," she pointed to the one she called Oliver. "Leave the ones closest to the 'coons. Get a bucket and start collecting live ones. Don't get too close. You," she said to the other male. "Keep the perimeter clear."

Racoons could be nasty, but he agreed with the woman. It was rare for them to show themselves in the daylight, especially around humans swinging brooms.

Behind him, nails scratched metal. He glanced over as Bella leaned out of the open window, then slid right out and onto the grass. She ran toward the group. The fur on the back of her neck stood tall, but her tail wagged furiously. When she reached him, she kept going, heading for the racoons.

The racoons took one look at her, scampered for the nearest drain, and disappeared.

The dog ran from one volunteer to the next sniffing and pushing each one with her snout until she ended back at his feet. She turned her back to him with her tongue hanging out and panted heavily.

Matt patted her head. "How about tha—" he began to say, but then he noticed Raine.

One of the guys continued grabbing hatchlings as they emerged from the nest, but not Raine. This was the second time in two days he'd seen her like this, knees dug in the sand. She sat on the backs of her feet with her head low and her hands clutching her thighs.

He looked at where the racoons had been. The morning donuts threatened to return. At least two dozen headless hatchlings lay dead in the sand.

With hands shaking, the female took out a plastic grocery bag and started collecting them.

Raine lifted her head but didn't get up. "Stop it, Mary Jane. I have to. There's a report."

Mary Jane hesitated. Tears streamed steadily down her face and off her jawline. "I'll take the pictures." She nodded and dropped the bag.

Bella sprinted away from Matt's feet toward the sea oats. She barked, ran in a circle, then sat and faced the foliage.

At this, Raine lifted one foot, then the other. She pulled her shoulders back and walked like a zombie to where the beast barked and danced. Reaching down, she pulled a hatchling out of the oats.

"Is it alive?" he asked.

Raine nodded. "The racoons won't be back with the dog here." Holding the hatchling above and below the shell, it moved its flippers as if it didn't know his brothers and sisters were dead in the sand.

"We'll put it with the rest." She stopped and looked up at him. Her eyes were dark and cold. Like a recording, she added, "Dusk. You're welcome to come watch."

The dog stepped to Raine and sat on her feet. Raine didn't take notice. The muscles in her jaw flexed and released. Her lungs expanded. She rolled her shoulders back, turned to face the carnage, grabbed Mary Jane's discarded bag, and began collecting the dead.

He wasn't sure if it was okay to ask but he did anyway. "Does that happen often?"

Raine's eyes were glossy. She didn't answer and kept sticking those damned corpses in the bag.

"This end of the island attracts 'coons and crows," the one with the bandana answered for her. Raine had called him Oliver. "They'll eat hatchlings if they have the chance. Some predators know when they're about to hatch and wait. We put the cages over the nests. It helps keep the predators from digging up the nest but still allows the hatchlings to fit through the slats."

Matt's phone buzzed. He stepped away and answered. "Chief Osborne."

"You're 10:30 a.m. is here, sir, over." Matt recognized the voice. Officer Paul Cummings, the rookie. "And, your 10:50 a.m. called to say he would be running late."

Blake Eaton interview. Matt checked his watch. 10:35 a.m. "Get Eaton some coffee. I'll be right there." He looked down at the beast. "I'm going to text you a list, Officer. I want you to pick up some supplies. Get the credit card from Glory. She has it at the front desk."

"Leave her," Raine said.

"No, I can—"

"Leave her," she repeated. "I want you to."

He stopped and stared in her eyes with his cell in his hand. She was sincere. "Call me if you change your mind. I'll come by for her this evening."

———

When Matt arrived at the station, two city guys stood on either side of the parking sign that read, 'Chief Roberts.' They were clearly having a debate.

Since it was Matt who called to have it removed, he wondered what the debate might be about. He pulled into a spot three down and shifted into park. He'd seen a lot in his days working in Reno, Chicago, and even St. Pete's. Yet, his stomach still roiled from the scene he'd just left. Stepping out of his vehicle, he silently thanked Raine he didn't have a giant dog to contend with.

"Morning, gentlemen. Thank you for coming," he said.

"You the chief?" the shorter one asked.

Matt held out a hand. "That I am."

"I'm Walter and this here's also a Matt," the man said and shook. "Just to clarify, you want the sign and the post moved or removed?"

Matt began to understand the confusion. "Removed."

Walter hit the other Matt on the arm with his shoulder. "Told you."

The other Matt squinted. He was dark and thick with long sleeves wearing a wide-brimmed sun hat. "Where you gonna park?"

Matt grinned. "Wherever there's an empty space." He decided an island this size couldn't have more than one Walter that worked construction for the city. "Did you hear about yesterday's turtle?"

Walter's eyes lit. "The big one that almost died? I heard about that."

"He was this big," Matt said, holding his arms out wide. "You almost had to dispose of him. Where does one dispose of a dead turtle that size?"

SEVEN

W alter looked from side to side as if someone might overhear. "We generally place them," he said softly as if that made it more humane. "At the bottom of new construction. It's nature, ya know. Ashes to ashes and all that."

So, Raine wasn't lying.

"People'd be surprised if they knew how many—" Walter looked around one more time. "—are, ya know, in the ground."

He knew his expression must say otherwise, but Matt nodded. "Makes sense. I've got an appointment, gentlemen. Nice to meet you."

"You, too, Chief. Have a good day, now," Walter said and wrapped a chain around the parking sign.

It was 10:45 a.m. Good. Eaton might be better angry.

Both of Eaton's feet were propped on the corner of Matt's desk. He wore a short-sleeved, white polo that was a size too small. His receding hair was cropped short and Matt barely smelled the inland chain coffee to-go cup over the overt smell of cologne. He didn't acknowledge Matt as he entered and thumbed through his phone.

So, maybe he wasn't angry. Matt ground his teeth and smiled. "Morning, Blake. Thank you for coming."

Eaton didn't get up. Matt wondered if it was because his leg was hurt from a stabbing in the Gulf or if he was just an ass.

"What is it now, Osborne?" Eaton asked, still scrolling. "Zoning? My new place? 'Cause I already told you everything about Seth Clearwater."

Matt sat behind his desk and thumbed through a few of the files. "It's Chief Osborne, and after the recent events, I'm interviewing the six of you."

"You're not chief yet," Eaton mumbled. "And it's five of us. Roberts is dead."

So, it was going to be that way. He was past done with island cliques and hazing. Swiping Eaton's Sperry's from his desk, his feet landed with a thud on the floor. He noted his legs were fine and sat a hip where the feet had been. Eaton didn't wince. He could be considered tall and thin. He might be the man spotted at the scene when the vandalized porch awning fell on Willow Clearwater.

"Now, you could say, 'Chief for the time being,' or even, 'Interim Chief,' but until I'm told otherwise, I am the Ibis Island chief of police, and I have questions. I have the murders of Seth Clearwater and Chief Neil Roberts to solve. So, unless you'd like me to drag this out twice as long as it needs to be, put your phone away and let's get started."

With an eyeroll worthy of junior high status, Eaton stuffed his phone in his shirt pocket, slouched lower in his chair and folded his hands over his abs.

"Two years ago, you invested in extensive renovations and expansions to Show Me's."

Checking his manicure, Eaton yawned. "We've had this conversation, Chief." He put emphasis on the last word.

Matt chose the wait strategy.

Eaton sighed and, for the longest time, Matt thought he was going to wait it out, but then he added, "Yes. I expanded. People do that when business is good."

Nodding, Matt flipped through a random file on his desk. "You never mentioned the property you bought two years ago."

That got Eaton's attention. "Do you know that I just moved into the top fifty in high-stakes poker? Where do you think I've been all week?"

Matt knew where he'd been all week and ignored the comment. He added, "The one you started work on just this summer. Why wait?"

Eaton sat up. "Do you know who my father is?"

"Are you saying your father paid for the new construction?"

"I have a trust."

"I'll need the paperwork on this new trust."

"It's not new."

Setting the file down, Matt leaned back in his chair. "I'm not here to cause you grief, Blake. I'm here to gather facts. Something you know may inadvertently help solve two murders. Your 'already told you everything' didn't include any trust or a new business location."

Eaton placed his folded hands on Matt's desk and leaned in. "Seth and Roberts were my friends. I want to see the murders solved as much as anyone. That's the truth." He looked up and to the right before setting his eyes back on Matt. "One minute Seth was there, then he wasn't. I feel awful about it, but I don't have to share with you every business decision I make. The last we spotted him, he was at the Crystal Springs cavern. He loved it there."

The knock on his door broke the awkwardness. It would be Cummings. Right on time.

"Excuse me, Mr. Eaton." Matt rose and answered the door. It was the rookie all right. With Mayor Green standing next to him. "Thank you for coming," Matt said to Eaton. "I'll keep in touch."

Matt stood tall as Eaton passed the mayor. "Mayor," he said and nodded.

The two of them looked between one another, then to Matt. It was quite satisfying. The mayor recovered quickly, sat down, and said, "What you did for Owen Branch. It was brilliant."

"Well, thank you, Mayor," Matt started as he walked around his desk and sat.

The mayor held up a hand. "Simon, please."

Nodding, Matt continued, "Simon. Sure. Change is hard. Compromise helps as long as it doesn't hurt the innocent."

"You still working the seat belt angle?"

"Seat belts save lives," Matt answered.

"Yes, sir." The mayor sat tall in his chair. "How is the investigation going?"

No question about meeting with Eaton. Smart guy. "It's going. One step at a time. It was brought to my attention that you and Glen Oberweiss rented a boat the day before Tropical Storm Ernest came through." The day Miriam Roberts and an unknown diver attacked Liam Morrison, Dane Corbin, and Zoe Clearwater underwater.

The pause was slight, but the pleasant expression on the mayor's face remained. "The wildlife under the water is especially interesting right before a storm, yes."

"Did you see the Coast Guard work the scene of the crime that morning?"

The mayor's shoulders fell forward. He nodded. "It would be impossible to miss. We kept our distance so as not to get in the way."

Matt rubbed his hand along the back of his neck. "You know I'm not an island guy. Help me understand why you would rent a boat from Big Joe at Yo-Yo when you have one of your own that seems like it would handle pre-storm currents much better than a rental?"

The mayor laughed. "That boat is not something you take out for a few hours."

"Right, right," Matt agreed. "That makes sense. It's more like a yacht. When did you acquire that, again?"

He recovered fast enough, but if looks could kill. "Do I need my attorney?"

"That's up to you."

"Two years," the mayor said. "I bought it two years ago. I own the supermarket, as you know."

The intercom buzzed. Glancing over, he saw it was Glory, the City Hall receptionist. He clicked over. "Good morning, Glory. What can I do for you?"

47

"Mornin', Chief. Dane Corbin and Liam Morrison are here to see you." Two guys who worked outside on boats for a living? Matt imagined Glory swooning over them.

"Tell them to have a seat, will you? I'll be out soon."

All the muscles in the mayor's face seemed to drop. He closed his eyes and added, "You know I liked that boy. Seth Clearwater, I mean. There was nothing we could have done. One minute he was there and the next he wasn't."

Tilting his head, Matt asked, "And, where did you see him last, again?"

"The Crystal Springs cavern."

Matt took a deep breath and stood. "I should get to the boys. They've been through a lot, with the recent attack on them and the youngest Clearwater, and all."

The mayor stood. "Any, um, luck with the search for the rest of the treasure?"

Matt waited several seconds before answering, "You'll be the first to know, sir."

As Raine bumped over the end of her parents' drive, she noted the goats were already in their enclosure on the roof for the day. They stood in a line peering over their fence and bellowed like they knew she had a dog with her.

Bella sat in the passenger seat of her truck as if she was human. That is if humans stuck their faces in the vents, letting the air conditioning blow their giant ears.

"Now, listen," she said and turned to face the girl. "Harmony is old. You are supposed to be a gentle giant. Everyone says so."

Tilting her head, Bella seemed legitimately frustrated at the human talk she could not understand.

Raine traveled around the car and contemplated. She decided on sticking her arm through the window and clicking on the leash that way before opening the door.

It was pointless, really. Bella could rip it out of her hand with little effort. "Come on, girl." She opened the door and, to her surprise, Bella stepped out with ease. "Who do you belong to?" Raine asked as she secretly hoped there were no critters in the front garden that might cause Bella to bolt.

They passed the giant mural of a goldfish circling a mermaid as she guided her around the side of her parent's home. The mural was chipped and made Raine's heart hurt. It wasn't like her mother to let things go without upkeep. The recent discovery of her only son's murder wore on her soul.

"Oh my," the object of Raine's consideration squealed from the backyard. Her mother wore a long, baggy floral blouse over orange leggings. "Is this her? She's a beauty!" Harmony Clearwater loved animals of any kind.

Her mother dropped to one knee and opened her arms. Bella took the bait and trotted over to the new willing target.

The tail with hair longer than Raine's whipped around. She nearly knocked over Raine's mother as the girl twined her head around Harmony's neck.

"Aww." Her mother grabbed hold of a nearby firepit seat to keep from falling. "Aren't you just the best girl? Let me take a look at you." Harmony escaped Bella's grasp and sat on a nearby bench. The girl turned in a circle, then sat on Harmony's feet. Her mother ran her hands down her back, then inspected each paw.

Brows above eyes lined with the age of time dipped low. "She is thin. Not emaciated, but she needs food and exercise."

Raine winced as her mother spread open the giant lips and ran her fingers along the top and bottom gums. Bella acted the same as if she were having her belly rubbed. "A little love and you'll be good as new."

Wrapping her arms around the dog, her mother asked, "How in the world did Chief Osborne talk you into watching her?"

There was a question. "I offered."

Her mother looked up at her. "Well, I'll be. Just look at this beauty. Is she chipped?"

"Chipped, yes, but not registered." She scratched the dog behind her enormous ears.

R. T. WOLFE

Bella's eyes rolled in the back of her head.

Raine said, "I wonder where she came from."

Her mother stood. "Matt just found her on a beach in Florida?" She faced Bella and looked her in the eye. "Sit," she said with purpose.

Bella wagged her tail and bumped her snout on her mother's thigh. "Not even 'sit?' This poor girl needs a loving home."

Raine and Harmony sat on the logs that served as benches circling the fire pit. "Thank you for meeting me out back. I didn't want to bring her inside with all of the breakables in there."

Her mother waved a hand like she was shooing a fly. "They're just things."

Raine shrugged and glanced over to the new pine in the corner of the yard. Bella rolled on her back. "We went to visit Miriam this morning."

Rubbing Bella's stomach, her mother glanced up at Raine. "Willow is good about those kinds of things."

"Who said it was Willow's idea?" Raine laughed at her own joke.

EIGHT

Raine's parents had lived in the house as long as she could remember. Mature pines created almost complete shade. Her father kept them trimmed at the bottom in order to allow the Gulf breeze to flow over the property.

It didn't seem to help Bella. She lay on her side and panted with her tongue hanging so far out of her mouth, it touched the sea shell mulch. Harmony rubbed her belly.

"Matt found the original poem in Miriam's apartment."

Her mother's arm stopped. Her chin dropped to her chest. She stayed like this long enough that Bella sat up and put her snout on Harmony's lap. "I feared that may be the case."

Seth had purchased plane tickets to run away with Miriam just before he was killed. "I'd like to shake the bitch," Raine said honestly.

Her mother nodded and didn't even scold Raine for the language. "I bet you would. Hopefully, she'll wake soon and Chief Osborne can get her to tell the truth."

"Maybe being stabbed in the Gulf by the guy she was scheming with will scare the truth out of her." Raine sighed. Bella whimpered, then yawned with a noise. It sounded human. "There is a third person in on this, you know."

"Maybe," her mother said.

"Someone had to man the boat when Miriam and whoever dove the morning they tried to kill Liam, Dane, and Zoe."

Her mother shivered.

When would Raine learn not to be so blunt? "I'm sorry."

"I know, dear." Her mother slid an arm around Raine's back, and Raine rested a cheek on her shoulder.

She smelled like raspberry tea and hibiscus flowers and mom.

Her mother spoke into Raine's hair. "We don't know for sure about that. The boat may have been empty." She kissed her on the side of the head.

Like clockwork, early afternoon storm clouds blew in. Raine could smell them as well as see them. "I don't think so. The man in the Gulf was stabbed as he attacked Dane, Liam, and Zoe. He would need help getting back in the boat. Getting back to shore. That was the day before tropical storm Ernest. The Gulf was very choppy."

"Chief Osborne is going to find who killed our Seth."

Raine hoped so.

———

Dane and Liam were not sitting when Matt came out to reception, and they weren't talking to Glory. Poor girl. They both stood in front of the waiting room chairs, Liam with his hands in his pockets and Dane with his arms crossed.

Each wore Sun Trips Touring t-shirts and frowns on their faces. Matt stepped toward them and held out a hand. "What brings two of Ibis Island's finest to City Hall?"

Liam offered his hand. "It's been a while since we've gotten an update on Seth Clearwater's case. We are here for you, Chief. What can we do to help?"

Matt would have expected Dane to serve as spokesman.

"How about you come on back and have a cup of coffee?"

Matt chose the rarely used conference room. He sat at the head of the table.

Dane sat to his left and crossed his arms again. He used his left hand to ring the barbed wire tattoo that circled his right biceps. Liam sat across from Dane with his hands palms down on the table.

Treasure hunter. High school teacher.

The teacher voice of reason continued the line of questioning. "How is everything going, Matt? Are you adjusting?"

Matt didn't see that coming. He realized they weren't here to see how he was adjusting, but damn it if he didn't appreciate being asked. "Small island."

"Ouch," Liam responded. "We so get that."

Dane didn't appear to be getting it.

"I like it," Matt confessed. Since the former Chief Roberts tried to murder Dane's girl, Zoe, along with his wife, Miriam Roberts, Matt decided not to prod. "I'll like it a lot more when Seth's murderer is behind bars."

"We recognize," Liam said, "that you're not accustomed to small island life. You might not understand that while Miriam and the unknown man were in the Gulf trying to scare the hell out of Dane and Zoe and me, or kill us and take Seth's treasure—"

"Luciana Bezan's treasure." So, Dane could speak.

"Luciana's treasure," Liam qualified. "A third person would need to man their boat in the pre-storm winds."

"Would likely have a third person," Dane corrected again.

Liam nodded. "It's possible the boat was unmanned, yes, but not likely."

"I'd do it alone," Dane said. He hadn't uncrossed his arms.

"We heard you found the original poem in Miriam's apartment."

"Original map," Dane corrected.

Liam craned his head to Dane. "Would you like to do the talking?"

"Yes," Dane said.

"We agreed that wouldn't be the best—"

"Miriam is part of this." Dane turned to Matt. "Someone

should be stationed at the hospital, waiting to question her when she wakes up."

"This isn't a movie," Liam argued.

Matt interrupted. "Did you two need me here for this?"

"See?" Liam said. "Now you've got him pissed off. That's why I was gonna do the talking."

"Liam," Matt said as sincerely as possible. "Dane. This isn't nearly as personal for me as it is for you. But, believe me, this is personal. Miriam lied to all of us. I've been assigned as Ibis Island Chief of Police and more than just Miriam Roberts has lied to me.

"I suspected Miriam was crooked since the beginning. Now, we have proof beyond a reasonable doubt. But, she didn't kill Seth Clearwater. It took force to shove that knife through his skull. I may not be an island guy or a diver, but I do know it would take additional strength to do so under water."

Matt pointed to the white board behind him. "That." He pointed to his copy of Seth's poem.

Her Legacy
The wet uncharted
The cornerstone that is Home
The under under

"It shows there were three places Seth hid the treasure he discovered. We assume the murderer found the treasure in the wet uncharted. You two and Zoe found the under under. That leaves the cornerstone that is Home, whatever the hell that means. Right now, we have every treasure hunter and their brother on this island looking on land and under water for this cornerstone that is Home, if there even is such a place. The hospital staff knows to call my personal cell if and when Miriam wakes up. I am questioning persons of interest and general islanders who might give me a clue as to who killed the Clearwater brother. The rest I am not able to share regarding an active investigation. While I appreciate your concern, I'd like a little trust, here."

Sometime during Matt's rant, Dane had uncrossed his arms. "Okay."

Okay?

"He came after us and the people we care about," Liam amended. "Isn't there anything we can do?"

"Yes. Yes, there is. Keep close to the Clearwater family. Someone tried to kill, or at least hurt, Willow when they booby trapped the awning that fell on her. The man who attacked you in the Gulf likely killed two people and will have no problem killing again. Keep your eyes open. Keep your ears open. This is public, now. The killer will be on alert. He, and I do mean he, is going to slip."

Dane leaned forward. "Treasure hunters are mostly addicts. They don't think or see like you do. Both the hunt and the find are nothing less than a drug. Killing could be justified in their minds. People you wouldn't think could be capable of murder or theft are just that—capable."

"Thank you," Matt said. "Good to know. I mean that."

Raine was right. It was condescending to ask the rookie to deliver the stuff for the stray. Her home was only a few feet off the street. Her truck wasn't there, so Matt began hauling the crap around to the back. Giant bed, enormous food and water dishes, industrial strength chew toys, treats, and a crate the size of a shed. All for a day at Raine Clearwater's.

It wasn't his first time at Raine's home. He'd already searched it, inside and out, when the crooked former Chief Roberts ransacked it, and again for the cornerstone that is Home.

It was clean, organized, and might be the smallest home he'd ever seen. He stopped to consider the outside rinse area. Uneven wooden slats surrounded the outdoor spigot. She didn't have a pool. No need to rinse off before getting in.

He thought he saw something between the wooden slats and swung open the door. Shampoo and conditioner sat on a tall shelf, along with soap and a razor and one of those puff things girls used in the shower. This was her shower.

He looked around at the neighbors' homes, judging who would be able to see what.

This couldn't be her only shower. Had he seen one inside?

Tires crunched over the seashell mulch that served as her driveway. "Chief?" she yelled from the front of the house.

"Back here," he answered and turned to get the crate out of the box.

Bella made her way back, trotting like a horse. Her entire body wagged. She cried and did circles around his legs. Holding up his arms, he regretted that more of the lint roller things weren't on the list. "What's the matter with her?"

Raine latched the door to her shower. "She seems to have missed you," she said and lifted on her toes to look in the shower.

Rubbing her face over Matt's legs, he thought this was more like a military reunion after six months on a tour of duty.

"Did you take a shower?" Raine asked.

"Oh, that. No. What? No. I was just looking."

"In my shower?"

NINE

"Why do you have a shower outside?" He realized that was more condescending than anything he asked of the rookie. "I mean, the slats."

"The slats?"

"You can see through the slats. That neighbor," he said, pointing next door, "can see when you are showering. What do you do in the rain? No pun intended."

"Howard is tired of watching me shave my armpits. Rain just adds to the cause." She picked up the directions to the dog crate.

It took him a long minute to recover from the mental visual.

He put a hand over the paper. "Thanks, but I'm a guy, and it's just a crate."

"Chauvinist." She crossed her arms. "As PPH, I need to tell you she needs shots to be on the island."

He lifted a single brow at her as he juggled the massive crate. "I thought you were Raine Clearwater of Ibis Island Turtle Watch," he said, emphasizing the word turtle.

He may have been mistaken, but he thought the ice princess may have smiled.

A few maneuvers and click. "See? Now, we stick the bed in, and

57

she's all ready for our girl." His back stiffened and chills ran down his spine. Correcting the word *our* would make it worse.

"She is definitely ready for a nap. How do we get it in the door?"

Looking at the crate, then toward the back door, he said, "Right, then." And, collapsed it back flat. "Back door?"

She walked to the back and opened it without using a key.

"I told you to keep your doors locked."

"You also told me to stay with Willow for the time being."

He set down the crate and laced a hand around her upper arm. "Your brother may have been a crime of passion, but Chief Robert's murder while in jail was premeditated. This guy must be taken seriously."

She set a hand over his, then pushed it away and held the door open wide for him. "I'm sorry."

He lifted his brows.

"Truly. I usually keep it locked. Any leads on a man with a limp?"

After lunch, he had appointments with the last three of the original six divers who dove with Seth the day he was killed for just that reason. "Not yet. You didn't tell me that you met Harriet."

She looked at him straight in the eye. "You heard about that? It was Willow's idea."

"Small town." It was the first time he'd been able to use the phrase. It was going to be a good day.

The only school on the island was the elementary school. The junior high and high school students took the bus inland for classes. Timothy Hart worked as superintendent for all three and was Liam Morrison's boss. "I taught social studies when I started with the district. Seth was one of my students back then."

He sat tall in one of the guest chairs across from Matt's desk. A straight part separated his dark hair, and his tie matched the color of his navy blue suit jacket and pants. Could he have killed Seth Clearwater? Stabbed him through an eye socket?

Hart added, "You know you're not making friends around here."

Fuel for Matt's fire. "I'm not here to make friends. I've been hired to serve as Ibis Island chief of police and to solve two murders."

"Interim chief."

A duly noted condescending reminder.

Maintaining his posture, Hart scanned the walls of Matt's office. "Seth was a good boy. A good man. We were his friends. We all feel deeply about what happened to him."

"Can you tell me when you last saw Seth Clearwater?"

Hart's eyes landed on Matt's. "You've already asked me that."

He wasn't wrong.

"The Crystal Springs cavern. Seth loved it there." His eyes moved to a spot on the carpet and fixed there. "He was a good student. Eccentric, but a good boy. His sisters were much younger than he. Unlike most high schoolers, Seth wasn't embarrassed by them." Hart's lungs expanded. "It all happened so fast. One minute he was there, and the next he wasn't."

"You acquired a vacation home in upstate New York a few years ago," Matt said as a statement and not a question.

Hart blinked and looked at him. He nodded. "My father passed away. There was an inheritance."

A knock on the door turned Hart's gaze in that direction. As Matt had instructed, Officer Cummings opened the door without being invited in. "Mr. Beckett is here to see you, Chief."

Matt stood and held out a hand. "I'm sorry for your loss, Mr. Hart." He meant it.

Hart looked between him and Cummings and back again before setting the palms of his hands on the armrests of the chair and pushing himself up.

Twenty minutes was short enough to take Hart by surprise. Good.

He recovered fast enough. "Let me know if there's anything I can do, Matt. Chief. There isn't a local on the island I don't know."

Matt nodded. "Come on in, Mr. Beckett."

"Tim." Beckett looked to the floor as the two of them turned sideways to pass.

"Richard."

"I'm a busy man," Richard Beckett said as he sat.

"This won't take long." Or, it could take the rest of the after-noon just for saying that.

"Do you have a new lead in the case?" Beckett asked. Sunglasses propped on the top of his head. They may have cost more than his linen shirt. "These tourists here searching for treasure have been excellent for business." Beckett rubbed his hands together like he was warming them in front of a fire.

"I'm not allowed to share details of an ongoing investigation," Matt responded. "And, while I'm happy your businesses are doing well, two locals have been murdered."

Beckett curled the corners of his lips and scratched an ear. "Bah. Seth was probably killed by a stranger we'll never find, and Chief Roberts hung around bad people long enough that it caught up with him."

This guy really thought he had it all figured out.

"Dane Corbin, Liam Morrison, and Zoe Clearwater were attacked in the Gulf," Matt added.

"That's very bad, yes." Becket leaned in. "But the treasure. The pictures were unbelievable. What I would have given to see it up close and personal."

This guy was incorrigible. "How's business?"

"Like I said," Beckett answered and rubbed his thumb and fore-fingers together.

"I was told you bought up a number of properties a few years ago?"

Tilting his head, Beckett stared Matt in the eye. It was a stale-mate, but Matt would win.

"What are you getting at, Osborne?"

Matt leaned forward over his desk. "It's Chief. Ibis Island Chief. Answer the question please, Mr. Beckett."

"I buy up property all the time." He shrugged and leaned back in his chair.

It reminded Matt of Blake Eaton.

"Ninety-five, now."

"Ninety-five," Matt repeated. "Impressive."

"Meeting with the owner of the lot south of Sun Trips after this."

"The one next to the parking lot you're constructing for Show Me's valet parking?"

"Blake told you that?" Beckett seemed honestly disturbed. "That's the one, yes."

"The lot with the leatherback nest?"

"Listen, Osborne," Beckett said through his teeth.

Matt was pleased to have hit this unexpected nerve. People always show their true colors, good and bad, when caught off guard.

"Those turtles have been nesting on this island long before those Clearwaters took over." Spittle sprayed on Matt's desk.

"Took over?"

Beckett leaned back and his chest heaved. "Putting turtles over people."

He was honestly confused. "Putting turtles over people?"

"Lights out at dark. Clearing the beach of chairs every night. Renter turtle notification. The light thing." He waved his arms in the air. "None of it makes a damn bit of difference."

Matt was definitely missing something but needed to stay on topic. The knock on the door helped.

"Good to know, Beckett. It's all good to know." He stood. "I appreciate you coming by. Best of luck with the sale this afternoon."

And just like that, Beckett changed back to jovial. He wiggled his eyebrows and corrected him. "Purchase."

Matt pointed a finger at him like a gun. "Purchase. Right."

The knock on the door this time would be Cummings with Glen Oberweiss. Matt worked to look surprised.

Cummings opened and stuck his head in. "Glen Oberweiss here to see you."

Matt stood. "Thank you for coming, Richard. I'll be in touch."

Beckett didn't get up. His eyes went between Oberweiss and Matt like a tennis match. "That's it?"

Beckett scratched behind his ear, then stood. "Yep. Tomorrow night. Board meeting."

Beckett was the only one who mentioned it. As he passed Oberweiss, he said, "Damn good to see you, Glen."

Oberweiss nodded but didn't speak.

Glen Oberweiss. Town historian and manager of the Ibis Island Museum. Current wife was a second-grade teacher at the island elementary school and volunteered with Turtle Watch.

"Good day, Glen," Matt said and held out a hand as if Beckett hadn't just been there. "Thank you for coming."

Oberweiss smiled. "Did I have a choice?"

"We're all working for the same cause, right? We want to find out who killed Seth Clearwater and former Chief of Police Neil Roberts. Please sit." Matt gestured toward his guest chairs.

As he sat himself, he asked, "You and Neil were friends, yes?"

Oberweiss lifted a shoulder. "We're both paid by the state. It gives a couple of guys something to bond over."

Matt nodded, but lowered his brows. "And Timothy Hart," he said as a statement.

Oberweiss lifted his chin. "Right. Yes. He is a state employee, too, but that salary is in a different stratosphere. It's our love of diving that made that friendship."

Matt nodded. "I get what you're saying. You live on a historian and a school teacher salary. No offense, but I'm impressed." Leaning back, he folded his hands over his abs. "No investments? Savings? A Trust of any kind?"

"Is there a reasoning behind this line of questioning? Again?"

Matt shrugged. "With the recent turn of events, I am interviewing each of you who dove with Seth Clearwater the day he was murdered. You understand."

"I want to find out who killed Seth just as much as you do.

More, actually. I knew him from the time he was a little boy. Jan and I are minimalists. One car. Our entertainment is the island. We have her teacher pension and that's it."

"The island is a beautiful place. I can see why people never leave."

"It can be a drug."

Interesting choice of words.

TEN

O ther than trying to drink from it, Bella seemed to appreciate the cool water pouring over her back. As cool as water from a hose on a Florida island could be.

Raine was determined to scrub every inch of her.

Oh no. She squinted. It was coming again. The dog started slowly, moving her head from side to side. Then, her shoulders. Until her whole body shook suds in a three-foot radius.

Rather than tasting shampoo, this time, Raine kept her lips closed.

The paws were caked with bits of shells from the mulch, but that couldn't be helped. She would figure out a plan for that later. For now, she scrubbed dog arm pits and behind ears the size of Raine's outstretched hand.

"You don't need to do that," a voice said from the street.

She looked up to see the chief's black and white SUV with the window rolled down.

Raine had taken off the collar. She hung on as hard as she could, but the dog slipped away and ran for the vehicle effortlessly. It took some wrestling, but she was able to get the dog away from the SUV long enough for the chief to park in the drive.

Strange noises came from the dog. She growled, moaned and cried louder than any canine Raine had heard before.

Hanging on around her belly, Raine said, "Are you going to get out or just make her suffer?"

"I'm not sure I want to end up like you."

Freudian slip. She looked down. She was completely soaked with water and bubbles. As if on cue, Bella's head started to turn left and right.

"Incoming," Raine called.

The shoulders, the body, and the door of the SUV were speckled with white bubbles, as well as the side of the chief's face.

Raine couldn't help it. It made her laugh so hard, she had to let go of the dog to hold her stomach.

Surprisingly, Matt braved the inevitable and opened the door. Bella rubbed against his navy dress pants and sat on the polished black shoes.

"Nice to see you, too, girl. Let's see if we can get you rinsed off." He looked up at her and wiped the soap from the side of his face. "I was planning on doing this tomorrow at my place."

She didn't know where home was for the chief. She shrugged. "My house smells like dog."

He took hold of the loose skin behind Bella's neck and led her over to the hose. "I'm sorry about that."

"I offered. Here. You hold her and I'll rinse."

It took a while and neither spoke. The silence was a pleasant surprise. She never liked social scenarios when small talk was required.

Bella rubbed her face over his shoulder as Raine worked on clearing soap from the thick fur.

"You're as soaked as I am," Raine said and finished with Bella's tail. "There are several mattes that will need to be cut out. I don't have an extra set of men's clothes here for you to change into." She didn't know where the last part came from and hated the layers of awful that surrounded that confession.

"I keep an extra set in my car."

Only to be trampled by his confession.

"Of course you do," she said and grabbed one of the old beach towels from the pile she had ready.

The chief stepped next to her and grabbed one as well. How could he smell this good after an entire day of working as chief of police on an island in Florida? It wasn't as if he stayed behind his desk like his predecessor did.

She looked up at him and caught him staring. His eyes. A thin, dark brown ring circled the lighter brown. It was an intensity of intelligence, world knowledge, and life. It poured out from his gaze and covered her with curiosity.

Shaking her head clear, she dropped her gaze to the dog. He'd worked in Reno, Chicago and St. Pete. Other than college, she'd never been off the island more than a week for a sea turtle conference. "And, you didn't have the exploited rookie get a brush."

He nodded and returned to rubbing legs and paws. "I'll get one in the morning."

"I've been thinking," she said.

He lifted his brows at her as he discarded a drenched towel and grabbed another. Bella pressed her forehead into the center of his white buttoned-down shirt, smearing multicolored dog hair all over it.

She grinned and continued. "We should set a trap."

"A trap," he repeated. It was condescending.

Her brows dropped and she stood. "Bait. Whoever killed my brother did it for treasure. Whoever killed Chief Roberts in jail did it to keep him quiet about said treasure." It was difficult to sound smart drenched in water and soap. Taking the next towel from the stack, she wrapped it around herself like she was getting ready to exit her outdoor shower.

The chief put a towel under the dog's belly. Bella looked like a baby carried by a stork. "Hold this for a minute?"

Raine complied and took the towel from him. "Are you even listening to me?"

"Very much so, actually," he said and opened the back door of his SUV.

The after-an-all-nighter-at-a-woman's-house clothes. She almost forgot.

He came back and looked around at the ground. Bella's giant, red collar lay next to the dwindled stack of folded towels. He clicked it on her and opened the front door. "How about a beer, and you can tell me about your ideas?"

Wait. What? Her eyes darted around her yard as his backside walked into her house. He couldn't do that.

"Tell me about being a Primary Permit Holder," he said as he literally rummaged around her fridge in her kitchen in her house.

Tapping her foot, she said, "Well," and then lifted on her toes to see if she had any moldy pizza in there. "Most PPHs are run by cities or counties. We are a non-profit, grass roots program. Do you need help in there?"

"Bud Light?" he answered her question with a question again. Bella sat next to him, following his every move.

She could play that game. "Do you have the nerve to question my beer choices in my fridge?" she asked, emphasizing the word 'my.'

"Choice singular, and I'm just asking if you want one."

"Oh." Heel. Soapy, wet heel. "No. I have Turtle Watch early."

"Right. I shouldn't stay." He put the can back and shut the door. "I'll just go change." He turned in a circle.

"First door on the right." She pointed to the bump out next to the living room/kitchen nook.

"You're not coming with?" he said.

She was sure the look of rage that overtook her face was loud enough to hear until she realized he was speaking to the dog. Spinning on her heels away from him, she waited until he disappeared into her no-shower bathroom/laundry room.

She put the last of Bella's things into one of her reusable grocery bags and pulled her towel closer around her wet clothes.

He came out wearing an army green Henley, leather sandals, and pair of faded jeans with a hole in the knee. It was the kind of hole made from wear, not from the manufacturer.

She almost thought he was sexy. Eww. Quickly blinking that away, she held out the bag.

"I'll get the crate and come back for that." He turned and reached in to pull out the bedding. The muscles in his back flexed beneath the Henley.

She turned away and ducked her chin to pet the dog.

"I do appreciate you taking her today. I have a plan for tomorrow. I expect the shelter will call within a day or two."

"You are taking her to the vet, though, right?" she asked with her back to him.

He walked by with the crate in hand. "Yeah. I should do that."

She followed with the bag, staring at the floor.

He loaded the crate and turned to face her. "I'd like to hear your bait ideas."

She would not fall for that. "Don't patronize me, Chief."

"There she is." The corner of his mouth lifted into a half-smile. "I hate to call you Ice Princess after you watched the stray for today."

She crossed her arms as she pulled the towel tighter. "Good night, Chief." She bent down to Bella as he opened the back of his SUV. "And, good night to you, girl. You are going to find your furever home and make someone the luckiest human ever."

Standing, she found him leaning an arm against his vehicle with one ankle crossed over the other. "An ice princess who speaks baby talk to dogs." He shook his head and whistled for Bella.

She trotted like a horse to the back tailgate, lifted her front legs on the bumper and looked up at him.

Raine turned to go inside just as the chief lifted her in.

"Bait," Matt said to the dog as he pulled into his apartment parking lot.

He needed to listen to the locals more.

As he parked, he rifled through the bag Raine prepared and

found Bella's leash. She'd rolled it in a tight spiral and placed it in a spot next to the stack of the water dish and the food bowls.

Clicking it on, he opened the side door for Bella.

As she did her thing in the grass, he thought of Dane Corbin. "I'll need him to help come up with a plan," he said to the air.

They walked up the flight of stairs to the first door on the left. "Now, this is just for a few days, girl. You'll get a good home with a big yard. I'll make sure of it." He opened the door. She walked in and went right to sniffing everything. "I'll be right back."

He heard her whining as soon as he shut the door.

As he jogged back to the SUV, he added a call to Dane Corbin and Liam Morrison first thing in the morning on his mental to-do list. Hauling the bed and Raine's bag in first, he decided that, unlike Raine, the two of them likely didn't actually go to bed at 9 p.m.

When he opened the door, the dog did that thing again. The one where she acted like she hadn't just seen him three minutes before. The whining and circling and sitting on his feet.

"Here you go, girl." He laid out the bed, stood back and considered. "Oh, and this." Rummaging through the bag, he found a bone bigger than his head. "Don't eat the apartment," he said and handed it to her.

She took it from him, walked to the bed, circled, and lied down.

One more trip to get the crate. He texted Dane as he walked.

have some time in the morning?

I could use a treasure hunter to bounce an idea off of

And, then Liam.

you work in the morning?

hoping to run an idea by a local islander

The book said to use the crate until one year old. The shelter estimated her at seven months, but he decided she wasn't like most pups. He hauled it into his place, set it in the living room and kept the door open.

"You can handle this when I'm here with you, right girl?"

His phone buzzed. That didn't take long. He pulled it from his front pocket. It was Dane.

i will make time

you say when

He had his meeting with the code enforcement officer at 8 a.m., but that could be moved back if needed.

He decided to wait and see if Liam answered and put his hairy, wet uniform in the washer.

Tossing in a detergent pod, his phone buzzed again.

I lead a scuba group at noon.

What did you have in mind?

Matt grinned at the school teacher texting grammar, then answered them both.

how about 10

I'll bring the donuts

Sitting down at his kitchen table, he powered up his home computer.

cops and their donuts

It was Dane. The banter was actually appreciated.

Bella trotted over with the bone in her mouth. She sat at his feet as he checked his email.

Flipping on the light next to her bed, Raine wondered when the last time was she had a full night's sleep. Caller ID said it was Oliver, section three coordinator. The red numbers at the side of her bed read 5:30 a.m.

"This is Raine."

She heard heavy breathing. Not the perverted kind, but the upset kind.

"Oliver?"

"They're gone." It was difficult to listen to an elderly man sob.

Flipping back the sheets, she set her phone on speaker. While pulling off her night shirt, she replaced it with the sports bra waiting on her nightstand for this kind of call. Her feet fell into the shoes ready at the side of her bed.

"What's gone, Oliver? Where are you?"

Her automatic Keurig had her coffee ready. She secured the lid as he found his voice.

"The nest."

How could a nest be gone? "I don't understand, honey. Just breathe. I'm on my way."

A stick of gum would have to replace a toothbrush. She'd backed her truck into her tiny driveway for the same reason she set a pair of shoes by her bed each night. "How can a nest be gone, Oliver?"

"Those fuckers!" he yelled. The line disconnected.

ELEVEN

Oliver was a recovered alcoholic. A veteran who came to her a few years ago trying to escape his nightmares. She hoped he wasn't in the midst of a flashback.

She tried to call him as she peeled out of her drive. He'd never given her his location. She pulled into the beach access at Cavern Ave. It was about the middle of section three.

She heard him before she saw him.

"Where are you? You cowards!"

Throwing her cinch sack over her shoulders, she ran as fast as she could, not even stopping to ditch her shoes at the beach end of the access.

Oliver darted up and down the beach, yelling at random points. She saw why almost immediately.

Clutching the middle of her shirt, she sucked in air.

Walking like a zombie, she made her way to the wooden stakes wrapped in orange tape—the ones she'd placed two months before—and dropped to her knees several feet from the nest. Or, where it used to be.

Someone had dug it up. Someone human. A deep hole in the sand lay where the eggs had been.

Ignoring Oliver, her nails dug into her thighs. She recited stats out loud. "Stake read 3/48/V. Section three, the forty-eighth nest laid, and verified." Wiping her nose with the back of her hand, she moved to her cinch sack and stuck in her arm.

A hand touched her shoulder.

Jumping, she smacked it away. It was the chief? "What are you doing here?"

"I got a call. What can I do to help?"

She stood. "What can you do?" She pushed him in the center of his chest with both hands. "What can you do?" She pushed him again. "Look at this!"

He grabbed both her wrists. "I need you to back away, now. We're going to take care of this."

She yanked on her hands, but he ignored her and added, "Together."

"There is no 'together,'" she yelled. Her head pounded. "This is my turf. Why won't you leave me alone?"

His long body pressed against hers, guiding her away from the nest. "You are disrupting a crime scene, Raine. See? Those are knee prints, and they aren't yours."

"There is," she choked as she finished. "Nothing you can do." If she let one single tear spill, she would never forgive herself.

"This is poaching. On our island." His voice was too calm. "We're going to find who did this, and they're going to pay."

"Like you found who killed my brother?" she yelled and regretted saying it almost before it came out.

His lips closed and his grip released. She didn't want it to. She wanted him to shake her or cuff her.

Instead, he pulled out his walkie. "This is Chief Osborne. I need an officer with a crime scene kit out to the Cavern Ave. beach access, and why the hell don't we have Humvees?" he barked to whoever was on the receiving end. "We are a police department on a damned frigging island."

He took out his phone and started taking pictures. Oliver stood next to him, apparently done with his ranting. "I arrived at oh five hundred, sir. No sign of the mother fuckers, but those tracks are not from the Turtle Watch four-wheeler as Raine just arrived."

"Are … they all gone?" Matt asked.

Oliver continued in his military register. "Won't know until the full evacuation is complete, but we have two visuals."

She didn't want to hear Oliver speak like this.

"I'm okay now," Raine said and stepped forward. "Chief, while I appreciate the sentiment—"

"No sentiment, Raine. We're going to find who did this. We're going to create a damned nighttime beach patrol." He was the calmest pissed off person she'd ever seen. "This is not going to happen again. Not on my watch."

Her family had been involved in Turtle Watch on Ibis Island for as long as she could remember. There had never been a nighttime beach patrol. A traitorous tear spilled over her lid. Ducking her head before she was caught, she took out her state-issued tablet and pulled up the data on the nest. She heard a new set of tires at the beach access. It was whatever officer had been called to come out with the crime scene thing.

He was right. It looked like two sets of knee prints. Each dug deep in the sand. A circle print the size of a five-gallon bucket marked the spot between the knee prints.

Who could do this? Why would anyone want to do this? Where were the eggs now? "Hatchlings that already have only a one in a thousand chance of surviving to adulthood."

"What did you say?" Matt asked.

Had she been thinking out loud? She shook her head. "Nothing."

"Officer Paul Cummings, this is Raine Clearwater and Oliver—" Matt paused for Oliver's last name.

"Lindenwood, sir."

"Raine is the PPH on this island, Primary Permit Holder. Oliver is a volunteer."

"Section Coordinator," Raine amended.

"I want you to get pictures of everything before Raine starts excavation of the nest. Bastards drove a four-wheeler on the beach and did this sometime between dusk and 5 a.m. When you're done taking pictures, get Oliver's statement, and then knock on these doors to see if we have any witnesses." He waved his arms inland as he gave orders.

She found the data on the nest as Matt's phone buzzed.

His eyes went right to her.

"It's Miriam. She's awake."

For a situation like this, Matt would have preferred someone he trusted like Officer Pence, or at least someone with a pulse like Officer Cummings. Since this was Pence's day off and Cummings was with Raine, the next in line was the code officer.

Officer Rodney Sheridan. He may be consistently angry and generally lazy, but Matt hadn't learned exactly what a code officer on an island did, and since his 10 a.m. meeting with Liam and Dane was postponed, maybe Matt could interrogate a suspect and question a code officer all in the same morning.

Sheridan stopped before he entered the room. He shoved his hands in his pockets and curled the corners of his lips. "What do you want me to do, Chief?"

Definite distain in the last word. "Follow my lead. Be my witness. I'll tell you if I want more."

Two nurses and a doctor stood around Miriam, replacing some equipment with others and asking a litany of questions. "Can you feel my pen?" The doc tapped each finger with the tip of it.

Matt had one chance at this. As he entered the room farther, he spotted Miriam's mother. Matt wondered why she would still be in the chair and not by her daughter's side, but that wasn't pertinent or any of his business. She stood when she noticed him and Officer Sheridan. This made her stand?

"I believe that can wait," Harriet said to Matt and stepped to the end of the bed. With the doctor at Miriam's side, the woman blocked Matt.

Stepping to Harriet, Matt said as gently as he could, "This is a murder investigation. Officer Sheridan, here, will escort you to the waiting room for a few moments."

Sheridan's eyes grew as big as saucers. "Do you think that's necess—"

"I'll call you when I'm ready," Matt interrupted.

"I'll be speaking to your supervisor." Harriet jerked her arm away from the hand Sheridan offered and marched out of the room with purpose.

As Matt stepped to the end of the bed, Miriam's eyes found him. She was lucid alright. If looks could kill.

The doctor waited for Miriam's mother to leave. "Good to see you, Chief. I'm at a stopping point. I can finish up after you're done."

"Thank you, Doctor."

Doc turned to Miriam. "I'll be back soon."

Standing at the end of the bed, Matt took out the notebook he kept in his back pocket. "Miriam Roberts, you are under arrest for attempted assault with a deadly weapon."

She closed her eyes.

"You have the right to remain silent. Anything you say can and will be used against you in a court of law. You have the right to an attorney. If you cannot afford an attorney, one will be appointed for you. Even with all of this," Matt said, waving an arm around the hospital room, "you're the lucky one."

She opened her eyes at that.

"Your accomplice is out there somewhere with a stab wound to his thigh minus proper medical assistance. You're here in the position to cut a deal."

She took a deep breath and closed her eyes once more.

"This is the only time I'm going to offer this, Miriam. You lied to me." He waited purposely for a few moments before continuing. "I don't like to be lied to, especially when someone's been murdered. Now, I don't know if you had honest feelings for Seth Clearwater, and at this point, I don't care. I want names, Miriam. Yes, I said names, plural. We know you have more than one accomplice in all of this."

Her eyes remained shut and so did her mouth.

"I used a warrant and searched your apartment. I found the original poem. Haiku, I think Seth Clearwater's family called it. The map is what I like to call it."

Tears fell freely, but the only words she offered were, "I want a lawyer."

Still in the Turtle Watch four-wheeler, Raine bumped over the hump at the end of her parent's drive. No extra cars. It was a relief as she hoped to speak with her mother alone. Her mother stopped picking whatever it was she gathered from her garden, looked up, and waved. Her smile was like a cup of late afternoon raspberry tea.

Leaning over, Raine took out the gloves she kept under the passenger seat for just this occasion.

"Peppers today, dear," her mother called. She waved toward the north side of the garden. "Reds and yellows are ready."

Raine spotted them. She used her shirt like a bowl and picked in silence. Her mother may be used to working in this heat, but most of Raine's Turtle Watch work was mornings. Twist and pull. The sun beat on the back of her neck. She gathered more than two dozen before her mother spoke.

"I might bring some of these to Dane and Zoe. Maybe the chief."

It's like she was reading Raine's mind, but Raine wasn't sure how to say it. Or if she should say anything.

Her mother let her not speak. "Let's wash these up."

Raine followed through the front door behind the long blond/gray ponytail.

"For money, your father and I used to sell the extras at the farmer's market there in the field next to the elementary school. I don't know why we still grow so much."

The object of the conversation sat in his recliner reading *Moby Dick* and drinking out of a Stay Wild, Moon Child mug. She loved this man.

"Hello, Dad," Raine said as she juggled the peppers.

He lifted his mug with one hand and turned the page with the other.

Her mother dumped the green peppers in the sink. "Wash your hands," she said like only a mother could. Raine complied.

"I heard about the stolen eggs," her mother offered.

Raine knew better than to ask how she knew about that.

"They took half the nest," Raine croaked.

As her mother rinsed, Raine sat at the small kitchen table in one of the mismatched chairs. She looked around this place she still called home. White painted cabinets with glass doors displayed neat stacks of dishes and coffee mugs. A few dozen miniature toy animals lined the windowsill. "Matt says he's going to start a nighttime beach patrol."

"Hmm." Her mother finished rinsing the peppers, then filled the teapot.

"Why would he say that?" Raine asked. "He's only interim chief of police on the island. He can't say that."

Raine looked over the many photos covering the walls in frames, each a different color and style. She took a deep breath. "He does get out of the police station. That's something Roberts never did."

Her mother chose two mugs, one was in the shape of a pig and the other read *Ibis Island* on it. She took out two tea bags from a manatee canister on the counter and sat at the table with Raine.

"I guess," Raine continued. "He came out when the awning fell on Willow at the restaurant." Even though it was empty, she chose the Ibis Island mug and cradled it between the palms of her hands. "He also came to the hospital to tell us the roof awning had been rigged. I just don't get it. He bags sand." Now that she'd started, she couldn't stop. She stood and began pacing, mug still in hand. "He answers calls late at night about someone or something bobbing in the ocean. Himself." She stopped to say with emphasis, "Not a deputy. I heard he got frigging Owen Branch to pay the Yancys for the shit he breaks."

"Language." Now, her mother speaks?

"I even saw him directing traffic." She turned to face her mother fully now. "What the hell is that? Is he just trying to get the board to vote him in as chief permanently? Is the promise of nighttime patrols a ruse? Should I offer to help with how to do that? What if it's not true?"

The teapot screamed. Raine looked around, her chest heaving in and out. Ducking her head, she slipped back into the mismatched chair.

Her mother rose to get the water. "It's okay, dear. This is new for you."

Raine nodded. "A cop who actually does stuff."

"Crushing on a boy," her mother corrected, pouring hot water in the mugs.

TWELVE

What? Eww. No. Raine tried to spout a retort, something clever and sarcastic, but when she opened her mouth, nothing came out.

"Hello, Henry." It was a male voice. Dane. Followed by the slamming front screen door.

"Please be alone. Please be alone," Raine chanted under her breath. It was not like she wasn't happy for Dane and her baby sister. She was. Very much. But, they were newlyweds, and the PDA had been bad enough when they were dating.

"Hi, Daddy," Zoe said. "What are you reading?"

Her mother dipped tea bags in the hot water. "Hello, Dane. So good of you to stop by. Raine, dear. Get two more mugs and tea bags out."

"Hello, Dane," Raine said through her teeth. "So good to see you. Would you like some tea?"

Tilting his chin away from her slightly, Dane kept his gaze on Raine as he skirted around the perimeter of the kitchen. "Great, Raine. What's the matter with—?"

"Hi, Mom." Zoe walked in before he had a chance to finish. She inhaled deeply. "Mmm. What's that smell?"

Dane walked over to Zoe and kissed her long and hard.

"Oh," Zoe said and smiled wide. "It's you." She kissed him again.

"Oh my gosh," Raine moaned and threw back her head. "Isn't that supposed to stop after you're married? Mom and Dad don't do that."

"Yes, we do, dear," her mother said, refilling the tea pot.

Raine covered her ears. She stopped by for this?

"Newlyweds tend to have frequent intercourse," her mother continued. "It's like a celebration of legal sex."

"Sex before marriage isn't illegal," Raine argued with her, hands still over her ears.

Her mother sighed. "Just remember, however, that hard to get is a good thing."

Raine darted her eyes between Dane and Zoe.

Zoe looked to her mother, then Raine and back to her mother again. "Does Raine have a boyfriend?"

"No," Raine said too loud. "Not legal, illegal or anything in between."

"Why invest in the cow," her mother added as if Zoe and Raine weren't talking, "if you can get the milk for free?"

Raine lifted her arm and checked a pretend watch on her hand. "Look at the time!" She spun on her heels and headed through the front door.

Sliding into the four-wheeler, she paused as the keys reached the ignition. Of course, she was okay with the chief. Anyone would be better than Chief Roberts. Turning the ignition, she looked over her shoulder to back out but stopped before she pulled out onto the street. It wasn't as if she liked him, liked him.

Her eyes opened wide. Forcing them shut, she covered her mouth with both hands and yelled, "No!" into her fingers.

––––––––––

It took nearly fifteen minutes to get from the grass in the back of Matt's apartment to the top of the stairs. For the tenth time, Bella pulled on the leash. Matt halted his feet and waited for her to stop. She looked up at him and tilted her head.

"Don't look at me like that. You're the one pulling. The Dog Whisperer site says I'm supposed to stop when you do that." He was talking to a dog. There was no breeze that morning, the sun was up, and he was talking to a dog.

Normally a patient man, he checked his watch also for about the tenth time. It took three more stops before they made it to the door.

She galloped to her water bowl, rattling the pictures on the walls as she passed. After drinking possibly her weight in water, she collapsed on the kitchen tile as if she'd just ran a marathon in the desert.

"Oh, no you don't. I have a job, and you need to go back to bed."

She was like a wet noodle. He tugged on the massive collar that cost him about as much as the Cubans. With a heavy sigh, Matt headed for the top cupboard where he kept the bones.

Keeping her head on the tile, she lifted her brows to get a view of him from under the sagging lids. As he chose one of the Saint Bernard-sized bones, she seemed to find a second wind and scrambled to her feet.

Wagging her entire body, he rubbed her cheek with his free hand. She pressed into his palm and closed her eyes.

"Bella," he said clearly like the website told him to. "Time to get in your crate." It didn't mention what to do if one was relatively certain the dog didn't know her name. He tossed the bone toward the back.

Losing all interest in him, she scrambled into her crate and stuffed the bone in her mouth.

"Don't get too comfortable, girl. Our landlord agreed to allow a temporary stay. This is a small-dogs-only place. You are the opposite of small."

On his way out, he grabbed the lint roller and used it on his pants as he jogged down the stairs. Driving two blocks would be cause for ridicule in most places. Since walking the two blocks from his apartment to the station would end with him covered in sweat, he drove. Most of the guys wore police issue shorts. Matt couldn't bring himself to do it.

He stopped for one of the dozens of weekly rented golf carts before pulling out of his lot. Two small boys rode in the far back. Choose his battles. Choose his battles.

Six men dove with Seth Clearwater the day he was murdered. Five were still alive. At least one of them had to know something. Someone was lying. Matt was going to find out who.

Without anything on his calendar for the next hour, he passed the station and headed to the Ibis Island Museum.

The lot to the museum was in desperate need of gravel fill. Matt's SUV rocked as it splashed in deep depressions filled with water from yesterday afternoon's rain. Like many of the island structures, this one was made of concrete brick covered in stucco. It might have been white at one time, or maybe Oberweiss purposely painted it a light gray.

As Matt entered through the heavy wooden front door, the cow bell above rang. Jan Oberweiss came from a room behind reception.

She wore those short teacher-like pants called something he couldn't remember, sandals, a light blue V-neck t-shirt, and small hoop earrings.

"Good morning, Mrs. Oberweiss. How does this day find you?"

"Call me Jan, please. How could we be better?" She held her arms out wide. "We're living on this beautiful island."

It was a common island answer, and he had to agree. "It most certainly is. I'm looking for Glen. Is he here?"

Her smile was warm and simple. "I'll get him. Be right back."

A rack with pamphlets advertising local parasailing and boat tours, strip malls, and the ferry taxi that took customers to and from the island south of Ibis. It was pushed against the wall behind him. He strolled to the first room that displayed island history. Large ancient pictures of settlers and black and white photos of the beginnings of island structures hung above cases of artifacts. No displays of priceless sunken treasure. As if he could be that lucky.

"There you are, Chief." Oberweiss came in out of breath. Had he been outside?

Matt held out a hand. "Good morning, Glen. Thank you for seeing me."

"Anytime." Oberweiss pointed to the case in front of them. "Island swimwear from the early 1900s."

They looked more like frilly t-shirts and long shorts. "This is some place you have here, Glen. How long have you been the manager?"

"Since the beginning of time," Oberweiss said with a smile.

Matt didn't press him on it. That wasn't what he was here for. "You live frugally."

Dipping his head, Oberweiss nodded. "We've been through this, Chief. Jan and I are both paid by the state. We have to. No need to rub it in."

Matt leaned his backside on the display case. "I have a feeling you would be much the same if you owned Show Me's or Beckett Realty."

Oberweiss stiffened. It wasn't slight. He scowled but quickly recovered. "Please don't lean on that," he said and pointed to the display case. "I might indulge a bit more, yes, but nothing like Blake or Richard. Don't group me in with those two. Not for money. What can I do for you?"

Fair enough. "I always learn something new when I come in here." That wasn't a lie.

"But, you didn't need to ask for me to help you look around."

Caught. "Do you own a boat, Glen?"

"All long-time islanders do, yes."

Matt repeated what Oberweiss had said. "Since the beginning of time," he said again and walked to the next room. Here were mostly sea turtle displays and information about conservation and Turtle Watch. The ancient wooden floor squeaked behind him as Oberweiss followed. "I keep wondering why a boat owner would rent a boat from Big Joe the day before a tropical storm." And, why you are such a glaring anomaly in the group. He turned to judge Oberweiss' expression along with his answer for the question that was actually audible.

"Ah," Oberweiss said. "I'm a historical artifact enthusiast." He held his arms out much like his wife had done. After a distinct pause, he added as if thinking out loud, "I assume you've spoken with Mayor Green as well." Oberweiss looked him in the eye now. "Like many, the thought of Luciana Bezan's treasure is like a drug. We didn't know Miriam and the others would hurt anyone over it."

"Others plural?"

"Sir, I respect that you're a city guy, but you might have much to learn about diving. Someone had to man their boat while they were down there assaulting those kids."

"Did you see the boat?"

Oberweiss shook his head. "Visibility was very low."

"But, you saw the Coast Guard?"

"Of course. Red and blue swirling lights are hard to miss."

Matt didn't miss the fact that Oberweiss had, now, leaned his butt against the sea turtle display case.

Oberweiss scratched his chin. "Chief, I want to find who killed Seth as much as you do. Probably more so. He was my friend. We shared a bond of both the love of diving and of the hunt for a piece of history."

"And you're both minimalists," Matt added.

Oberweiss' chest expanded and released. "Yes." His mouth opened again, then closed. Oberweiss turned away from him and glanced up toward a poster on the wall that read, "Turtles Dig the Dark."

Oberweiss had given Matt more that the rest of them put together. Matt wouldn't press him any further. For now.

THIRTEEN

Thick patches of six-foot tall grasses created tall dunes at the northwest end of the island. They helped prevent beach erosion. And, sometimes entangled sea turtle hatchlings on their way to the Gulf.

This portion of the Ibis Island beaches was extensive and the access paths lengthy. Raine spotted the two women long before she reached them. They stood halfway between the access entrance and the Gulf.

As their eyes met, the two of them waved like shipwrecked sailors who spotted their rescuer. In return, Raine lifted an arm and hiked her cinch sack up on her shoulders and juggled the bucket she brought with her.

One of them yelled as Raine reached earshot. "Are you Mrs. Clearwater?"

Mrs.? Not nearly. Regardless, she nodded.

"We knew not to touch them," one said like she'd just earned a badge.

"I appreciate that," Raine said as she approached the spot.

"My name is Emily and this is my sister, Amelia." Each wore swimsuits under cover-ups. Loaded beach bags rested next to them.

They shook hands as Raine scanned the sea grasses.

"This guy was walking by, pointing and staring. We offered to be the ones to wait for you. They are right through there," said Amelia. "There are two of them. We looked around for others but kept away from the sea grasses. Those are protected."

Raine smiled. "Good work," she said and, as expected, the sisters smiled from ear to ear.

The hatchlings were lethargic. They must have been stuck for a while. Raine placed them in the bucket, then did a search for any others.

Visuals of yesterday morning's headless hatchlings, of the stolen nest of eggs, kept flashing through her mind. Her stomach churned as she attempted to assess which nest these two could have come from. A morning rain at this end of the island covered any newly emerged turtle tracks.

As she woke her tablet to check data for nearby nests, the one named Emily chattered.

"We've always wanted to meet you, Mrs. Clearwater. We've heard so much about you." Emily's arms flailed through the air with every syllable. "If only our kids could be here for this."

Picking up the bucket, Raine held it out to her. "Holding the hatchlings without certification is illegal, but not the bucket. How about I get a picture?"

Amelia squealed and dug out her cell. She tilted the bucket toward the cell phone, and Raine took the picture. Pulling out the coloring books she carried in her cinch sack, Raine asked, "How many kids?"

"Oh! They will love this! We have three between us."

As Raine handed over the souvenirs, she said, "I should get these two to bed."

"Where will they be released?"

"Not sure yet. These are the only two so far today." Taking a deep breath, she sighed. Public hatchling releases were almost guaranteed to be disastrous. No one listened. They were all too mesmerized with the turtles to follow directions. Stand back, no flashlights, don't touch them. "How about you watch our social media page? I'll post a location when I know one."

Two grown women. Cheering.

"We'll bring the kids. Oh! This is the best day ever."

That was because they didn't find a nest of stolen sea turtle eggs that morning. Raine smiled and said her goodbyes.

Two quick, then one slow buzz. A text. She read it as she put the bucket with the turtles on the floor of the passenger side of her truck.

guard station six

family way too close to a nest

She pulled out onto Beech Street. She would drop off the hatchlings in Mary Jane's garage on her way. How many PPH's had a Mary Jane's garage? The shower stall in the garage stayed warm enough to put the hatchlings back to sleep, but not so warm they might overheat.

Her phone buzzed. Again. This time, Caller ID said Matt.

Goose bumps erupted on her arms. She dropped her phone and had to pull over to dig it out of beneath her seat. This was several levels of wrong.

As she retrieved it, she turned it over. Missed call. It was for the better. Pulling back onto the road, she concocted a bait plan in her head. She would need Dane, of course. Raine wasn't too proud to realize that was his thing.

Glancing down at her phone, she rolled her eyes and dialed the chief, then put it on speaker.

"Raine," he said as he answered. "I was just trying to get a hold of you."

"Oh?" Raine said and tapped her thumb on the steering wheel.

"Can we meet to discuss a nighttime beach patrol?"

Her face grew warm. She could feel the heat as it moved up her neck. No, no, no.

"Hello?"

"I'm here. When? I'll check my calendar." I'll check my calendar? She ran her free hand over her face. "I mean, what day?"

"Ten a.m.?"

She sighed. "10 a.m. as in today?"

"Yes, ma'am. Dane and Liam are coming in to kick around your idea about bait. I thought we could take out two birds with one stone."

"That's in an hour."

"Yes, ma'am."

Her left eye twitched. "Fine. If I don't have anything else come up, fine."

Pulling into the City Hall lot, Matt noticed the old chief of police parking space still sat empty. He passed it and parked five spots down.

As he turned off his vehicle, he looked out his windshield at the sky. It was the most brilliant blue he'd ever seen. And, one he got to see each morning when he pulled into work. The short, afternoon rain would hide it later on.

Good thing his bag of donuts was sealed. The breeze created from opening his door caused Bella hair to swirl like a small tornado. He guessed three more days before she was adopted. He could do three more days.

The City Hall receptionist sat behind her desk filing her nails. He walked straight toward her rather than heading for the hallway that led back to PD. "Good morning, Glory."

She looked up and tilted her head. "You already said that to me today, Chief."

She wasn't wrong. He stopped and crossed his arms. "When you come back after lunch, I want you to park in the old chief of police spot."

Her eyes grew wide, and she dropped the file. She opened her mouth enough for him to see her gum. It was blue.

He smiled. "That's an order, Miss Studebaker."

A series of mumblings trailed behind him as he headed for his office. The scent of burnt coffee and stale donuts blew through him. He wouldn't trade it for anything. Glancing down at his bag of fresh CJ's long johns, he felt a quick twinge of guilt that they weren't for the staff.

He liked that there were no cubicles in the PD common area. Metal desks faced each other in twos. At a corner desk, Officer Sheridan sat pecking away at his keyboard. Matt's brows lowered.

"Officer Sheridan," he said as he passed him. "As soon as you get to a stopping point, I'd like to see you in my office."

"Yes, sir," Sheridan answered without looking up from his screen.

Matt passed the conference room. The schedule was listed on a piece of copy paper. As it always did, it included a single event. The second Wednesday of the month Board Meeting. That would be tomorrow.

That might be pushing his plan, but he didn't know how much time he had left as interim chief and decided he'd better get done what he could.

The notes on his desk included a complaint from a resident about repeated late night noise from the rental next door, a threat from another who heard Matt was considering banning golf carts from city roads, and a thank you from a local for busting Owen Branch.

He worked some on his presentation to the board, then checked his watch. Nine forty-five. No Sheridan.

The intercom interrupted his frustration. He lifted the receiver and pressed the flashing button. "Chief."

"Your ten o'clock is here," Glory said as she chewed her gum. "Or should I say ten o'clocks plural?"

They were early. It didn't seem as if Officer Sheridan was planning on showing up anyway. "Thank you, Glory. Send them back and Raine Clearwater when she arrives."

Dane wore his Sun Trips shirt, but Liam was in jeans, a buttoned-down shirt and a tie.

"Oh, boy," Matt said in place of a greeting. "Liam, I seem to have forgotten that you are no longer putting in summer hours."

"This is important. I got a sub."

Matt nodded and turned. "Let's go to the conference room. There is more space in there." He held his arm out for the two of them to lead the way.

They complied, but Dane asked, "You invited Raine?"

"I did, indeed."

"Well, that's a relief," Dane said as he made his way through to the conference room door. "I may have mentioned something to Zoe, who may have mentioned something to her parents."

Liam stopped his feet and looked from Dane to Matt.

"You, too?" Dane asked.

Liam shrugged and sat.

Matt said, "Good thing I bought extra donuts." He opened the bag and set it on the table. "Let me just tell Glory."

When he returned, Matt sat, leaving the seat at the head of the table empty. "How's business?"

"You said you needed a treasure hunter to bounce ideas off of."

Liam leaned toward Dane. "He told me he needed a local." He pointed to himself.

"Raine had an idea. It might be a good one. I think we should wait until she gets here," Matt said. "How's business?" he repeated.

"This cornerstone that is Home thing has the island packed with tourists and Sun Trips packed with customers." Dane leaned on the two back legs of his chair. "Heard you want to ban golf carts."

Why was that such a big deal? "From the public streets, yes. They're dangerous."

"Good luck with that," Liam said.

It was like a parade. Glory led the way, scooting in her impossibly tight mini-skirt and even more impossibly high heels. Following her was the Clearwater family. In order. Henry, Harmony, Raine, Willow, then Zoe. No one chose the head of the table.

Liam leaned over to Willow, kissed her on the mouth, and whispered, "Where's the shrimp?"

As everyone looked at her, she dipped her head and said, "Paula."

Matt let out a heavy sigh. "Here I was hoping to keep this on the down low."

"We are Clearwaters," Zoe said. "We know all about secrecy."

"Raine?" he called. She nodded but didn't look at him. "Would you share your idea with—" He shook his head and looked around. "—everyone?"

FOURTEEN

Raine sank lower in her chair. "I got thinking about what Dane keeps saying over and over again." The last part may have come out too slow.

"Hey," Dane interrupted.

She shrugged. "It makes sense. Look at what's happened to the island."

"What makes sense?" Dane asked.

"Treasure being a drug. Whoever murdered Seth also had Chief Roberts killed while in jail awaiting trial. He or she rigged the beam that fell on Willow. If he's mesmerized with treasure, or whatever, maybe we can set a trap. Bait."

Dane nodded. "That might just work."

Willow leaned forward. "Like fake treasure?"

Raine shrugged. "That's Dane's department. It was just an idea."

Dane got up and walked to the end of the table.

Harmony lifted a pointed finger. "According to Dane, everyone who is looking for the rest of the treasure is crazed. Bait would attract all of them not just Seth's..." She took a deep breath and finished. "Killer."

"Not all of them are watching us." Dane pointed his finger around the table. "If we kept it on one of our properties..." He paced the back of the small room, then turned and placed both hands on the table, palms down. "Sun Trips is near the top of the island. If we set up a perimeter, not a big flashy one, but a perimeter on the north side, brought some heavy equipment, Seth's killer might come sniffing around."

Two short, then one long buzz. Raine read the text under the table. It was the sixth one in the hour they'd been scheming the bait plan. The plan she regretted mentioning.

"We could covertly close Sun Trips," Zoe offered. "The murd—" she started to say, then corrected herself. "The one who killed Seth might be even more curious."

The last text was from Mary Jane.

thirty-five hatchlings for release tonight
seven more dropped off this morning

The previous record for a single day was fifteen. She responded with a thumbs up emoji, then looked to the group.

They all stared at her. "Yes," she said, hoping that fit with why they were staring.

Matt stood. He pointed to each Clearwater as he gave directions. "Zoe, you get going on closing Sun Trips starting Monday. Dane and Liam, you do whatever you need to do to make the north side of your business look like you're hiding something. Henry and Harmony, you'll take over some of the more public Turtle Watch duties—"

"Hey!" Raine interrupted. "I never—"

"Yes, you did, dear," her mother said matter-of-factly. "Letting go will be good for you."

Raine put her elbow on the table and her face in her palm.

"Willow and Raine, you'll help me with anything suspicious. You'll spot it easier than I will."

Willow lit up like a light bulb. "You mean like a stakeout?"

"Don't you have cops for all of this?" Raine barked.

Matt nodded much too patiently. "If that's what you want, but we will look suspicious. You won't."

Damn. That made sense. One by one, they shook hands with him like a receiving line. She was not going to be any part of that and dug her hands in her pockets.

She and her mother were the last to leave. As Raine came to the door, Matt put his arm across the opening. "Can you stay a while longer?"

She looked behind her to see if he was talking to her mother.

Until he added, "Or, do you have to get to one of the text messages you've been taking care of?"

No words would come, so she shook her head.

He pulled his chin out. "No you can't meet, or no you don't have to go take care of one of the text messages?"

The red. It was coming. Please, no. "The second one." She forced herself to look at him. Her eyes went right to his lips. She squinted and turned, then pretended to have something in her eye.

Her mother leaned in and kissed her on the cheek. "Cows and milk, honey," she whispered in her ear.

This was not happening.

Her mother passed, leaving her alone with him. Her stomach growled. Minus the squinting, she kept her eyes closed. It was easier that way.

"Let's make this fast so you can get to lunch."

Yep.

"I know we haven't hashed out night patrols. I assume there are turtle things to consider, but there is a board meeting tomorrow night. I don't know how much longer I will be interim chief of police, and I want to do what I can before I'm gone. I am going to present some purchase requests. I'd like to include what we need for night patrols. Would you come to the meeting?"

Sometime between kicking her out for lunch and asking her to attend the meeting, her eyes had opened. He was for real. The light brown eyes that were smart and creative. The short haircut that was always trimmed and tight. And the scent. What was that scent?

"Raine?"

What had he asked? "Shit."

"Shit?"

95

She looked at the wall behind him. "What are you considering?"

"Two Humvees, a half-dozen night vision goggles, and one more hire to rotate the graveyard shift."

It made her smile. "Humvees? Whoa, cowboy. How about four-wheelers? Night vision goggles aren't necessary either. Sight over the light-colored sand is surprisingly clear."

He nodded, pulled out his notebook, and wrote. As he wrote, he said, "Humvees scratch. Four-wheelers." He looked up at her. "The night vision goggles stay. You will be amazed."

She shrugged and looked at the wall on the other side of him.

He continued. "I'm going to train four of my guys, plus one I'll hopefully be approved to hire. They will need instruction on what to do and not to do regarding the sea turtles. Can you provide me the information to share with the new night guys?"

"I train entire police departments." It sounded pompous, but hell. It was her job.

"There she is." He smiled.

The ice princess thing. Why wasn't that funny anymore? She stood now and looked him in the eye. "I'll be at your board meeting, and I'll train your guys. If the new hire goes south, you could have the code enforcement officer do it since he doesn't enforce any codes anyway. You tell me when you're ready, and I'll give you some times I have available. I'll need one entire morning and one two-hour evening session."

He faced her completely. The beautiful light-brown eyes were nearly eclipsed by his brows.

"What?" he said at the same time she did.

She lifted her brows. "You first."

"What do you mean, 'doesn't enforce codes?'" He said that last part slow.

Heat started again, only this kind was straight up mad. "I mean all Code Enforcement Officer Sheridan does is smile and make nice."

His expression was unreadable other than he was not happy. He dropped back into his chair.

"What codes are we talking about?"

"What codes?" Her voice grew louder. "Parking lot, street, business, and residence lights that are not turtle friendly. Beach front residents with lights on after dark. Rentals without the proper notification about lights off after dusk. The size of wedding tents, number of people, flooring used and loud music. Trash pick-up, putting away or stacking beach furniture at night—"

Matt held up both hands, palms out. "Okay, okay. What makes you think Officer Sheridan isn't doing his job?"

"I call them, email them, then turn them over to Sheridan. He fines them. They complain and don't pay the fine or change their violation. He smiles and makes nice. Rinse. And. Repeat."

"How serious are we talking?"

Her eyes grew wide. "Even if the lights aren't beach front, if they shine in eyeshot of the beach, hatchlings and even full-grown turtles will mistake it for the horizon and follow. The hatchlings get lost, use precious energy and most of the time get killed by a predator or car or, or, or raccoon! Only one out of every thousand sea turtles makes it to adulthood. Light should point away from the beach, be shielded, and be amber in color."

She looked at her phone. It was off. "Oh, look. I'm needed on the beach."

He grabbed her upper arm. "I want a list."

"A what? Let go of my arm."

He let go, but stepped so close, she could smell that damned sexy scent. "A list of who's violated codes."

Her knees. They were growing weaker by the second. She couldn't utter even a single syllable.

"You bring the paperwork," he growled. "I'll bring the gun."

Matt would deal with Sheridan. He would give him a chance to explain himself, then he would deal with him. He had a plan.

This, however. Hunting down property owners for code infractions on an island in Florida? How many times since he arrived on

Ibis did he find himself dumbfounded? He waited in the micro-
scopic driveway for the ice princess.

Raine told him the paperwork would be easy to find. It had
been fifteen minutes. He supposed easy to find was relative. It was a
good thing his tank was full, because he was not about to turn off
the air or roll down the windows.

They would need to make a stop at his apartment and let out
the beast. The thought reminded him to check his email for any
interest from the animal shelter about an adoption.

A miniature lizard leapt on his windshield. Matt jumped and
almost dropped his phone. A quick glance from side to side said he
saved losing man points as no one was around to see. The thing did
miniature lizard pushups in front of Matt's eyes as its neck blew up
and deflated over and over again.

No emails from the shelter. He would call before closing time if
he didn't hear anything by that afternoon.

A group of giant pelicans flew in V formation high above. He
had museums to inquire with regarding treasure they might have
acquired two years ago that matched what the Clearwaters discovered in the Gulf. He had a board presentation to practice and a
code officer to put in his place.

Deciding to check and make sure she didn't fall and break her
neck, he opened his door. Just as his foot touched the seashell drive,
she appeared. In her arms was a manila file folder packed with
papers. A lot of papers.

"Where were you headed?" she asked as she walked around to
his passenger door.

He didn't answer and stared at the file folder.

Looking over at him, she must have read his expression, because
she looked down at the file and said, "Don't get your panties in a
bunch. We're just talking to the heavy hitters."

"How many heavy hitters?"

"Two. Take Beech Street north."

He shifted into reverse and looked both ways. "Let me guess,"
he said, pulling onto the road. "Eaton and Beckett."

"I don't know what you plan to do different from Officer Sheridan."

"First we'll talk nice, then we'll slap people around." Even though she stared out the window, he could tell from the side of her face that she didn't laugh, or even smile at his joke.

"Can I try out my board proposal on you?"

She inhaled and exhaled. "Sure." She kept her gaze out the window.

The muscles in his face fell. He didn't want to anymore after she said it like that.

"Show Me's first?" he asked.

She nodded. "This is the time of day he's there. He usually leaves before the lunchtime crowd gets there."

A family of five, each riding a rental bike, rode on the sidewalk next to a construction site. Each basket was full of supplies for a day at the beach. Concrete for three separate in-ground pools was poured behind the new multi-rental construction. Although he was glad the board declared long before Matt's time that structures over three stories were off limits, he wondered what it was like before builders like Beckett bought up so many spots for rent.

"That's one of Beckett's," Raine said. "It used to be a tiny cottage on a large lot. Large for Ibis, anyway. A widower lived there forever and a day."

It was as if she read his mind. "Tell me about Eaton's code infractions."

She nodded and opened her folder. "His are just for Show Me's. His lights are responsible for over a dozen nest disorientations."

His expression of confusion must have been evident.

"Remember that a disorientation is a term used to describe when a sea turtle or turtles become confused, mostly due to artificial lighting, and head away from the water rather than to it. It can happen to adult turtles and hatchlings."

Tilting her head only slightly, she glanced over at him, then turned red. He didn't know ice princesses could blush.

FIFTEEN

"I guess that's more than you wanted to know. Show Me's lights are not turtle friendly. They cause disorientations. Eaton thinks hatchlings are good for business, even changed the lights to amber only to change them back again."

"Amber?" he asked as he turned into the Show Me's lot. A boy he remembered named Wendell Hopp worked valet.

"Morning, Chief. We're not open just yet, but I can park your vehicle for you in our remote lot."

"Hello there, Wendell. That won't be necessary." He pulled away and double parked by the front door. Keeping the car running, he turned to her. "Amber?" he asked again.

Her lungs expanded and released. "Light created from the horizon has a shorter light wavelength. It is a blue green. White lights have blue green in them. Amber lights do not. He's had this many tickets." She picked up nearly half the stack of papers. "He ignores them."

"Not anymore," he said under his breath.

"Umm. Sir," Wendell called from the entrance to the lot, "there's no park—"

Matt had already turned off his vehicle and was halfway out.

Raine wouldn't look at him. He wouldn't push it. "Ready?"

Nodding, she let herself out.

The foyer was more of a small gift shop filled with polos and t-shirts that read, "Show Me's," mixed in with floral gowns and linen shirts.

The hostess's nametag read, "Lisa."

"Chief Osborne," she said with glee and then turned to Raine. "Hello, Raine. I like your hair today."

"Thanks?" Raine said as a question. "Boss here?"

Glancing over her shoulder toward the back of the bar section, poor Lisa's entire posture sank. "He doesn't like to be bothered when his office door is closed."

"It's the chief of police," Raine assured her. "No one can blame you."

The regular bouncer was a man named Eli. Eli was more like a house. It was too early for him to be working. That was a shame. Matt really liked Eli.

Nodding, Lisa led them through the dark bar area. Overly padded bench booths circled three sides of the perimeter with a long bar the fourth. The bar back and the entire ceiling were covered with smoky mirrors. It smelled like someone lit too many floral candles.

Lisa walked to the door in the back. She knocked as she opened it. "Mr. Eaton, Chief Osborne is—"

"Blake. Long time," Matt said sarcastically.

Eaton sat behind a giant mahogany desk. His eyes darted between the three of them. Poor Lisa.

"I wasn't—" Lisa started to say before Eaton held up a hand to her.

"Have a seat, Chief."

Matt did not sit. "This won't take long. I'm here to deliver a few citations." Purposely, he looked to Raine's folder. "It looks like quite a few."

He would be lying if he said it didn't give him pleasure to see Blake Eaton speechless and turning several shades of red.

"Raine?" Matt said.

In slow motion, she handed them over.

Transferring them from Raine's hand to the middle of Eaton's desk, Matt said, "These here are overdue, Blake. I'm sorry that you previously had a chief who didn't enforce island code and assure you that I'll fix that."

Eaton stood but stayed behind his desk and jabbed a finger in the air. "If you think you're going to walk onto this island and expect me to suddenly respond to any of these useless codes or pointless threats, you have a lot to learn about Ibis Island and about me."

Ignoring Eaton's rambling, Matt said, "I'm not versed on island code. That's why I have Miss Clearwater here with me." Raine Clearwater who was uncharacteristically quiet. "You'll find I'm very careful to follow laws. Unfortunately, if these fines are not paid and codes adhered to, I will be forced to not only put a lien on your place of business, but notify the Ibis Island Sun Times that Blake Eaton, owner of Show Me's original and soon-to-be-built restaurant and bar may be responsible for the loss of a Florida State Wildlife Conservation Commission multimillion dollar beach renourishment project for Ibis Island."

"You. Who do you—?" Blake's cheeks kept puffing in and out like the lizard's neck from Matt's windshield. "We'll see about this."

"Ten days, Blake. We'll be back."

Raine's eyes were as big as saucers. Stiff as could be, she turned and followed Matt's lead as he gestured for her to lead the way out the door.

He passed poor Lisa who had to turn her head to keep from smiling.

Matt felt like he had gotten to know Dane, Liam, and the Clearwaters. Even Raine. But, this was confusing. She walked in small, insecure steps all the way to his SUV.

"You okay?" he asked her as they climbed into his black and white.

She nodded quickly, which solidified his confusion.

"I just don't have any other copies, that's all. I didn't know … I … I just didn't know that was what we were going to do."

Giving Wendell a two-finger salute, Matt pulled out onto the road. "To tell you the truth, I didn't either."

"You remembered about beach nourishment?"

He winked at her. "I surprised myself with that one."

"You know, the Wildlife Conservation Commission isn't going to do anything about any local code violations."

"Blake Eaton doesn't know that. Let's give him his ten days and see what happens. Where to next?"

"Richard Beckett."

"Ah. Save the best for last."

"His office is the other direction."

"Yes, but my apartment is this direction, and someone I know mentioned buckets of Saint Bernard-sized urine. It's not a visual I'm willing to risk."

Her phone buzzed again. Raine kept forwarding the calls to her sisters. She'd worked for years trying to beg, bully, and threaten Eaton into installing turtle-friendly lights. His place was located on the west side of the island. It was a populous spot for sunset watching, for dining, for dancing, and for disorientations.

Could this work? Bella came through the door before Matt. The leash was taut and Matt had to jog to keep up.

Bella peed a bucket, all right. It took a full five minutes for Matt to walk her the short way back to the door of his apartment building.

He stopped each time Bella pulled. She paused and looked up at him as if she was asking what the hell he was doing.

What would the inside of the chief's place look like? Was it organized and decorated like his office? She shrugged and opened her file. The rest of the code violation copies she'd brought with her were for Richard Beckett. She could think a lot more clearly with the chief out there and her in the SUV.

Show Me's may have the most disorientations, but Beckett had, by far, the most code violations. He wore them like a badge.

Matt jogged out of his door, rolling his pants with a lint roller as he went.

"Hey," she said as he opened his door. "What have you heard from the shelter?"

He shook his head and started the vehicle. "I haven't."

She couldn't help it. She started to laugh. It got louder and louder until she was more like a junior high school girl than anything else. "She is so yours."

"What are you talking about?"

"They aren't looking for anyone else to adopt her." She clutched her stomach. "They have you."

"What? No. I told them I can't keep her."

"Uh huh."

"I told them I was only going to serve as a foster."

"Uh huh."

"I told—" He rubbed a hand over the back of his neck. "I'll call this afternoon."

Beckett Realty and Construction was located in a small strip mall next to the local bank. The modesty of the store front didn't fool anyone.

The oldest of Beckett's daughters sat behind the reception desk. Lou Beckett's hair was purple today. One never knew.

Lifting her eyes, Lou peered through the longest fake lashes Raine had ever seen. Through a heavy sigh, she spoke. "What can we do for you, Raine? Oh, hello, Chief Osborne."

Raine felt a hand rest in the middle of her back. Waves of heat built from her toes all the way to the top of her head. It was like everything went black. This was becoming a problem, one she needed to fix.

"Excuse me, Raine." Matt stepped in front of her and then released his hand. "We're here to see your father, Lou."

"Do you have an appointment?" Lou answered. Raine wasn't sure if she had something in her eye or if Lou was batting her fake lashes at him.

She had some nerve. Raine stepped in front of the chief. "Is he here or not, Lou?"

Matt set his hand on her back again. Oh, boy. "I believe he is, Miss Clearwater." He led her toward the back. "We'll find our way, Miss Beckett. Thank you for your help."

Except, she wasn't helpful. Fortunately, he left his hand there and knocked on Beckett's door with the other. Clutching the file folder with both hands, she gave herself a small pep talk.

Beckett wore his signature linen shirt. His sunglasses still rested on his head. For most, it meant someone was on their way in or out. For Beckett, it was just where he kept his sunglasses.

"Good day, Richard," the chief said as he entered the open door. "What a lovely day we have going on out there."

Beckett looked up, then to Raine and Matt and stood. "Didn't you just have me come to the police station to answer questions?"

Matt nodded. "Yes, indeed, but this has nothing to do with that."

She wasn't entirely sure why, but the way he dipped his head raised red flags. She didn't even care that his hand was gone.

"We're here," she interrupted, finding her nerve, "because you're going to fix your code violations. The chief, here, may care about the fines. That's on him. I just care about code."

Beckett looked between her and Matt.

"You have ten days to pay your fines and thirty to fix your violations." She slammed the file on his desk. "Or else we're putting liens on your rentals." As long as she was taking dialogue from the chief, she added, "Or would you rather be the real estate broker who trashed the prospect of beach restoration for the island because of your code violations?"

Both of them stared at her with their brows lifted high. Damn straight.

"Chief," Beckett said as if Raine wasn't standing there. "The turtles have been using this island to lay their eggs long before humans settled here. Lights or no lights, beach furniture or no beach furniture, they survive just fine."

She could feel the heat begin at her neck and cover her face. This time wasn't anything about a useless crush she had on the new guy.

Stepping between them, she started, "You listen here."

The hand was back. This time she reached behind and swatted it away. "Your neglect is directly responsible for the deaths of countless highly endangered animal species!"

Beckett curled his lips, turned his head and let out a distinct, "Psht," as he dismissed her with a wave of his hand.

She raised both arms and leaned over the desk. "I have the data."

This time the hand did not go to her back but around her waist. Leaning over, she was able to swipe the files at Beckett before the un-assuring hand pulled her back.

"How many years—?"

The chief held her back with a single arm. Was it legal to bruise a police chief in the ribs?

"Richard," he said as she ranted. "This is law. Thirty days. We'll…I'll be back."

He used his very unsexy body to push her out the door.

SIXTEEN

Matt leaned over his steering wheel and checked as mid-afternoon dark clouds eclipsed the sun. Right on time. They helped to tamper the blistering afternoon heat. Either that, or his blood was thinning, as they say happens, and he was adapting to the climate.

He rolled down the windows and opened the sunroof as he headed for the station. Bella hair swirled like a hurricane reminding him to call the shelter.

Punching the virtual assistant button on the dash, he said, "Call Grouper Animal Shelter."

"Calling Grouper Animal Shelter," the system responded, and the number rang through the Bluetooth.

"Good afternoon. Grouper Animal Shelter. This is Bella. How can I help you?"

"Bella?" Matt said. He couldn't help it.

"Yes, sir. How can I help you?"

He slowed down around one of the two sharp curves on the main drag. "Yes. Good afternoon. I'm calling about the Saint Bernard."

"I'm sorry, sir. We don't have a Saint Bernard."

He rubbed a hand along the backside of his neck.

"You're welcome to stop in and put your name in our system for anytime we might get one. However, this is Florida. That doesn't happen often."

The golf cart in front of him did not slow down for the curve. His eyes darted from one side of the road to the other.

"Bella, this is Chief…This is Matt Osborne. I brought in a Saint Bernard?"

Two pedestrians were halfway across the road, making their way to the beach. Matt stopped his vehicle. The golf cart had to slam on its brakes, causing the passengers to fall forward.

He was tempted to flash his lights, but it wasn't like the golf cart was speeding.

"I'm sorry, sir. I'm confused."

He let his foot off the brake and took a deep breath. "No worries, Bella. I brought in a Saint Bernard a few days ago—"

"Oh! I remember. Yes! How is she? What a cutie."

Rubbing a hand over his face, he answered, "I'm still waiting for a call regarding adoption interest for her. Any word?"

"Oh. Oh!" said Bella. "Right. Yes. Well, no. Not yet. If you would like to keep her—"

"No, thank you. If you don't get any bites." Any other day and the unintended pun might be humorous, but he'd had to deal with poached turtle eggs, rejection from a suspect waking from a coma, an unexpected meeting with the entire Clearwater family, a crazed ice princess, and two code violation addicts. "I'll tell you what. Please let your supervisor know that I'll keep the dog for three more days, and then I'm dropping her off."

By the time he pulled into the City Hall lot, it started raining. He didn't get his moon roof closed fast enough. His right arm was soaked. Good thing Glory had her car in his … in the old chief's spot. There was a paper taped to the back window. Unlike him, Glory was not a new islander. She understood the afternoon rains would come and had the note taped to the inside.

He cursed the spot four spaces down and grabbed his umbrella. By the time he reached her car, the rain had stopped. Damned if he was going to take down the umbrella he'd just put up. He stood at the back of her car with it over his head.

This close and minus the rain, he could read the note plain and simple.

'The chief ORDERED me to park here."

Placing a hand over his mouth, he laughed all the way to the front door.

Glory looked up from her magazine long enough to see it was him, rolled her eyes, and started reading again. "Your arm is wet," she said as she read.

"You're not wrong."

He pulled up a waiting room chair from along the wall and sat in front of her desk.

Pulling her chin back, she said, "Girl problems?"

Furry girls. Turtle girls. "Oh, it'll be all right."

She put her nose back in her magazine. "I'd believe you, Chief, if you weren't sittin' here with the receptionist."

"I want you to call the *Ibis Island Sun Times*."

"Me?"

At least she put down her magazine. "That's right."

She jumbled through a drawer and pulled out a pad of paper and a pencil. "Shoot."

A grin spread over his face. "I'm going to send you a street camera shot of a man standing in the rain. I want you to send it to the paper and tell them to put out a wanted ad for anyone with information aiding in the finding of this man."

"Will do, Chief. I'll get right on it."

As he put back the chair, Glory scrolled through her phone. "*Ibis Island Sun Times*. There it is. You know, Chief. I haven't seen the morale around here this good in … ever."

"It is indeed a good place to work, Miss Glory."

The morale was good almost everywhere around the island. Officer Sheridan sat at his computer, busy as ever. "I'd like to see you in my office."

"Yes, sir," Sheridan said without looking up from his computer.

Matt stopped in front of him. "Now."

He looked up at Matt and repeated. "Yes, sir."

Looking over the commons area, he noted it was close to shift change. "I'd like to have your attention," he announced.

Scattered heads popped up over monitors. "Staff meeting at 4:05 p.m. I need first and second shift both in attendance." Not a single moan from first shift. Impressive. "I trust you'll let second shift know as they arrive. I have a short meeting, then we'll gather in the conference room."

It was good to be in her own vehicle again. This was normal. Riding in a cop car? Not normal. Raine sat in her parent's drive running the air conditioning. Okra and kale blew in the island breeze. The goats called from the enclosure Eli Murphy built for them on top of her parent's home. Normal and normal.

The chief's damned plans for Eaton and Beckett had better work. She'd routed six Turtle Watch calls to her sisters, and she handed over her only copies of Blake Eaton and Richard Beckett's code infractions.

She repeated the thought, but this time out loud. "I gave my only copies to Eaton and Beckett." Dropping her head, she let her forehead rest on the steering wheel. "Not normal."

The knock on the passenger window made her jump. Willow stood with her arms crossed. Rolling down the window, Raine asked, "Is Zoe here yet?"

"Why are you sitting in your truck?" Willow asked.

"Everyone is answering questions with questions these days," Raine said and put her head back on the steering wheel.

Willow opened the door and got in. "Zoe's inside. Talk to me."

Raine didn't remove her head from the steering wheel but rotated it to face her sister. "What were the Turtle Watch calls I forwarded you about?"

"Zoe and I were wondering why you did that. Did the earth stop rotating?" The muscles in Willow's face dropped. "Oh. That's a question. Right. More hatchling calls. What do you think is going on with that lately?"

"I don't know," Raine said to the dash.

"Mom!" Willow's daughter came running out of their mother's front door. "Grandpa says it's time to feed the goats!" She ran to the driver's side, so Raine rolled that window down, too.

The miniature Willow wore leggings and a baggy shirt like her mama and grandma. Raine waved.

Willow spoke to her through Raine's window. "Who's sweeping the goat poop?"

Chloe and Raine put two fingers to their noses.

"Well darn," Willow said and opened the passenger door. "I'm it."

The kid held the paper bag of food under her arm. "Grandpa says we have to make Bertha wait until the others get some chow." She spoke the last half of the sentence in a Grandpa Henry voice.

Raine stepped out and put her hands on her hips. "Did someone lose a front tooth?"

Standing a bit taller, Chloe smiled and pushed the tip of her tongue through the space created from the missing tooth.

The goats knew what time it was. Along the front edge of the enclosure, they created a noisy line, Bertha in front.

"See you inside, Aunt Raine," Chloe said as her bob bounced on the way to the ramp that led to the goats.

Of all of her father's goats, Bertha was the biggest, bossiest one Raine had ever seen. She didn't know how they were going to pull off making her wait. The two of them made their way up the ramp that led to where the goats waited impatiently.

When she made it into the house, she noted it smelled like … vegetables? She walked into the kitchen to investigate and found her father kissing her mother against the counter.

Oh, damn. They still do that. "Ahem."

"Oh, hello dear." Her mother turned on the water and sprayed green peppers.

Raine was scarred for life.

"We decided to set up a table at the farmer's market Thursday. You inspired me."

Her father placed tomatoes into a cardboard box lined with newspapers.

"That's a really good idea. Can you use some help?"

"Relax a bit, dear. I'll call when we do."

Raine stepped into the sunroom, and then stretched out on the padded bench. Opening the Turtle Watch social media page, she thought about the two young mothers who had guarded the hatchlings until Raine arrived.

Publicly announced hatchling releases generally turned into minor disasters. Observers never kept the proper distance. No matter how many times Raine said to. Someone inevitably forgot to turn off the flash on their cellphone camera, and sometimes the public couldn't keep themselves from helping a stray and illegally picking it up to help it to the water.

She typed out the post anyway.

Sea Turtle Hatchling Release

Come by the northwest corner of the island at dusk to watch as around forty hatchlings are released into the Gulf to brave the journey miles out in search of the sea grasses they need for nourishment and protection.

Squinting her eyes, she pressed Enter and closed the app.

The sunroom windows were open. Screens kept bugs out but not the heat. She let her eyes drop for just a moment.

Zoe came with a pan full of snap beans needing to be bagged and sat at the other side of the enclosure. She didn't notice Raine. Raine was glad Dane wasn't with her. She wasn't in any mood to deal with their making out.

SEVENTEEN

After such a firm directive, Matt half expected Officer Sheridan to follow him back to his office. No such luck.

Lucky for Sheridan, Matt wasn't the temperamental type. Except, Sheridan didn't know that, and the last chief made 'temperamental' an everyday word.

After fanning through the old school paper messages on his desk, he was close to stepping out and humiliating Sheridan in front of both the first shift as they came back to the station as well as second shift as they arrived.

Sheridan must have gauged how long he could hold off and met Matt in the hallway.

"Am I in trouble?" Sheridan asked as they walked into Matt's office.

The guy was about as bland of a human as imaginable, both appearance and personality. Although the former could be a result of the latter.

Matt walked around his desk and sat down for the second time in the last fifteen minutes. "Why would you be in trouble, Rodney?"

"Right. No reason." He sat down and thrummed his fingers on the armrests of the guest chair.

"So, we've decided to look into a firewall for our internet system. I'll need a list of any and all sites you've used on your machine to ensure we don't inadvertently block any."

Sheridan turned as red as the lobster Matt had for dinner last week.

"How long have you been with IIPD, now?" Matt asked.

Sheridan straightened in the chair. "Fourteen years."

Matt nodded and glanced out his window. "Pence made it through Chief Roberts' entire tenure due to a stack of stellar evaluations and thirty-five years with the force. How did you manage it?"

"I know how to keep people happy. It's my specialty." He wagged his brows up and down twice.

"Tell me all about code enforcing on Ibis Island." Matt leaned back and folded his hands over his abs.

"What for?"

Matt's voice dropped. He didn't want to sound condescending, but... "To learn about code enforcement on Ibis Island."

Sheridan shrugged. "A complaint is made. If a code has been broken, I send out a notice, notifying the person or persons who did the violating."

Matt nodded and looked him in the eye. "That's helpful. Please go on."

"I, uh. If said person or persons don't resolve the violation, we fine them."

Folding his hands on top of his desk, Matt leaned forward. "And what if the fines aren't paid?"

Not a muscle moved on Sheridan's face. "That's not my part."

"Not your part? Help me with that. Your job is as the Ibis Island code enforcement officer." He enunciated the word enforcement.

"I've been doing this for fourteen years."

Right to defensive. Predictable.

"The union will back me," Sheridan added. He crossed his arms over his chest and added, "I saw a man with a limp when we were at the hospital."

The muscles in the back of Matt's neck stiffened. "Why didn't you tell me?"

"You said I was there only to serve as your witness with interrogating Miriam Roberts." The smug expression on Sheridan's face was paramount. "And, that you would let me know if you wanted more."

Taking a deep, cleansing breath, Matt said calmly, "Where exactly was he? Was he coming or going? Give me a description."

"Third floor. Going, and I didn't see his face. He was over six foot, wore jeans and a white t-shirt. His hair had lots of braids that were tied in a ponytail. Are you going to order me on leave? That would be paid under the contract."

The corners of Matt's lips turned. He didn't stop them. "Instead of wading through the muddy waters of failing to complete job description and insubordination—who needs that union mess?—I'm going to transfer you to the new graveyard beach patrol."

Sheridan's eyes darted around the room. He stood and raised his voice, "You can't do that. That's a demotion."

"I can and I will. That is a lateral move, and it's an order."

"I'm not doing it. You can't fire me."

"I can fire you for insubordination, but again…so much paperwork." Matt stood and walked nose-to-nose with Sheridan. "I know the contract, too. Under this scenario, if you choose to refuse the transfer, it will be an unpaid leave."

Nostrils flaring, Sheridan stood and grabbed the door handle.

"Training is Thursday, oh seven hundred. Mandatory."

The slam of the door was textbook.

Willow joined them in the sunroom. Raine noted that she sure finished feeding the goats fast. She should have laid in the other direction. From this angle, she could see her parents in the kitchen. The visual of them against the kitchen counter would be forever etched in her brain.

"You should be on a honeymoon," Willow said as she and Zoe tied blue curling ribbon at the tops of the bags of green beans.

"And, Willow, you should be booking a venue for your wedding. I think we both are waiting for the same thing."

"What do you think Raine is waiting for?" Willow asked. "She has a man just right for her and she pushes him away at every turn."

The conversation chased the tired away. She thought about lifting her head and telling them she was right there. Curiosity beat out better judgement.

Zoe ran scissors along the ribbon, making it curl tight to the bag. "He wouldn't take her anyway. She works hard at keeping everyone an arm's length away, not just him."

Beads of sweat dripped down Raine's temples. A shower might be called for both before the hatchling release and after.

"It nearly killed her just to let us retrieve a few disorientated hatchlings," Willow said.

"As if she wants it any other way?" Zoe asked. "She left my wedding reception."

Willow said, "There would be no Turtle Watch without Raine."

Her father stepped in and rested a shoulder on the doorjamb. "We will love her unconditionally, even if she is a bitch."

The sunroom bench shook as Tropical Storm Ernest blew sheets of rain through the screens.

"Raine, wake up."

Her eyes opened to Chloe shaking her with both hands. "You're crying, Raine. Wake up."

She sat and, blinking, gained her bearings. Tears that had been falling over her temples, now flowed down her cheeks.

Willow followed close behind Chloe. "Oh, Raine." She came and sat with her on the sunroom bench, wrapping an arm around Raine's shoulder and squeezing. "What is it? You've been working so hard. Why don't you let Zoe and I do the hatchling release tonight?"

"How did you know—?" The post. Raine realized the answer before she finished the question.

Rubbing both hands over her cheeks, she wiped the tears away. The backs of her eyes still burned, but she would be able to cover for it.

"I'd like some help at the farmer's market on Thursday, Raine." Her mother set a giant bowl full of bite-sized squares of watermelon in front of her father on the kitchen table next to a plate of pineapple slices.

"Mom." Zoe sat next to him. "She is way too busy for any farmer's market."

Henry placed a hand on Zoe's forearm.

Zoe looked at it, then him, and sank in her chair.

Taking Raine's hand, Willow stood. "Watermelon is your favorite. Come."

It just made the backs of her eyes burn more, but she followed.

"Do you want to talk about it?" Chloe said.

Raine smiled down at her. "I threw a file at Richard Beckett and crawled halfway on his desk before Chief Osborne pulled me down."

Elbows out, her niece covered her mouth with both hands. Her beautiful brown eyes were as big as two moons. A six-year-old snort came out of her mouth and she laughed.

Raine lifted her brows and swayed her head from side-to-side. Her shoulders jiggled. The laugh started deep in her gut. She rested one hand on Chloe's shoulder and one on her stomach as they laughed together.

Some sat. Some leaned against the walls of the conference room. Even including Lucy Green and Glory Studebaker, there were barely enough to fill the conference room, but they were there.

Matt stood behind the chair at the head of the table. Officer Pence sat at the other end. He nodded and Matt began. "Thank you for coming with such short notice. I didn't want to send this in an email, and I didn't want you to hear it from anyone else. Ibis Island PD is going to start a night patrol of the beach."

A pin could of dropped.

"I've already called third shift but didn't want you to hear from anyone else. It will simply be an extension of their territory.

Training will, of course, be needed. I am requisitioning the board for a new hire to cover the extra beat. That part is confidential until after the board meeting. If anyone of you would like dibs, let me know now."

Officer Graham slowly raised his hand.

"Officer Graham," Matt said. "Check."

He wasn't much older than Cummings, no young kids at home to keep him up sleeping days. Two more hands went up. "Galloway, Boyer. I'll keep you all apprised."

"I am putting a wanted ad in the Ibis Island Sun Times for information leading to the whereabouts of the gaper who stood across the street during the Waterfront awning collapse on Willow Clearwater. I'm including the street camera pic, as distorted as it is."

Placing both hands flat on the table, he dipped his head low. He nodded three times, then lifted his head. "The perp who earned himself a knife in the leg in the Gulf last week was possibly spotted early this morning near Miriam Roberts' hospital room."

A few heads leaned together and grumblings began. "A man with a limp was seen walking away from Roberts' room. He is said to be over six foot with several braids tied in a ponytail. I found this out just a few moments ago."

Squealing on Sheridan would be unprofessional and might cause an issue with the union. However, Matt didn't need to actually say it. "With our new changes, I've transferred Officer Sheridan to join the graveyard shift."

"Oh, man."

"Shit."

"Sucks."

Sucks as in for Sheridan or for those who had to work with him? Matt held up a hand. "He declined, and instead chose an unpaid leave of absence to consider this option."

"Keep your eyes and ears open for anyone fitting the description of the man spotted at the hospital. I'll have our witness work with a sketch artist once I figure out how to get one to Ibis. I'll be headed out to the hospital in the morning to talk to the day shift." He took a deep breath. "I need to tell you that I've worked with my share of cops." He shoved a finger around the room. "Your sense of honesty and work ethic is unmatched. I am honored to work with each of you."

"Right, right, right," Galloway called from the back. "But, who's next up for your parking spot?"

The round of laughter helped ease the tension from the changes, from the news of Sheridan. It didn't hurt the frustration of the island's unsolved murder either.

EIGHTEEN

Raine gave honest consideration to taking the night off. But, after losing her temper in front of Richard Beckett and the chief, and then that nightmare, she needed some semblance of normal before she was going to get any sleep.

The sun hit the horizon. Enough scattered clouds provided a breathtaking skyline. Yet, few ventured out this far. The northwest side of the island meant lengthy beach access trails. She passed the tall grasses where she'd retrieved the hatchlings that morning. The eyes of a ghost crab peered from its hole.

"You're early," she said to it.

Her sisters were there. Her mother and Chloe, too. She felt much lighter as she walked.

About thirty spectators. Kids, too. Not an opportune time to turn over lead to her sisters.

Willow spotted her first. As Raine made her way to them, she watched as Willow held out a hand to Zoe. Zoe dug in her front pocket and retrieved a bill, then slapped it in Willow's hand.

"What's that all about?" Raine shouted as she came within earshot.

Next to them, a five-gallon bucket sat covered with a towel.

"Zoe bet me you wouldn't show."

Raine set her hands on her hips. "How much?"

"Twenty." Harmony made two long lines in the sand with a stick.

Raine turned to her mother. "You didn't bet?"

Her beautiful brown eyes looked up to her and smiled. "That wouldn't be very motherly, now would it, dear?"

Raine called out to the bystanders, "Good evening, and thank you for joining us." From the corner of her eyes, she spotted Willow's shoulders falling as she slapped the twenty back into Zoe's hand.

Squinting at them briefly, she continued. "My name is Raine Clearwater, and I am part of Ibis Island Turtle Watch. Boy, do we have a treat for you tonight."

Willow and her mother sat, facing the multicolored skyline. They crossed their legs and pulled out tattoos for the children. Zoe guarded the hatchlings.

"How many do we have?" Raine asked her.

"Seventy-two."

Raine's jaw almost hit the sand. "How?"

Zoe shrugged. "Crazy day."

"Lines are drawn in the sand," Raine announced to the crowd. "Pun intended."

Chuckles came from the crowd as each stepped to a line.

"They are to give you a general idea of where not to step. Parents, please keep your children an arm's length away. Sometimes they lose self-control."

Although, mostly, it was the adults.

"In a few moments, we'll give you the signal to sit like this." She kneeled close to the line without touching it, and then sat on her heels. "The hatchlings ought to, and I emphasize the ought to, crawl within the lines to the water.

"These are live creatures, however. They have minds of their own and may stray. Please do not touch or pick them up. That is not permitted. One of the certified Turtle Watch volunteers will—"

Over the crowd, awkward movement caught her eye. She

121

squinted and craned her head around the tallest guest. The sun was in Raine's eyes, but she thought she saw...she did see.

She took off in a full sprint. Her toes dug into the sand, left, right, left, right. He locked eyes with her almost immediately. Even with the limp, he ran. Did he think she wouldn't know who he was from this distance? She would know him anywhere.

Matt sat on the floor of his apartment with a beer in one hand and Bella's paw in the other. Even with the unsolved Clearwater murder, today was a good day.

Holding up her paw, he put his hand next to it. "You're going to be a big dog."

The furry skin above her eyes lifted. Brown eyes looked up to him.

"Yes. I am talking to you."

As he scratched around an ear, she moaned and crooned.

From the small table near the entry door, his walkie buzzed. Someday he would turn the thing off when he got home. That day was not today.

"Drunk reported in the street at Palm and Beech, over."

In the street? He stood and waited for a response.

"Officer Pence. Still with the disorderly conduct, over."

Matt dug a bone from the pocket of his jeans and threw it in Bella's crate. "Time to get in your crate."

"Officer Boyer. I'm at the south end finishing up a speeding ticket, over."

Stepping into his slip-ons, he grabbed the walkie with one hand and his holster with the other. "I'm three blocks out. Over."

"Chief?"

"That's right. On my way. Over."

He dug the fob from his pocket as he clicked the walkie to the holster. It was early for a drunken call.

Angry car horns blasted. He heard them all the way from his apartment parking lot.

His tires cried as he rounded onto the road. He flipped on both the lights and sirens. Tires screeched from the site.

He heard her before he saw her.

Raine Clearwater.

Traffic backed up five cars deep and was growing. Even with the red and blue flashing lights, a driver in a Kia accelerated around the stopped cars.

"No!" Matt yelled as she stepped, barefoot, in front of the moving car.

She screamed and waved her arms at it, then smacked the window as it drove past. The sirens didn't seem to faze her.

He, too, veered his car around the line and pulled in horizontally ahead of the car in front. As the beams from his headlights scanned the pavement, he saw them. Dozens of them. Sea turtle hatchlings carpeted the street.

Throwing the car into park, he flipped off the sirens and called for back-up. Torn between reaching Raine and securing the scene, he chose cop autopilot. He grabbed a few flashers and a stack of orange pylon cones from his hatch and began placing them in a line directing traffic away down a side street.

Seconds after he flipped on the first flasher, she charged him.

"Turn that off!" Her face was as white as a sheet.

He was wrong. There may be hundreds of them. He was a fast learner and grabbed her wrists as she reached him. Hers were cold and clammy.

"Raine. Stop." He looked straight into her light brown eyes. They were glossy and red. "It's going to be okay."

"Okay? Look at this! I've got to—" And just like that, she pulled away and ran for a Smartcar that drove between the pylon cones. She banged on the hood with her fist. "Get the hell out of here!"

Matt heard the passenger. "She's insane."

Or going into shock.

He needed reinforcements, not of the PD kind. Pulling out his cell, he dialed.

"This is Henry."

"Mr. Clearwater, this is Chief Osborne. Raine is in trouble. She needs help."

"Where?"

He heard rustling on the other end of the phone. "Two blocks north of City Hall near the northwest access."

He hardly had time to hang up when Harmony Clearwater's voice came from the beach access. "Willow, use the release bucket to gather the live ones. Zoe, go get that damned rental to turn off their deck lights!"

Matt looked to where Harmony pointed. He hadn't noticed it before. White lights had been left on around a deck on top of a rental. The live ones crawled over the dead ones and headed straight for the light. The sign in the yard read Beckett Rentals.

Dodging hatchlings, he directed traffic as Raine and her mother exchanged words he couldn't hear.

Sirens came from the south. Officer Galloway. Matt spotted Henry Clearwater on his tail as he approached. Matt locked eyes with Galloway and gestured toward the north line of stopped cars. Galloway nodded and took that end.

Henry parked on the wrong side of the road and got out of his ancient Camry. "What's going on?"

"She can't take much more and needs to get out of here." Matt pointed to Raine.

She didn't respond to him talking about her like she wasn't there. She wasn't doing anything. Just standing. In the middle of the street with turtles crawling around her feet. "Get her home."

Henry walked up to her and circled his hand around her arm. Looking down at the hand on her arm, she began to pull away until her gaze saw her father.

"They aren't answering," Zoe hollered as she returned from the rental.

That was an easy one. "Get her something sugary to drink," he said to Henry as he guided her like a zombie toward his car.

The brick layout created an easy climb to the second story. Matt used a sleeve to unscrew the bulbs. Pausing before he descended, he looked down at the scene. The ground. Turtle pancakes dotted it like the face of a heavily freckled redhead. Zoe had joined Willow in gathering the live ones. Harmony pulled an arm out of a cinch sack with a plastic grocery bag. She picked up a dead turtle and placed it in the bag.

"Stop right there, Mrs. Clearwater," Matt yelled from the deck. He climbed down and jogged over to her.

Waving Galloway over, he said, "Harmony, do not pick up a single one of those. Officer Galloway, I'm going to text you the number of Richard Beckett. I want him here ASAP."

NINETEEN

Raine's clothes were drenched in sweat.

Her father tightened the blanket wrapped around her.

"The chills are going away, Daddy." She curled up tighter on the couch and took a sip out of the can of soda he'd found in her fridge. "You don't have to stay." She desperately wanted him to.

He sat in her recliner and crossed his ankles on the footrest. "Your mother's rekindled fixation with the farmer's market is something I'll gladly escape. I could use a break from tying bundles of okra. 'Why wouldn't we, dear? We have plenty.'"

His spot-on impersonation of her mother made Raine chuckle.

"Chief Osborne took me out—" she started before realizing what that sounded like. She closed her eyes at the visual of her losing her temper in front of him. "Chief Osborne," she corrected. "Had me bring copies of code infractions to our two heaviest hitters."

He slouched in her chair and folded his hands over his stomach. "Blake Eaton and Richard Beckett."

She didn't know he knew that.

"He said he would put liens on their businesses if they didn't comply."

"Do you think he means it?"

She found herself nodding. "I do, actually. I lost my temper."

He laughed.

"It wasn't funny."

"I have a feeling it was."

"Lucky Nemo is the man who held a knife to Dane's neck in the Gulf."

He turned his head to face her fully.

"He is the one Dane stabbed."

He didn't ask how she knew. She hadn't seen Lucky's face, but with the long salt and pepper braids, earring glittering in the sunset, and tattoos covering one forearm and a single calf, she would bet her life savings on it.

The turtle release, her mother drawing lines in the sand, that incredible sunset. Chasing Lucky. Before she knew it, she'd replayed the entire evening in her head. The entire evening until the road in front of the Beckett rental.

"When you're quiet like that," she whispered. "I never know if it's because you understand the rest of the story, or if it's because you're waiting for the rest of the story."

His smile was warmth. It was safe. It was light.

"If I ask you something, Daddy, will you answer me honestly?"

"Of course."

"Do you think—? Do other people think—?"

"Nope and nope. And Turtle Watch will continue when you move on." He winked. "You talk in your sleep, you know."

She did not know. It was mortifying.

"You have many people who love you just the way you are. They are ready and waiting for you—"

"To love them back," she finished his sentence for him. "I know."

"That's not what I was going to say. They are ready and waiting for you to let them."

Her chest expanded slowly before she let it out all at once.

Tomorrow was a new day. "I'm going to take a shower. Thank you for taking care of me."

His eyes opened wide.

She smiled. "I mean it."

Detours were marked and traffic flowed safely away from the scene.

The Clearwater women waited with him, all of them except Raine. He wondered if she was okay. He already had every member of the board steaming mad at him. He had just added the island PPH.

They sat next to the beach access without even covering their mouths from the stench. He didn't either. It seemed disrespectful somehow.

The black and white rounded the corner. No sirens. No lights. Matt hadn't given that directive to Galloway and didn't know if he was relieved or disappointed.

He stood in the middle of the carnage, legs shoulder-width apart and arms crossed.

The passenger door opened the minute Galloway stopped the vehicle.

"You'll pay for this one," Beckett yelled, breaking the silence. "You turtle freaks humiliated me in front of my date. Sending an officer in full uniform without a warrant? Oh, you'll pay all right. You can kiss your job good-bye."

With a pointed, shaking finger, he stomped toward Matt and crunched a dead sea turtle hatchling. Halting to see what was under his shoe, he lifted his foot like a stork. Gently, he set it down in one of the few empty spaces.

His jaw dropped. His gaze traveled over every inch of the wreckage.

The stench from the mass death setting on asphalt in Florida heat was something Matt would never forget.

Beckett's hand lifted and covered his open mouth. "What?" he said so Matt could hardly hear him. "How?"

Matt pointed over his shoulder at the deck of his rental. "Lights left on. I'm going to go out on a limb and say there are no reminders in that rental about lights out after dark during turtle season."

Beckett kept staring from side to side and all over the ground. It was as if he was scared to move his feet. "The lights did this?" He said it like he was dazed.

"Climbed the brick and unscrewed them myself."

Beckett's eyes met Matt's. "Matt, that rental is empty."

Empty?

"That makes sense," Matt said. He closed his eyes and shook his head. "Damn it. Follow me."

Walking around the entire perimeter of the carnage, Beckett did as he was told.

"May us turtle freaks start cleaning this up?" Zoe asked.

Beckett jumped like he'd seen a ghost.

"That is part of what we do," she added.

Matt nodded as he and Beckett headed for the front door. The knob didn't budge.

"Should I," Beckett stuttered. "I have a key."

Shaking his head, Matt headed around back. "Let's take a look back here, first." It was a single residence home on stilts. Like most of the homes on the island, the ground floor was the garage. The front door would open to a set of stairs that led to the living space.

Just as he'd expected. They rounded the back to a broken door leading into the garage entry.

"I swear that wasn't—"

Matt held up a hand. "I know, Richard." Or, at least he did now. "I have an idea who."

———

The knock at the door made Raine roll her eyes that she'd locked it.

"Daddy," she said as she opened it.

Except it wasn't her father.

The heat. It started at her neck and traveled over her cheeks. She was too exhausted to care.

As he stepped in, Matt said, "What good is locking your door if you just open it without asking who's knocking?"

Her hair was dripping wet, and she was still in the towel from her shower. "I don't have the energy, Matt. If you're coming to check on me, thank you. I'm fine."

"I am. Glad to hear it. You're not ghostly white anymore, so that's a good sign."

"Listen—" she started to explain. Forcing herself to look him in the eye, she noticed that he wasn't looking at her eyes. He was looking at her.

He covered her mouth with his. His hands ran across her cheeks and his fingers laced into her wet hair. The room went black, or maybe that was because her eyes rolled into the back of her head. His tongue moved with just the right amount of sexy she always dreamed there would be.

She wasn't sure if she was responding. There were no parts of her that could move. Her arms hung limp at her sides. She wasn't entirely sure if she was kissing back.

As fast as he started, he pulled away. "I'm sorry," he said. "I—"

Fear of losing the moment woke her arms. She grabbed his shirt with both hands and pulled him in. Her mouth covered his and was lost in everything that was now.

His long arms wrapped around her backside and lifted. As her legs wrapped around his waist, their lips tested and their tongues explored.

He carried her. She didn't care where. As long as he didn't let go. Her hands responded to her brain and other parts of her body. They grabbed and kneaded. His arms and back flexed as he carried her. Things dropped on the floor as they went.

Letting go of her backside, she hung on with her thighs. He used both arms to pull his shirt over his head. It dangled from the fingers on one hand as his eyes traveled over her face. His other hand wiped away strands of wet hair that had fallen over her eyes.

Beneath her thighs, his chest expanded and released. Her hands clutched his bare shoulders as he stared at her lips.

He turned around and sat on the bed with her legs wrapped

around him and her feet locked behind his back. He watched as his thumb traced a line from one side of her mouth to the other. The storm that brewed inside her shook deep in her core.

She closed her eyes expecting his lips to replace his thumb but it didn't stop. It trailed over her chin and down her neck. A sexy chill covered her body as the towel released and crumpled around her waist. Her fingers dug into his back. His thumb circled one side of her then the other. She could have lost it then and there.

When the circles made their way beneath the white cotton, a noise came from deep in her throat she didn't recognize.

Beneath her, he struggled to be free. Lifting on her knees, she pressed on his chest until he lay flat on his back. She released him as he cupped and molded.

When her hands found him, he stilled. His eyes opened wide before dropping to half closed. Heat grew as the last piece of fabric flew somewhere she didn't know or care.

Hands that were slow and confident matched everything she knew about Chief Matt Osborne. Mercilessly, he kneaded and explored until he found her center. Her breath caught. Clutching his back, she dug her cheek into his neck and cried out as she went over. She hung on and on until she came down, an entirely different need erupting.

She wasn't sure how long it took her before coherency returned, but she pulled back to read his expression. That corner of his mouth that always lifted smiled, and he said, "More."

TWENTY

The tone from a text woke her. Lifting a single lid, the red numbers at the side of her bed read 5:12 a.m. She rolled over and let her hand fall on her phone.

It was Mary Jane.

got a sick kid

She forwarded the text to Willow before remembering what had happened the night before. Clamping her eyes shut, she slowly lay back down. With the one eye, she turned to glance at the place next to her in bed.

It was empty.

What had she done? She sat up straight in her bed. She was still naked. "Oh my gosh," she said out loud, pulled the pillow over her lap, and covered her face with both hands.

Punching the pillow with each syllable, she yelled, "I. Am. So. Stu-pid."

"Hello?" It was him.

She covered her mouth. He wasn't gone.

He had four drinks in a carrier from C.J.'s in his hand and stopped short as he entered her bedroom. A smile spread over his face.

Looking down, the pillow she had assaulted was in her lap and nothing else covered her. She yanked the sheets over her.

"Hello," she barked. "I mean, hello," she said more like a normal person.

"I had to let Bella out."

He was in full uniform other than his shoes and had obviously showered while he was home.

"I wasn't sure what you drink, so I got tea and regular coffee." He held up a small paper bag that was in the extra drink spot. "The tea was because you're a Clearwater and I thought … well, anyway, Clarence gave me some creamers."

Her voice didn't want to speak. She forced it. "Regular is fine."

He sat in front of her. The scent of sandalwood cologne made her dizzy.

Covering her hand with his, he said, "I have a lot to tell you about last night."

She pulled the sheets higher and forced her eyes not to clamp shut.

"Not about that," he said and laid his smiling mouth on hers. "About Beckett," he said around their lips.

"Can I, um? I should probably shower." She willed her phone to buzz with a turtle emergency, but it failed her.

"Right. Of course." His expression didn't match his words. Taking a deep breath, he explained, "I didn't like the idea of your neighbor watching you shower before. After what we shared last night, I really don't like it."

And, the heat. It was more like an erupting volcano this time rushing up her neck and over her face.

"I'll make something to eat," he said and stood.

He left with the coffee. She sure could use the coffee. Grabbing her robe, she sulked out back.

Opening the wooden shower door, she glanced over her shoulder at Howard's house. No time for that worry. The water helped. A lot. She had lost all of her senses at the turtle disaster and again with— She clamped her eyes shut.

She had to tell him about Lucky Nemo.

This time, she wrapped the towel around her wet head and the robe around herself.

Dressing as fast as she could, she opened her bedroom door and paused halfway through. He sat in her chair at her ridiculous excuse for a kitchen table, humming as he thumbed through messages on his phone.

At her table barely big enough for two, he'd set a bowl of scrambled eggs. A couple pieces of toast and the only jam she had in her fridge. Marmalade.

He had been warm and attentive and selfless. And, not just in her bed. The scents of toasted bread, warm butter and scrambled eggs loosened her shoulders and woke her stomach.

Barely moving his head, he glanced up to her and lifted a single brow.

This time what filled her chest and cheeks wasn't heat, and it burned the backs of her eyes. She stepped out and looked at the ceiling. Not allowing her gaze anywhere near him, she dipped into her chair.

He touched the back of her hand with the tips of his fingers. "Why do you do that?"

Tears had threatened to come more in the last few months than in her entire twenty-nine years. Shaking her head, she forced a smile and picked up her coffee.

"You're acting like what we shared was something isolated."

That was presumptuous and helped her find her voice. She sat up in her chair. "What makes you think I am interested in more than one night?" She ran her fingers through her wet hair, shaking it dry.

This time, he smiled with both sides of his mouth and began to spread her marmalade on his toast. "From nearly crawling over Richard Beckett's desk to scratch his eyes out to pounding on the hoods of passing vehicles that might run over a sea turtle hatchling, you're not exactly one to hide your feelings."

And the heat kind of heat. It spread up her neck and covered her face. He knew. How long had he known?

He took a sip of coffee and leaned back in his chair. "And,

you're not the one-night stand type. If you were, I wouldn't be here."

"What about my job?" she argued.

He lifted a corner of his mouth. Her eyes were stuck on it for too long.

"How do you and I hurt your job?"

She closed her eyes. At least for this moment, she allowed herself to dwell on his words, 'you and I.'

"People will think I slept with you—"

"Singular?"

She shook her head. "You're confusing me."

"I apologize. People will think we are seeing each other," he corrected. "Please continue."

"People will think I'm trying to get you to … I don't know … enforce code."

He shrugged and took a bite of his toast.

"And that you are trying to get an in with the PPH."

That damned sexy corner of his mouth lifted for the third time. "I am."

This was hopeless. "Lucky Nemo is the man with the limp."

The muscles in his face dropped.

"I saw him last night. I was chasing him when I ran into the turtle mess." Lifting a hand, she set her forehead in it.

The food tasted better than it should, but they ate in silence for far too long.

"The rental was empty," he said. "Someone broke in and turned on the deck lights."

"Beckett, that bastard." She pushed her chair back and started to stand.

He grabbed her wrist. It made her forget what they were talking about.

"He didn't know."

Rolling her eyes, she sat back down.

"The lock on the back door leading to the garage was broken."

She nodded. "Beckett would have used his key."

Her eyes grew wide and her mouth opened.

"I think it was broken into for the same reason the eggs were poached. Someone is trying to distract Clearwaters from looking for the cornerstone that is Home."

"Lucky wanted me to see him," she said. "He knew I would run after him."

He nodded and took a sip of his coffee. "It makes sense that it's Lucky, but it doesn't make sense that he killed your brother. That was before his time, and if he knew there was more treasure, he would have been on the island more than a few days a year since Seth's murder."

"We've had exponentially more disorientation calls." She hit her forehead with the palm of her hand. "And, the women at the northwest corner of the island yesterday said a man had pointed them out to them."

"Beckett was wrecked at what happened in front of his rental. He cried."

Her mouth dropped.

"I'm not making that up."

"Wow. So what's next, Chief?"

"We have a board meeting."

It was her turn to smile. "Are we having an actual conversation?"

That corner of his mouth. It lifted and the ring of brown around his eyes shone.

It was almost eight o'clock. Raine grabbed her keys and shoved her phone in her back pocket. She couldn't remember the last time she'd left the house this late. Or, the last time she left her bed unmade and dishes in the sink.

As she hustled out the door, she spotted Matt's walkie on her kitchen counter. She would drop that by the station.

On second thought, she would call him to meet her on the beach to get it. Raine clipped it to the pocket of her jean shorts.

The knock on her door brought a smile to her face. It opened before she reached it. Standing in her living room was not Chief Osborne coming to get his walkie.

Zoe strode in followed by Willow.

Stepping to Raine, Willow's arms wrapped around her and squeezed. "How are you doing?"

Patting her back with the tips of her fingers, Raine watched as Zoe stepped past the embrace and into the kitchen.

"Thanks for stopping by." Raine's bullshit radar woke. "I'm fine. Really."

Willow pulled away. She pushed a strand of hair from Raine's forehead. "I wasn't able to walk the section you texted about this morning."

"What?" Raine's chest tightened. "And, we're standing here talking?"

"Mom covered it." Willow said quickly and joined Zoe in the kitchen. "She told us to come check on you."

Raine started scanning possible scenarios and reasons for her mother to give that directive. "In that case, I feel like I should take back the thank you."

"See?" Willow said. "You're smiling and making jokes while late getting out to the beach."

Damn. Caught.

Zoe crossed her arms. Willow stood next to her with her hands folded low.

"You've been letting others take Turtle Watch calls," Zoe said and squinted her eyes.

Willow added, "We understand last night you left us with the release because you spotted the disorientation."

Or Lucky Nemo limping away.

"But call after call." Willow lowered her brows.

Zoe craned her head over the kitchen sink. "You don't eat breakfast."

Oh, no. The heat. Not now. Please not now.

TWENTY-ONE

Willow scooted next to her. "There are two plates in here."
Willow faced Raine. She lifted her chin. "Someone slept here last night."

The heat cleared Raine's jawline and threatened her cheeks.

"Who was it?" Zoe ordered, cocking her hip.

Raine shook her head back and forth like she was shivering.

Willow's eyes dropped to the walkie.

Raine closed her eyes tight.

"You had a police officer stay the night?" Willow asked.

Raine could hear the smile on Willow's face, even through her eyelids.

"You had sex with Chief Osborne!" Zoe yelled.

Willow said, "Raine slept with Matt."

"It was an accident!" Raine said as her eyes flew open.

Her sisters stood with their mouths shaped in little Os.

Of all things, Zoe laughed. She laughed until she held her stomach and buckled over. Willow did too. She even snorted. Raine couldn't remember the last time Willow snorted from laughing.

A smile spread over Raine's face. Just as Chloe had done, she covered her mouth with both hands. She couldn't stop the laughter. She laughed so hard, she had to sit back on the arm of her chair.

"Are we laughing," Willow said between gasps, "because Raine had sex with a cop, or because she said it was an accident?"

"I have," Raine said, "no idea." Sucking in air, her eyes watered from laughing.

"No wonder Mom sounded so happy when she told us to come by," Willow said.

The muscles in Raine's face fell. She stood. "How does she know?" Raine checked the time on her phone. "He barely just walked out the door."

"What did he drive?" Zoe asked. "Where did he park?"

Raine fell back to the arm of the chair. "Well, shit."

"Did you use protection?" Willow asked.

Zoe rolled her eyes. "Sheesh, Willow. Do you have to do that?"

Crossing her arms, Willow said, "Mom's going to ask. I can either tell her, or she can ask at the most inopportune time."

Raine held up a hand. "We didn't actually get to that."

"Oh," Zoe said.

She wasn't sure when it happened, but Raine found herself sitting in a circle on the floor with her sisters.

Willow put a hand on Zoe's leg. "It's not a requirement. It was their first ... Was that your first?"

"We didn't have any protection, and why do I feel naked again?"

Another attack of uncontrollable laughter went around the circle until Willow sat up straight. "Raine," Willow said with an expression as if she'd just had an epiphany. "He's perfect for you."

Dipping her chin, Raine shook her head. "I know."

"That's not how you're supposed to say that," Willow said.

"I don't really know him."

Zoe held up a hand. "Or you've known him since the day I found Seth's remains."

"It's been a long time since we've been like this." Willow tilted her head.

Raine nodded. "Seth would be sad if he knew how few and far between this happens." Regardless, Raine had to tell her family about Lucky. "We'd ... I'd like to have a family meeting today. Luciana's around 1 p.m.?"

Willow lifted a finger. "Remember that Liam is a school teacher. It's hard for him to rearrange his schedule at the last minute like the rest of us can."

"We do that to him much too much," Raine said and paced the floor. "You are way too patient about that. Can he get someone to fill in for him tomorrow? Same time?"

Zoe waved an arm between the two of them. "What about tonight?"

"The chief ... Matt has a board meeting, and we're scheduled to do a night patrol briefing after that."

"I'll tell Mom and Dad," Willow offered.

Raine sat in the parking lot of his apartment. It was not like she hadn't been here before. She had. A few days ago, even.

But not inside.

It was like she was sleepwalking and would wake any time now.

Taking a deep breath, she opened the door of her truck. She looked around to see if anyone was watching. Sand from the morning's nest excavation fell from her knees. As she walked to the door, she lifted her shirt and sniffed. Could be worse.

His place was on the second floor. She knew this apartment building. It was behind the county jail side of City Hall. Willow's high school friend, Tony Gravatt, lived here after graduation.

She climbed the stairs, then knocked on the first door on the left.

"Don't knock," he called from inside.

Did that mean don't knock and don't come in, or don't knock and come in? She erred on side of caution.

When the door opened, he was frowning. "Don't do that again."

So, don't knock and come in. "Okay."

He stood in full uniform. Holster, shiny shoes, gun. Leaning in, he kissed her forehead. It made her eyelids close. Bella whined and pushed her snout between them.

Dropping to one knee, Raine rubbed foreheads with her. With a free hand, she released his walkie from the waist of her shorts and held it up.

He took it and secured it to his equipment belt. "Thanks. Watch this trick." Taking her hand, he pulled Raine in and shut the door. He sat on his living room floor and leaned his back against a wall.

Bella trotted over to him like a pony in a hurry. Matt covered his jewels as she danced in a circle, then stepped in the center of his lap and sat.

She pulled out her phone and took a picture.

"She won the heart of my landlord."

"Does that mean she's yours?"

"Ours," he corrected. "And no, it's not meant to be. Not like you and I."

The skin on her arms tingled. "How can you do that?"

Bella leaned into him and dug her snout into his shoulder.

"Do what?" he asked as he ran a hand over Bella's head and down her back.

"Be so casual." She shook her head. "And confident."

He stood, making Bella do more circles. Somehow, the dog sensed they were leaving. She walked over and stood at the door.

"Sometimes you just know."

"But—"

"We'd better get going," he said. "Not that I'm in a hurry, but your family needs to know that people are using Turtle Watch to distract them from finding Seth's treasure. And, they might not like it if you don't tell them about Lucky."

She liked that he said Seth's and not Luciana's. "Tomorrow at Luciana's. 1 p.m.?"

After clicking on Bella's lead, he locked the door behind them. "I can switch some things around and make that work."

"You're not a school teacher," she mumbled.

Bella stood on the console between their seats, stuck her head out of the sunroof and rested it on the top of the SUV.

"Does anything get you mad?"

141

R. T. WOLFE

"Hmm. There's a question. Trafficking children, killing puppies and your brother's murder case."

"Angry? Why angry?"

"I assume you're not talking about trafficking or puppies." He smiled and twined their fingers together.

He turned onto Pelican Bridge. Kids in cars pointed at Bella.

"Dead end after dead end. Don't get me wrong, I focus on the facts only. If I didn't, anything I put my hands on that ended up in a court of law would be tossed. But, I don't have a gut feeling about who the bad guy is, and that never happens."

She looked out the passenger window. "I miss him."

"I know," he said and rubbed his thumb on the back of her hand.

"I think it's Blake Eaton." She turned to look at him. "Why does that make you smile?"

"Because you don't like him."

"That's an understatement."

"Agreed."

They turned into the parking lot.

Bella pulled her head out of the roof and danced in circles in the back. "You don't even know where we are, girl," Raine said.

A gentle hand turned her chin to face him. "I know where I am," he said and kissed her.

Matt held the conference room door open for Raine. All five of them showed. Blake Eaton leaned on the back legs of his chair chewing on a toothpick. Glen Oberweiss sat straight, clutching his thighs. The mayor folded his hands on top of the table, and Timothy Hart thumbed through his cell. Richard Beckett was the only one who offered eye contact.

Raine took a seat between him and Oberweiss, then fired up her tablet. One side of her dark hair covered her cheek while the other side was tucked behind an ear. Confident. Smart as hell. Beautiful.

"Chief?"

Matt blinked, then searched the table for who spoke. Mayor Green. "Yes. Let's get started."

Eaton interrupted before Matt had a chance to do the getting started. "You have interrogated us several times already. Now, you're bringing the family with?" He nodded the side of his head toward Raine. A rare breeze of rage blew through Matt.

"How about we let him tell us why she's here first?" Timothy Hart had put his phone away.

The mayor covered the minutes from last month. Big Jo at Yo-Yo Rentals was denied extending hours of operation on the water. Mrs. Oberweiss had her request to freeze the farmer's market table fee.

After a round of, "Ayes," the mayor asked Matt to explain the budget requests he added to the agenda.

"Thank you," Matt said. "As a new chief—"

Eaton mumbled, "Interim chief."

"I've noticed a few safety concerns I'm sure you'll be interested in." He passed out copies of his proposal. "You'll see first and foremost, I would like to enforce the state law banning golf carts from streets."

Eaton threw back his head. The mayor's mouth hung open. Hart held up a hand. "Let the man finish."

"Speed limit marquises are needed along the thoroughfare. As we all know, speeding along that road is too easy. Ticketing doesn't help since most of the speeding is done by the rotation of tourists. With the proximity to the beach, pedestrians are in grave danger."

Eaton mumbled, "Grave danger."

"Large mirrors north and south of the two bends in the thoroughfares adjacent to the beach accesses will help with pedestrian crossings at these locales. Finally, I am going to extend the territory of the third shift to include the beach in order to catch and prevent more poaching. This will include the need for two four-wheelers, six sets of night-vision goggles, and a new hire. Miss Clearwater?"

She cleared her throat. "I spoke with the FWC, the USFWS, and the DEP this afternoon. Ignoring the poaching could definitely keep us from getting the beach restoration grant."

Matt winked at her. She turned red. Man, he loved when she did that.

"In the off season, I train police departments up and down the Florida west coast and part of Alabama. This is important enough that I can make time to train our Ibis men in blue as soon as you need me."

"Thank you, Miss Clearwater," Matt said.

Mayor Green blew out air, making his cheeks expand like a chipmunk. Timothy Hart looked down and away. Blake Eaton, Matt believed, played cards on his phone.

It was Beckett who stuck up for him. "We have a budget for a reason. It hasn't been changed in years."

Everyone gawked at him, including Raine.

"This is more than two years' worth of line items," Oberweiss said.

This was like buying a house. Ask high, come down on your price, then make a deal.

"We can save 50 percent on the marquise speed limit lights by making them solar."

"Golf carts will cost us in the long run. They are one of the biggest attractions to the island."

Matt paused and sighed heavily. "It's a state law," he said, then nodded. "I might be able to bend."

Hart, the mayor, Oberweiss, and Beckett nodded.

Mayor Green lifted a hand. "I propose an approval for the budget items with the suggested adjustment for solar-powered speed limit marquise and without the golf cart ban. All those in favor?"

He needed a simple majority. Raine couldn't vote. All hands raised except Eaton. It took some work to keep from fist-pumping the air.

"Don't think this gives you an in to stay as chief," Eaton growled.

TWENTY-TWO

Matt parked next to her truck. Even in the dark, he could see it was her. It had been a long time since his heart skipped a beat.

The moonlit beach framed her silhouette. He sat for a moment. Her phone wasn't in her hand. Nothing was in her hands. They were in her pockets. She glanced up and down the beach as a light breeze blew her dark hair around her face.

He'd known he was sunk. This was the first time he realized he was lost.

"You're late," she said as he made his way down the beach access.

He stepped to her as miniature pine cones sank in the sand beneath his shoes.

"You're late," she repeated. "And, you're wearing pants on a beach."

He covered her words with his mouth. It was soft and inviting. Burying his fingers in her silky hair, he pulled her against him. She was warm and complicated, confused and confusing.

Her arms came between them and pushed. Her smile was brighter than the moon.

Taking her hand, he let her lead the way. "I was waiting at your house."

"Oh," she said barely loud enough for him to hear.

"We'll figure this you and I thing out. We've got nothing but time."

Pulling her hand away much too quickly, she dug it in her pocket. "First, I'll work with the night patrol officers on identifying turtle tracks, both hatchling and adult females. In order to not run over hatchlings, they'll need to keep it around five to ten miles an hour."

"Why do you do that?" he interrupted.

"Why do you always wear your gun?"

"Don't change the subject."

"Why do I do what?"

"Pull away from me."

"Anyone could see us."

"I don't believe you care about that any more than I do."

She pointed a few yards toward inland. "See here." Walking to a marked nest site, she squatted down. "This nest hatched earlier this evening. Do you see the tracks from the tiny flippers?"

They were tiny all right. Dozens of them.

"All tracks head straight for the water. No disorientations. This is the way it's supposed to happen."

"You're not going to record it?" He realized she didn't even bring her cinch sack with her.

"This is Zoe's section. She'll get it in the morning."

"Progress," he said mostly to himself.

"You're sure you don't care?" she said. "Because my sisters came over this morning and found two plates in the sink."

"I see."

"My mother told them you spent the night."

He shook his head. "Wait, wait, wait. Your mother?"

"Small town. Cop car. My driveway."

Taking a deep breath, he shrugged. "You might not have noticed yet, but I don't care too much about what people think of

146

me. I try to do what is right." He took her arm and guided her to a standing position. "And this is right."

"There's something else." She turned to face him. Her chest rose and fell.

Before she got to the something else, the focus of her gaze changed to the sand behind him.

"This," she said and jogged away. "Adult tracks." Her voice rose an octave like a toddler who just found an Easter egg.

"It is rare for a female to lay eggs this late in the season." She walked farther down the beach. He thought he could see the tracks, too. As they came closer he was sure of it. It was a giant replica of the hatchling tracks.

"This would be a false crawl, but still important not to tear up with four-wheeler tire tracks." Her head tilted and her brows dropped. "See how she came in, and then turned." Her feet stopped. Raine looked up and down the beach. "Something's wrong."

He didn't see anything and waited for her to explain.

"These tracks." She squatted again. "I've never seen them run horizontally along the beach."

The word, 'never',' coming from Raine Clearwater was enough for him. He unhooked his gun holster and clicked off the safety.

The tracks made a wide line and led down the beach. On either side, there were deep, alternating wedges made from the flippers. "Raine, look at this." He pointed inland a few feet. Footprints followed the path of the turtle tracks. The human kind.

She took off, jogging along the top of the tracks.

"No," she yelled as her jog turned into a full-out sprint.

He scanned the beach as he followed. It looked like regular beach to him.

Skidding to a stop ahead, she covered her mouth.

He had an idea of what it was but didn't want to go there.

When he caught up, there was a hole. A giant hole.

———

Raine paced around the hole, unable to pull her hand away from her mouth.

It was what she feared. An adult loggerhead. The hole was too deep. How could anyone possibly get her out?

"A ramp," Matt said. "We'll build a ramp."

She nodded. "Okay, yes." They had to try. "She needs water." She scanned the area. "I have a bucket and a towel in my truck."

"You go," Matt said like a cop. "I'm calling for backup."

"What are the police going to do?" she asked and sprinted down the beach before he had a chance to answer.

This was meant for Raine. Rage burned in her very soul.

She kept an eye on Matt as she ran back toward the hole, bucket and towel in hand. He circled the hole much like she'd done. The turtle was completely below the surface of the sand.

"What about a sheet of plywood?" he yelled as she came within ear's shot.

Shaking her head, she panted. "Too slippery." She dug the ark shell from her front pocket and tossed it to him. "We have to dig."

She stepped the few feet to the water.

"With this?" he said from behind her.

"Shovels are against turtle code. It's all I have." She filled the bucket with Gulf water and dipped the towel.

"I called Dane and Liam. Officer Galloway is on his way. Raine, we need shovels." Ignoring the shell, he dropped to his knees and started digging with both hands.

He was right about the shovels, but first she tossed the water on the back of the girl. Her flippers started moving uselessly as if she knew it was hopeless but had to try anyway. All it did was dig her in deeper. Raine tossed the towel over her back to help keep her hydrated, then pulled out her cell and dialed Dane.

Dane didn't answer until the fourth ring. "The chief already called. We're on our way."

She knew that. "We need shovels," she pleaded.

"I'll call Liam and tell him. I've got one in the back of my Jeep."

Matt's shirt and hair were already soaked with sweat.

"More on the left side," Raine said and dropped down next to him.

He didn't balk at her critique, just moved over and kept digging. "How long can she last like this?"

"Pretty long," Raine said, but how were they ever going to get her out?

Officer Galloway arrived. No greeting. Just, "Damn," and he started digging.

Two figures came out of the beach access path. "What the hell?" It was Zoe. Of course, Dane brought her. Raine should have known. Liam was close behind.

Matt stood. "Stop." It was his cop voice.

Raine interrupted. "Not far enough."

"We need to evaluate," he said.

"We need to dig," Raine argued and kept digging.

Liam didn't try to whisper. "We get that you don't like him, but he came out to help and brought Officer Galloway with him. Maybe give him a break?"

Out of the corner of her eyes, she noticed Matt glancing over to her. She did the same and shrugged.

Liam stood with his hands on his hips like a schoolteacher. "What if you soften the center of the slope there. Then, two of us can get in and push while two of you pull?"

"Good idea." The ends of Matt's fingers were raw. She could tell even in the moonlight.

Leaning close to him, she held out her shell. "It will help."

They dug and evaluated, evaluated and dug. She stood and wiped the sweat from her forehead with the back of her sandy arm.

Dane and Liam jumped in on each side of her. The turtle didn't move from the proximity, but she blinked and looked at them.

As they pulled and pushed, Zoe ran to the water and refilled the bucket.

"Not yet," Raine said, holding up an arm. "Wait on it."

Raine dug in front of the girl. Matt and Officer Galloway pulled. Liam and Dane pushed.

"Now!" Raine yelled to Zoe.

Zoe tossed the bucket of water on the turtle's back. Flippers started to move like she was swimming for her life. They hit Liam in the head. He bellowed but kept pushing.

"She's almost up," Zoe cheered, clapping her hands.

The turtle breached the edge, pulling herself the rest of the way out of the hole. She lay there looking at the humans, but not moving.

"Do we take her to Mote?" Matt asked.

"She's not injured."

"At least I'm not a dumbass this time," Matt said and smiled.

She closed her eyes and sighed. Taking the bucket from Zoe, she stepped her feet to the water and came back with it full. Gently, she pulled the towel from the shell and drizzled water over the girl.

She moved again, this time for the Gulf. The waters were calm. The sound of an enormous shell dragging along the ground was something she never wanted to forget. A few strokes of her flippers breached the water top, and as if nothing had happened, she disappeared.

Matt stood in the line of silent heroes. He lifted an arm high. "Yeah," he bellowed, three octaves lower than his normal voice.

Though dirty, exhausted, and sore, each still exchanged high fives and one-armed hugs.

All except Raine. Her gaze was stuck on the sand south of the hole. She hit Matt's shoulder with the back of her hand.

He turned to her. Raine pointed to the human footprints next to the long horizontal line of turtle tracks.

"No limp," Matt said.

Zoe stepped forward. "Where's the other set of prints?"

Matt looked between the two women. "Other set?"

"They washed away with the rising tide," Raine said.

Matt shook his head. "Help me understand."

TWENTY-THREE

"No sea turtle walks horizontally beside the water like this. It's either leaving the water or returning to it. That person," Raine said, pointing to the only set of human footprints still visible, "kept her from turning inland. The missing footprints are from the someone who kept her from turning to the water."

Zoe leaned into Dane. "I can't believe someone would do this intentionally."

Raine looked at Matt, then closed her eyes.

Dane said, "I'm driving Liam home and getting Zoe to bed … to sleep. She needs to get up early."

"I'm not sure if I can sleep after that," Zoe responded.

"Nest 62/6/V hatched earlier this evening," Raine said.

"You entered it, I assume?"

"She did not," Matt said. "I was a witness."

Zoe squinted at him, then picked up the shovels.

Dane took them out of her hand. "Call anytime, man," he said to Matt. "That was some stupid shit and incredible all at the same time."

"Thank you, Officer Galloway," Matt added. "Now, I know why you all wear shorts."

Galloway nodded as if he was still in awe. He reached out a hand and Matt took it. "I look forward to patrolling soon and catching mother fuckers like the ones who did this." His eyes went right to Raine. "Sorry, miss."

As the group disappeared into the beach access walkway, Matt whispered, "We're filthy. You should come to my house."

She looked up at him questioning.

"Your neighbor shouldn't get to see you shower tonight."

She stepped back.

"You did it again," he said.

"Did what?"

He collapsed on the sand and pulled her down with him. "Pulled away."

Rotating, she sat in front of him. Their knees touched. "We were just—" She looked back toward the beach access they had been kissing in an hour before. She turned to him, took a deep breath, and looked him in the eye.

It was like looking into her own, the color matched so closely.

"If we're going to do this," she said, pointing a finger back and forth between them.

"This?"

"Don't interrupt."

He held up his hands, palms out.

"Why do you keep an extra set of clothes in your SUV? How many women on Ibis have you been with?"

He sighed. "I have a dirty job. One."

"Oh," she said again, minus the mumbling.

She waited for him to ask. "Aren't you going to ask me the same?"

"Nope."

"What about now?" she argued. "What if someone sees us sitting like this? Aren't you the least bit worried?"

"Still nope."

As Galloway's black and white disappeared onto the street, Matt turned to Raine. "I told him to get a shower and change of clothes before finishing his shift." Matt couldn't quit shaking his head in awe. "This is something I'll never forget."

Hands deep in her pockets, Raine leaned against the driver's side door of her truck. Her smile was brighter than the moon. "You've said that once or twice already."

As fast as it came, her smile disappeared. "It was done on purpose."

He stepped to her and tucked a loose strand of hair away from her face and behind her ear. "Yes."

"I want it to be over, Matt."

"I know." He pressed his forehead against hers. She lifted on her toes and laid her mouth on his. Every part of him awakened.

She smiled around their lips. "You taste like beach."

He placed open palms against her truck, one on each side of her face. "Shower?"

"I don't have a toothbrush."

"I have an extra."

Her brows dropped, and she slid away.

He sighed and took her arm. "Again?"

"I don't want to doubt you." She waved her hands around as she spoke. Then, she swayed her head from side-to-side and said, "Not that I haven't done that since the day you arrived."

"Or the day Zoe came to my office in St. Pete."

The expression on her face told him she didn't think his joke was funny.

He took her hands and stopped her from pacing. This time, he leaned back against her car door and pulled her close to him. "Someday you're not going to do that."

"Do what?" she asked, looking up at him.

"Doubt us. I'm a patient man."

Her smile was slight, but it lit the night sky. "In the meantime, what do you want to know?"

"We're caked in sand."

"Hence the shower. Well, sort of hence."

"You'll have sand in your shower," she argued.

"Ah."

"Now, who's sorry they don't have an outside shower?"

"Definitely not me." He took her hand and pulled. "Come. We'll rinse off."

"In there? You're the one with pants on."

"They'll dry," he said and marched with her across the sand.

"I don't have people towels."

"Me either," he added.

She walked a step behind him, but at least she was still walking.

The water was warm and nearly as still as glass.

"Sharks like to hunt in shallow waters at night."

He paused, then glanced over to her. Her teeth shone in the moonlight.

"You grew up with a big brother. You should know that was not a smart joke." He grabbed her by the waist and threw her in.

She surfaced, gasping. He took the sides of her face and buried himself in all of the layers and mystery that were Raine Clearwater.

Her arms wound around his back and her legs around his waist. Together, they melded as his hands explored and memorized each dip and curve.

He took hold of the backs of her thighs, lifting her until heat met heat.

Her head fell backward. "Oh," she said long and throaty. Lifting her arms overhead, she leaned back until she stretched along the top of the water. He gripped her hips and drew her closer.

Her breath quickened. "We're going to," she said in short gasps, "run into the same roadblock we did last night, aren't we?"

"I'm no idiot."

She rose to a vertical position and set her feet in the sand. "Why are we here, then? Let's go to your—"

"Because we're sandy." He kissed her as he lifted her arms above her head, then ran his hands down her arms, around the swell of each side of her and over her waist.

The sound that came from deep in her throat sent him beyond the point of no return.

Wrapping her legs around him once more, she lowered one of her raised arms to rest on the top of her head and the other down the center of his chest.

As her hand explored over his abs and farther, he walked them deeper in the water. When she reached him, the air left his lungs. She maneuvered his pants until she freed him in the water and into her hands. Pressing his forehead against hers, he turned his head from side-to-side.

His hands became desperate, desperate to learn, to discover. He found what he was searching for as she cried out and shook in his hand. She clung to him as she moaned. Her teeth grazed his shoulder.

He lifted her chin to look at him. "Now," he said. It wasn't a question.

"Oh, yes."

He'd never put one on in the water before. It's amazing what desperation can do to a man. He had to see her.

"Look at me."

She did and he dove in. The light brown flickered and her lids fell closed. "Look at me," he said again.

Her eyes opened and nails dug into his shoulder blades.

They moved as one, deeper and deeper into the abyss that belonged to that moment.

Her hips were needy and reaching. Grabbing her backside, he reached as well, watching the moment she sucked air, and she clung to him. He let go. He let go into the woman who held his heart in the palm of his hands.

They clung to each other in the water through aftershocks. He held on with both arms, kissing the side of her head.

"How about that shower?" he whispered in her ear.

Raine helped Willow set folding chairs around the eight-foot plastic table Willow set up at the side of the dance floor in the back of Luciana's. Other than Willow, she was the first one there. "How's business?" Raine asked as she set up the last chair.

"Booming," Willow said. She carried a stack of cups with one hand and a pitcher of water with the other. "Not sure what it will be like after the rest of the treasure Seth found is discovered, but I'll take it."

The bell rang. Zoe and Dane walked in. Zoe wore her cowboy hat and Sun Trips work shirt. Dane, a tool belt.

"How is the house coming along?" Raine asked.

Dane sat and crossed a foot over his knee. "Just about ready for company."

Zoe hit him in the arm.

"Framing's done. The outside walls are nearly set," he said.

Liam came in next with his jeans, shirt and tie. He walked straight for Willow, took her hand low, kissed her cheek, and whispered something in her ear.

She blushed.

Dane and Liam shared the entire play-by-play of the turtle in the hole for Willow before their mom and dad arrived.

"Are we going to have to hear it all over again?" It wasn't Raine's favorite story by far.

"No, dear," her mother said and sat at the table. "Zoe already filled me in. Who would do such a thing?"

"That's part of why we're here," Raine said. Everyone became quiet and turned to look at her. "Chief Osborne called to say he would be late."

With an evil grin, Zoe mouthed the words, 'Chief Osborne?'

Dane lamented over the dead end that was the cornerstone that is Home and whether her mother would give away her garden overload at the market that Thursday. The bell rang again. Finally.

In full uniform, albeit soiled with something that looked like motor oil, Matt made his way to their table. Removing his hat, he sat in the only spot left at the head of the table between her mom and her.

Paula strolled over with a pad of paper and pencil in her hands.

"Well, isn't this just the best reservation of the day? What can I get for y'all?"

Everyone said water except Dane who wanted a draft and Liam peanuts.

"I'll be right back with that," she said and sauntered back behind the bar.

With the tips of her fingers, her mother touched Matt's forearm.

The hairs on the back of Raine's neck spiked and her eyes opened wide.

"Thank you for coming," her mother said to him. "Are you using protection?"

"Mom!" Zoe yelled.

Raine set her forehead in her hand, clamped her eyes shut, then lifted her head, letting her hand slide over her mouth.

Willow lifted both hands to Raine, palms out. "I didn't get a chance to tell her yet."

"What are we protecting?" Liam asked. He looked around the table. "What?" he asked again. "You mean Raine and ... Oh."

Dane smiled from ear to ear. "Oh, this is good. Do tell, Chief. And, welcome to the family, man."

TWENTY-FOUR

Matt looked to her. That damned sexy corner of his mouth lifted. How could he be smiling at a time like this?

She mouthed the words, "I'm so sorry."

"Why yes, of course, Mrs. Clearwater." He rubbed a hand along the back of his neck. "Shall we get down to why we're meeting this afternoon? At least I hope my relationship with Raine isn't the top of the agenda."

He said, 'relationship.'

He folded his hands and leaned over them. It was like a magnet in the center of the table drew everyone else in as well.

She may have been sweating by then, but she was more interested in solving her brother's murder than the mass embarrassment at hand.

"Although we have some answers to share with you, we still have more questions than answers."

"We believe you are being targeted. The purpose is likely to scare and/or distract you. Turtle Watch is experiencing a statistically improbable number of hatchling disorientation calls. Raine? You can explain this better than I can." He gestured a hand toward her.

She was still reeling about her mother's inappropriate question.

"Someone is snatching hatchlings, planting them and calling Turtle Watch. All. The. Damn. Time. Someone poached an entire nest of eggs and left lights on causing a massive disorientation."

Matt lifted his brows. "Succinct. Thank you. We have no leads on the tall, thin man spotted at the scene of the hacked awning that fell on Willow. I placed an ad in the paper."

He looked to Dane. "This is going to be hard news for you. I know you and Lucky Nemo are treasure hunting companions." He looked around the table. "It looks as if he is the prime suspect in the assault on you in the Gulf. He's been spotted lurking around two Turtle Watch events and … is walking with a limp."

"To hell with that," Dane said and pushed away from the table.

"It doesn't make sense that Lucky is Seth's killer," Matt added as Dane paced. "The motive is clearly the treasure, but if Lucky knew about the treasure before recently, he would have been searching the area more than just this last several weeks."

"Miriam Roberts has lawyered up. The five surviving divers who joined in Seth's last dive have solid alibis. Each of their eyewitness testimonies regarding the last time and place they saw Seth remains consistent. Some cavern named Crystal Springs."

This time, Raine pushed away from the table. She was followed by Willow and Zoe.

Since her sisters stood speechless, Raine spoke. "Seth would never waste his time in the Crystal Springs Cavern."

Matt nodded and held his hands out. "Okay, okay. But, we now know he was searching for this treasure. He could have been looking in there."

Shaking her head violently, Zoe leaned forward and pointed a finger. "That cavern is full of tourist traffic. Seth was looking for a hiding place, not one with thousands of visitors a year who could have found it themselves."

Dane marched to the table, turned his chair backward and plopped down. "We'll show these assholes a distraction. I've got two front-end loaders and two eight-foot-bed pick-ups ready for our diversion."

"Just stay clear of the leatherback nest," Raine reminded.

159

Matt nodded again. "Better sooner than later."

––––––––––

Since it was after school hours, Raine used the elementary school parking lot. She found a spot and hurried out of her truck. In the back were the two eight-foot folding tables she'd gotten from Luciana's.

Her father came walking toward her.

"It already started," she said as he neared. "I'm sorry. A juvenile loggerhead with something gastro was bobbing in the water. I fished him out, and now I'm late and smell like turtle."

"Island time." He released the truck bed door and slid out the first table.

She took the other one and carried it on top of her head. It was hard to believe. The people here. Many were the same from years gone by. They just had more wrinkles.

The strong scent of peppers, dill, fresh flowers, and fennel ignited a warmth in her soul and longing for a simpler time. Her mother sold a handful of okra out of a box on the ground. She, too, with lines drawing memories over her face.

It was like an old-time favorite record playing on a jukebox, and was scratched to a halt by Eli Murphy who stood at Mr. and Mrs. Henderson's table. His height and muscle mass made him stand out in the midst of the earthy, granola crowd.

"Eli," Raine said behind him. He turned as she walked toward him with the table on her head. Setting down his bundle of kale and blue potatoes, he took the table from her and set it up behind her mother in the grass.

"If it isn't Raine Clearwater." He wrapped his giant arms around her before she had a chance to warn him about her turtle perfume.

Three children stood next to them closer than personal space allowed. They stared up at the two of them. Raine was sure they were gawking at this giant, younger man shopping for kale at a farmer's market.

But then, their parents caught up to them.

"Emily," Raine said. "And, Amelia. How is vacation?"

"You remembered our names!" The one Raine remembered was named Amelia squealed. "Children, this is Mrs. Clearwater."

Even though her left eye twitched, Raine smiled.

"Are you the Turtle Lady?" asked the short girl with a ponytail high on her head.

"She sure is," Eli said. "And, I bet she has some turtle tattoos in her pockets."

As her parents arranged boxes of vegetables on the tables, Raine pulled out her rubber band full of tattoos. "What if I didn't?" she said to Eli as she bent down on one knee.

"These are the dampen and press kind," she said as she handed one to each of them. "Where are you going to put them?"

The oldest one made a muscle at Eli and pointed to an invisible biceps.

Eli threw back his head and laughed in the deep bellow only he could do.

Over his shoulder, Raine noticed a man in uniform across the street directing market traffic. Their eyes met and he winked. She didn't even care about the blushing anymore.

"Why don't the two of you come by Show Me's tonight?" Eli asked.

She stood to look at him face-to-face, but it didn't make much difference. "How does everyone know?"

"Winking?"

"Maybe that was for you," she said to him.

"Oh good. I'll wink back." And then, he did. "I close tonight."

Raine held up her hands. "Not that you're not my favorite bouncer, but your boss isn't too happy with me right now."

"He's in Vegas." Eli shrugged. "Again."

Now, he had her full attention. "Must be nice." She didn't know Blake Eaton went to Vegas ever, but, 'again,' could mean something." Rocking on her heels, she said, "Twice in one year. Must be nice."

"Twice? Not nearly." He shook his head. "I've lost track."

"No wonder he's rolling in it."

He shook his head. "Trying to make up for the Cowboy Crowne Casino debacle."

"I remember that." Or not. "A couple hundred thousand is change for a guy like Eaton."

Eli bent down and picked up his vegetables. "That's not enough zeros."

One more prod would seem too much like an interrogation. Which it was, but...

"Raine?"

Shaking her head, she looked up to him. "We might not be ready to move from winking across the street to out on a public date just yet. Really good to see you, Eli."

Looking up, she saw that Matt was gone. With her heart beating out of her chest, she walked around the two folding tables and tied one of her mother's aprons around her waist. "So, what's my job?"

Her mother pointed toward the scale and biodegradable plastic bags. "Take customers from that end of the table after you call Chief Osborne to tell him what has you all in a tizzy."

"I have got to work on my poker face," she mumbled as she stepped away.

He didn't answer until the fifth ring. She almost hung up.

"Hello, beautiful."

"I need to see you." Looking down, she noted she was shaking her hand like an author with writer's cramp.

"Thank you." His voice was happy enough that it took her aback.

"Not like that. I have information."

"What was that with Eli Murphy?" he asked slowly. "I can't tell if I should be worried about him flirting with you or flirting with me."

"He's married. So, neither."

"That doesn't necessarily make a difference."

"He wants us, you and me, to come see him at Show Me's. He's working tonight."

"That's ironic as I was just thinking about taking you out for a nice meal."

She may have stomped a foot. "Stop changing the subject."

"What subject was that again?"

"I can hear you smiling. It's irritating."

"Yes, but I make up for it with my good looks."

"Blake Eaton," she barked.

"What did you say?"

"I have information about Blake Eaton."

"I'll pick you up at seven."

"I'll meet you at your place." She had no time to explain why. "I have to go help my folks."

TWENTY-FIVE

Matt leaned against his SUV as Raine turned into his lot. The breeze was welcoming and the temperature refreshing. He might become a Floridian yet.

She parked next to him and was not smiling.

He'd barely opened her door when she started.

"Blake Eaton killed my brother." She got out and stood square in front of him, crossing her arms. The stance made her linen pants, strappy sandals, and strapless floral blouse look out of place.

"Eli Murphy told me that Eaton lost ..." She curled her fingers like quotations. "More zeros than $200,000 and that he's gone to Vegas more times this year than Eli can remember.

"He's there right now. Plane tickets are $82 one way. We leave tonight. If you can't, I understand, but I'm going."

He dared not to grab her wrists, so he linked their fingers together and held them near his shoulders. "First of all, you look incredible."

Her dark hair was smoothed flat and shiny, and she smelled like an ocean breeze.

"We can't arrest him for losing money in Vegas."

She took a deep breath and opened her mouth.

164

He let go of one of her hands and placed a finger on her lips. "I'll look into it. We'll look into it. But, we need proof that will hold up in court."

Her bare shoulders fell. He placed his hands over them and wasn't hungry for food anymore.

She turned her chin away. "I'm going."

"We'll go," he said matter-of-factly.

She did a double-take back toward him.

He took hold of her face with both hands. "We'll go when he's not there. Let's get some dinner, and we'll talk."

Her eyes rolled and her lids closed.

Dipping his lips to her ear, he whispered, "Why wouldn't you let me pick you up?"

He felt her inhale deeply as her shoulders lifted and fell. She leaned back against her truck and folded her arms. "Because I want to stay with you tonight but don't want you to have to take me home at 5 a.m."

"I'm not hungry for food anymore."

She laughed and stuck out a hand, palm up and placed a fist on top.

"Rock, Paper, Scissors?" He didn't understand.

"To see which car we take to Show Me's."

He won with scissors.

"Two out of three?" she offered.

"Nope. I drive."

"That's not fair." She grinned and headed for his SUV.

"It was bad enough spending the night at your place with my Ibis Island issue black and white in front of your house. Don't get me wrong. Worth it by far, yet unprofessional. But out to dinner?" He took her hand and headed for the other side of the lot. "We're taking my car."

"You have a car?" she asked and stopped a few feet before they reached it. "You have a fifteen-year-old Corolla with rust starting around the back tire wells?"

"Sixteen and be nice to her. You'll hurt her feelings."

"I'm impressed is all. Most men want their car to show their personality."

"Who says I don't?"

"I brought a toothbrush."

He stopped her at the passenger door and kissed her long and hard. He could have stayed there in the thick Florida evening air, losing himself in this woman. He heard what he'd learned to be a caw of an island raven somewhere behind him.

A small croon emanated from her throat. He set his forehead on hers. "You're making it difficult not to throw you over my shoulder and take you to my cave."

"You kissed me." She sighed and looked at him with soft brown eyes. "Are you sure you want to do this?"

"I remember being in your bed. I remember in the Gulf being in—"

Her expression was unreadable.

"That's not what you mean. I think I was sure the day you jumped in the Gulf with your bridesmaid's dress on." He closed one eye. "Or, when you nearly stormed onto Richard Beckett's desk."

She bumped him out of the way and opened the door.

Wendell Hopp was valet again. As Matt pulled to a stop, Raine got out. This was miles different from coming here with Matt in uniform and her with a folder of code violation citations.

"Wendell Hopp," Raine scolded. "Pick your jaw up off the gravel."

Matt handed Wendell a bill. "What she said." Matt pointed to Raine.

As he took her hand, she pretended to look somewhere behind him so she could inhale the clean scent he seemed to have even when sweaty and digging out a trapped loggerhead. Dress pants and a fitted shirt. What was she doing with a police chief? If this went south, she wanted to remember every moment.

They walked into a crowd of women wearing impossible heels

with all sorts of body parts peeking out of clothing. As they waited for their tables, each seemed to throw back their hair and smile like they were posing for a photoshoot.

Matt stepped to the hostess podium. "Osborne for two."

"Chief! Raine!" a deep voice bellowed from over her shoulder.

It was like an announcement over a bull horn.

Eli Murphy left his post as bouncer and hurried over to them. "I've got your table right over here."

Matt glanced to her. She shrugged.

It was a dark, corner booth in the back of the restaurant seating section. She would have preferred a table on the beach if only to show him the code infractions.

Sliding in, she picked up a menu.

"You said it was too early for this," Eli said and waved a thumb between the two of them, then took Matt's hand and shook.

She pointed over her menu at Matt. "It was his idea."

"I say it's a good one. It's busy as hell out there. Make sure to stop by and see me before you leave." Eli turned sideways, dodging bodies on his tiptoes as he made his way to his post in front of the bar entrance.

She glanced up to Matt through her lashes. "You're not looking at the menu."

"I like to choose from the specials."

Their waitress bounced to the table dressed in black slacks and a white blouse. "Raine," she said. "Good to see you."

"Kim Shelby, look at you." Raine looked up. "This is Matt. Matt, Kim."

"So, you're the new chief?" Dipping closer to the table, she added, "Everyone's talking."

"Nice to meet you. Do you have specials tonight?"

She turned over a single page and set it in front of him. "Stoned mushrooms. They're stuffed with a melted gouda cheese, red wine butter sauce, drizzled balsamic-pomegranate reduction and tomato-cilantro relish. Or, our Cajun catch. It's a blackened Island Grouper with shrimp tossed in a Cajun butter sauce, with a toasted garlic crostini sprinkle. May I start you two off with something to drink?"

He gestured to Raine.

"House red," she said.

"Whiskey on ice," Matt said, and Kim left.

She leaned in. "Blake Eaton."

He sighed. "We'll wait until he returns from Vegas, then we'll fly out and ask around."

She felt her mouth open in a little O. She couldn't help it.

Leaning forward, he spoke softly. "I need to be transparent with you. Facts help. They bring us closer to the truth, closer to an arrest. But, even if we find out he lost millions right after your brother was killed, that means little in court."

"Why were you in the parking lot?" She knew it was random but couldn't help that either.

His head shook back and forth. It was slight, but made his point. "I had a girl up in my apartment." He lifted the corner of his mouth.

She frowned.

"Someday you're going to stop doing that. I'm a patient man," he repeated. "Mostly. She is covered in fur and slobbers on my furniture."

"I knew who you meant."

"Listen, Raine. Since college, I've been with exactly one woman. We dated for eight years. The breakup was messy."

"I'm sorry."

"No need. It was the right decision."

"What happened?"

"We were young. In the beginning, we shared the same taste in music, the same type of vehicle and color of Skittles. As we grew, the important things were more important. I wanted kids; she didn't. I'm a homebody; she needs to travel. I'm frugal; she liked to spend it before she made it. I could have compromised. She didn't want to. That should have been my first red flag. Or, maybe the fourth. She moved with me from Reno to Chicago. She wanted Lake Shore Drive. I wanted stability, so she broke it off."

As Kim returned with drinks, Raine and Matt pulled apart like an opening curtain.

Raine took a sip as Matt ordered the Cajun Catch. "The Stoned mushrooms sound good. Thanks."

They spoke of high school and college, family and hobbies. Never once did he ask to reciprocate his love life history.

He dipped over the table, this time close enough for her to feel his crisp breath with a hint of whiskey. "The sun sets soon."

"It's cloudy," she said, regretting it before it came out. Rather than sticking her foot in her mouth again, she took a sip of her wine.

"Let's eat and then give it a try. You can show me those non-compliant lights."

TWENTY-SIX

Morning dawn streamed through the sky light in the conference room. Since Glory wouldn't arrive for more than an hour, Matt prepared the interactive smartboard and loaded the slide show for Raine.

He woke with her that morning. She'd dressed as fast as a fireman, brushed her teeth, and skipped breakfast. Stopping to help make the bed, she was so smooth, it was hard to tell she was rushed. Especially when he took her in his arms and kissed her before she left.

He knew everything he needed to know about Raine Clearwater. The rest was intriguing surprises.

Third shift would return soon. The two of them who were off last night waited in the breakroom eating the fresh donuts Matt picked up from CJ's and the coffee he had ready for them.

Raine's Vegas idea was a good one. He had Cummings monitor when Eaton returned. The kid would be on call during first shift for any progression with the bait set adjacent to Dane Corbin's Sun Trips locale and with the Seth Clearwater case in general. He would ask Pence to do the same for second shift and Galloway third.

His phone vibrated. Pulling it out, he'd be damned if his heart didn't do a little thing when he saw it was her.

going to be late

pit deep in sand proving a false crawl is not false

He had no clue what that meant. It didn't change the already knowing everything he needed to know about her.

"You get these from Clarence, boss?" Galloway walked in the room with Officer Cruz on his tail. "I'm gonna get fat if you decide to stick around."

"Not sure if that's a vote of confidence or not," Matt said and greeted them. "I'm going to need to see you in my office for a short meeting after the meeting."

Fleming elbowed him. "Oooo."

He could hear Boyer and Koch arrive through the back as they offered their regular passing-of-the-guard ribbing to one another. "Hope those traffic tickets aren't too much for you today." Sounded like Koch.

"I'm sure you had a major drug bust followed by murder one," another returned.

Galloway leaned against the back wall with a steaming cup and long john. "How long should I tell the missus before I'm home?"

Matt erased the board notes from the dry erase board. "Miss Clearwater said an hour."

"Miss Clearwater," Boyer muttered and lifted a brow to Koch.

Matt stopped and turned. "Is there something you'd like to say, boys?"

"No, sir," they said in unison and sat.

He finished with his erasing as he said, "And, no, I don't call her that when we're at dinner."

"Whoa!" Galloway hollered. "I did not see that coming." He looked around the table. "Did any of you see that coming?"

"Dude, where have you been?" Boyer leaned back in his chair. "They were at Show Me's last night."

"I can hear you," Matt said sarcastically.

"Right. Sorry. Really. But Show Me's? Do you think they spit in your food? Blake and Miss Clearwater, ya know, oil and water?" Galloway emphasized the word, 'Miss.'

"She got a call before we made it to food. Possible tragedy averted."

"Raine Clearwater. Smart and hot."

The room went silent. Matt lifted his brows.

"She's standing behind me, isn't she?" Galloway turned his head to the door. "No disrespect, Teach."

"None taken," she said, walking to the front of the room. Dropping her cinch sack on the table, she faced the group. "We at Ibis Island Turtle Watch honestly appreciate you stepping up for this addition to your job description. Today, we're going to cover some basic sea turtle code and law facts you'll need to know as you patrol the beaches."

She spoke as she picked up the slide show remote. "By the mid-nineteenth century, sea turtle numbers were critically low." She flipped to a black and white of a thin, gray man. "This is Dr. Archie Carr. He's the author of the award-winning book, *The Windward Road*, which first alerted the world to the plight of sea turtles."

She flipped to a photo of a Loggerhead. "A female sea turtle stores enough sperm from one mating to lay four to five nests of eggs."

"Ouch. That sucks," Koch whispered to Fleming loud enough for her to hear.

With a straight face, Raine said, "And like Officer Koch here, it takes a Loggerhead around thirty-two to thirty-five years to reach sexual maturity." She winked.

The room erupted in laughter, and Matt's heart fell out of his chest and landed at her feet.

"Conservation for this species began in 1983." She switched to a bar graph. "Close to thirty-two years later, nest numbers began to grow."

She turned and set both hands on the table. Dirt was under her nails and sand stuck to her Turtle Watch shirt. She leaned in and looked each one in the eye. "I realize this might not be your motivation for being here this morning. It might be because you're interested in catching the poachers, or maybe just because the chief ordered you here. We are … I am grateful either way."

Stepping to the side of the screen, she flipped to a new slide. It was a list.

"Ibis Island beach code infractions include beachfront properties with furniture left on the beach or chairs not stacked at night."

She passed around something the size of an index card with cellophane covering a hole in the center. "The lights in this room are made with white light. Turtles follow white light as it mimics the bands of color in the horizon. If you hold up your card, you'll see the ceiling lights. When you pull the amber cellophane over the hole, the lights from the ceiling disappear.

"This is why beachfront property is required to use amber-colored lighting that also directs the beam of light down or away from the direction of the beach."

Next slide.

"The reason I'm telling you this is because code infractions, therefore, also include leaving on lights visible from the beach that are not amber and facing downward. No flashlights, not even from cell phones."

She spent ample time covering each infraction and the reason for it, answering questions and turning him on all at the same time.

"The following are illegal rather than a simple code infraction." As she flipped the slide, she explained, "Poaching is obviously against the law, but much like our manatees, so is handling or even touching an adult or sea turtle hatchling. Disturbing a nesting female or disturbing a nest is also against conservation laws. Tomorrow morning, we'll cover how to avoid injuring or disturbing females as they make their nests or hatchlings as they emerge. Questions?"

"No, ma'am."

"Now, where can I find one of those donuts?"

Matt initiated a round of applause. "Breakroom. There's coffee, too. Can I see you before you leave?"

As she packed her materials, Fleming whispered something to her Matt couldn't hear before she headed for the breakroom.

Galloway followed him to his office. "Should I shut the door?"

Matt considered it, but with Raine on her way, declined.

"I'm going to be gone overnight for a day or two soon. I'd like you to be on call for me. I'll, of course, pay overtime if it falls on your day off."

"I can do that. Let me know when."

She stepped to his door and waited in the hallway.

"Come in, Raine."

He spoke to the two of them. "I have Officer Cummings watching for Blake Eaton's return from his latest out-of-state trip. Raine has a professional history with him, so she's going with me."

Galloway rolled his eyes.

"You have something to say, Officer?"

"No. No, sir." Galloway rocked on his heels. "Well, only that Eaton was in the Java-Java drive-thru this morning."

"Let's go," Raine blurted. "I'm going. Are we going?"

"Hold on, hold on." Matt sat and contemplated. "Yes, we're going. I need to make sure and have one officer per shift assigned for anything regarding Dane's bait trap and especially anything pertaining to the … to solving your brother's murder."

Galloway shrugged. "Consider it done."

"So, when's the flight?" Raine asked.

Without being able to think of anything holding him back, he nodded. "Tomorrow. I'll check departures. Thank you, Officer. Get home to that missus of yours."

Matt shut the door as Galloway left the room. "There's more."

"That sounds bad." Raine sat.

"I want you to control that quite nasty temper of yours."

"No promises," she said slowly.

"Dane found asphalt poured around the leatherback nest."

She barely had time for her butt to hit the seat before she bolted to her feet. "No. Matt. No, listen to me. The hatchlings. They have to feel— in order to know— Matt, sea turtles come back to within a few miles of where they were born to lay their eggs.

"After thirty-two years?"

"Yes. Part of the process of knowing both how to get to the

water and how to return involves feeling what it's like to walk over the sand."

"I'll take care of it."

"How?"

"I've got Beckett and Eaton meeting us there in an hour."

"Why Beckett?"

"Beckett worked the land transaction for Eaton."

"Of course, he did."

TWENTY-SEVEN

R aine couldn't decide whether to pry Matt's hand from her arm or be thankful he held her back.

Between Dane's front-end loaders and pick-ups and Eaton's mass of poured asphalt around the leatherback nest, she could hardly see straight.

"We are going to work this out," Matt said, with an emphasis on the word 'going.'

Lines of sweat dripped down her back, more from rage than the heat of the day. The nest. With her free hand, she grabbed the side of her hair. What would the FWC say? Could the hatchlings possibly make it with all of this?

Blake Eaton and Richard Beckett stood side-by-side, both dressed like idiots in the rising Florida sun. They looked like they were on their way to dinner and dancing rather than talk around a construction site at nine in the morning.

"We didn't break any laws," Eaton said like Raine was a bug on his windshield. "Or even any of your precious codes." He waved a hand around like a game show host. "See? I even left three-foot on all sides of the thing."

She stepped to him, Matt holding her arm back. "This, 'thing,' is a highly endangered leatherback nest. Not only does this interfere with the hatchling's ability to—"

"Fine me," Eaton said while checking his fingernails.

Heat filled her head and threatened to boil over. Yanking her arm from Matt, she spun and pushed with both hands. "I'll do better than that, I'll—"

"Whoa, now." This time, Matt grabbed her from around the waist.

She clawed and kicked as Eaton gathered his balance. "You'll pay for that, you freak."

Richard Beckett stepped between them. She could almost reach him when he said, "Blake." And held his arms out, palms down.

Eaton did a double take. Frankly, so did she. Matt didn't let go, but let her feet reach the ground.

"We don't need this," Beckett said.

"Damn right. That's what the hell I'm saying." Eaton straightened his blue button-down short-sleeve shirt. He craned around Beckett and pointed a finger to Raine. "Everyone saw that, you—"

Beckett put a hand on Eaton's shoulder. "We don't need the lot."

Eaton pulled his chin back and, with wide eyes, started at Beckett. "The fuck is wrong with you?"

"We can cut it off through here." Beckett encircled a large part of the lot with his arms. "You still add twenty-five parking spaces. It's fifteen extra spots. We don't need them."

"You can take your orders," Eaton said to her. "And your suggestions," he said, turning his gaze to Beckett. "And shove them up your asses."

"Dig it up," Beckett said to Raine. "I'll take care of him."

Raine stood with her mouth open as Eaton mumbled incoherently. "Why?" she finally said.

He sighed loudly. "Because I can."

On one side of Raine was Dane, the other Matt. With their knees touching, they sat in a circle on the concrete floor of the tiny Sun

Trips Touring registration booth. Outside, front-end loaders and extended four-by-four pickups parked around a circle of tarps.

"So, um digging up asphalt near the leatherback nest could—" she whispered.

Dane leaned around her with his attention pointed at Matt. "They never said a word about the machinery and tarps."

Raine continued, "If we could just dump sand over—"

"I noted that, yes," Matt answered. "And yet Eaton's gaze kept jumping back and forth in that direction."

Raine put one hand on each of their shoulders. "Okay, okay. They took the bait. And, by the way, why," she said to Matt as she pushed the shoulder under her hand, "did you just stand there when Eaton was all over me?"

Blinking, he turned his attention toward her. "I wanted to see what Beckett would do, if anything. He came through."

"Yet," Dane injected, "he couldn't keep his eyes off our fake dig site either."

Matt nodded. "Doesn't mean they'll show."

Dane leaned back and sat up straight. "They'll show."

Raine pulled her cell out of the pocket of her hoodie and texted Liam.

you good?

Sticking it back in her pocket, she leaned in. "Where do you want me?"

She still had a hand on her phone when it vibrated. Pulling it back out of her pocket, she noted.

Yes. Willow's texted us every ten minutes. This could be a long night.

Raine's shoulders dropped at the thought of Willow having to stay home for this, but their parents weren't willing to watch Chloe and miss out.

She messaged her mom.

how's life in the bushes?

"We're going to duck into the front-end loader closest to the nest," Matt answered. "Ready?" He stood but not tall enough to be seen out the reception window.

Raine nodded and checked her phone. Her mother had responded.

kinda busy right now

"Eww," Raine said.

He paused. "What's the matter?"

Raine shook her head and lifted a hand. He took it. They made it to the door and stopped.

Matt looked around and then pulled on her arm. She followed at a quick pace to the driver's side of the machine. He opened the door and let her climb up first.

"Where's the passenger seat?" she whispered before realizing that was a dumb question. At least it was a big seat.

The tarped-in area was only about as big as a large kitchen and ended at the water on both sides. "How long do we stay?" she asked.

Climbing in, he pulled her beneath his arm. "As long as it takes. Are you sure about this?"

"What?" Raine turned to look at him. "You mean the stakeout? Yes. I couldn't sleep if you all were out here anyway."

He kissed the side of her head. "Someday you'll be able to let go."

"Hey. I let my sisters take Turtle Watch calls, didn't I? And the hatchling release."

"That was because you were chasing Lucky Nemo."

She sighed and nestled under his arm. "When will you pick me up tomorrow?"

"Plane leaves at 3:30 p.m. I'll pick you up at 1 p.m."

"Clearwater or Sarasota?"

"Clearwater."

The comfortable silence that ensued was cherished. She should be helping him watch, but for just this moment, she let herself sink into the circle of peace that surrounded this man everywhere he went.

Whether it was wading through a pouring water main break with pylon cones or yelling orders over his walkie for backup to help with a poached nest. Coming to the hospital to make sure her family knew first that Willow's accident was no accident to manipulating a room of city officials into buying a new four-wheeler and hiring an additional officer for nighttime beach patrol. And, thinking they bargained a deal.

For the first time in her life, she had someone she could honestly say the words, 'I love you' to. It didn't terrify her or leave her insecure. Instead, she turned her head into his shirt, inhaling his scent of sandalwood and Gulf breeze.

His lips pressed against the side of her head and his voice was deep and throaty. "And I love you."

Her eyes flew open. Oh, no. Had she said that out loud? Her heart should be racing. Her back should be plastered against the door on the other side of the front-end loader cab. Instead, the corners of her mouth curled and she sank deeper into his arms.

And, at that, she let sleep take her.

Matt's eyes scanned the area from one side to the other. Raine was exhausted in his arms. Even though she refused to stay home and rest up for tomorrow's long and busy day, he was at least glad she fell asleep.

No movement could be seen from the Sun Trips hut, the bushes where Henry and Harmony sat or the pickup that held Liam and Zoe. They actually made a decent stakeout team. Galloway was on call and the light was—

"I love you," Raine mumbled into his chest.

His eyes closed and, even though her words were spoken in her sleep, he laid his lips on the side of her head and whispered back, "And I love you."

Something out of the corner of his eye made his gaze whip to a spot behind the Sun Trips hut. It was Dane. Was he taking a leak?

His muscles tensed as he did another quick scan of his surroundings. Dane squatted like a catcher at the plate. His stare was focused on the water.

As Matt rotated to that direction, he saw nothing. The water wasn't calm, but it wasn't choppy either. Regardless, there was nothing sticking up. No splashing. Trusting Dane, he ducked lower and eased Raine down to the bench seat of the cab.

A half a head encased in scuba gear appeared. He would have assumed it was a turtle if not for Dane's reaction.

Dane disappeared around the side of the hut. Just as Matt pulled his phone out to text him, his phone vibrated.

someones in the water

Matt responded.

i see him

there could be more than one

wait for my signal

He released the latch of the door, but kept it closed. Either the diver was three-foot tall, or he stayed as low as possible and approached the beach, because all that remained out of the water was his head to eye level.

The head scanned the beach, and then waited.

As he watched the head, he texted Liam and Henry.

man in the water

stay where you are

TWENTY-EIGHT

The moon was a sliver, and yet with the cloudless sky, it lit the light sand enough to see his outline. Matt white-knuckled the door handle.

Without letting go of the door, he did a 360 scan. It took him less than four seconds, but when he turned around, a body soared through the air and landed in the water on top of the diver.

"Aww, damn it, Dane." As he opened the door, he heard Raine ask something, but he didn't have time for that. It was clearly a man. Grabbing for his handcuffs, he reached the two in five strides.

"I'll stab you in the other leg, you stupid mother fucker."

A knife flew away from the two of them and landed close to the front-end loader. Oddly shaped, it reflected moonlight in strange patterns, but Matt didn't have time for that either. "Dane, let go!" he ordered.

Ignoring his orders, Dane locked the thrashing man's arms over and behind his head. Matt couldn't tell that it was Lucky but he trusted Dane with that, too. He knuckle punched the man's right thigh.

Lucky became limp and cried out in pain.

Reaching over their heads, Matt slapped the cuffs on one of

Lucky's hands. Like a dance move he'd used a hundred times, he twisted the arm down and around as he grabbed the other and locked the cuffs around the wrist.

Soaking wet, Dane bent over sucking air with his hands on his thighs. He lifted his head high enough to say, "Search him, Chief. He's got more hidden than just the one knife."

Matt pulled out his Swiss Army knife, cut the backpack off and tossed it toward the knife Dane had chucked. As he searched Lucky, he scanned his surrounding for others.

Circling the three of them was the whole group. Henry, Harmony, Liam, Zoe, and Raine. They weren't looking at Lucky but at the jewel-encased knife Raine held in her hands.

———

Raine stood at Willow's door. She didn't want to wake Chloe, so she texted her instead.

at your front door

open up

She must have been sitting in her front room because she opened immediately and threw her arms around Raine. The hug was long and tight and didn't even make Raine uncomfortable.

"I hated not being there," Willow said into Raine's hair. As soon as she said it, she pulled away. With large eyes, she amended, "Not that I would expect Mom and Dad to watch Chloe and miss it. I just—"

"I know," Raine said and stepped around her. Neatly folded laundry covered the couch and one of the cozy chairs. "The others are coming. Let's make some room for them to sit."

Picking up a pile that clearly belonged to Chloe, Raine said, "How much did Liam tell you?"

Willow followed with an equally tall stack of little girl clothing down the hallway to Chloe's room. "That you caught Lucky Nemo and that he was carrying a piece of Luciana Bezan's dowry. Another piece."

Succinct, but not all. Raine decided to wait for the others. "We were supposed to stay put."

Chloe slept with her little mouth open. She looked like everything that represented peace and innocence. So as not to wake Chloe, she set the folded clothes along the wall next to the only dresser in the room.

"We didn't," Raine whispered. "None of us. As soon as the commotion started, we all came running from our lookout spots, even Dad."

Willow set her pile next to Raine's. "And Matt?"

Shrugging, Raine headed back to the front room. "He will have an interrogation and paperwork. I don't expect to hear from him tonight."

"That would be difficult."

Raine paused. It wasn't. Even when they disagreed, even when they fought.

The front door opened. Liam stepped in and made it to Willow. Their kiss was deep enough that it was uncomfortable for Raine. It was rare for the two of them, so she decided not to razz them like she would Dane and Zoe.

"I'll make drinks," Willow said as she headed for the kitchen. Liam followed as three knocks rapped the door. It opened before Raine could answer.

Her parents and Zoe walked in. "Dane wanted to stick around and keep an eye on things," Zoe said.

Raine tried to focus as the play-by-play was told twice through for Willow and, likely, so others could speak it out loud. Better to organize their thoughts that way.

Her mother sat on the floor in front of her father. She crossed her legs like a teenager. Liam, Willow, and Zoe took the couch as Liam spoke animatedly with his hands.

This was her family, and she was loved.

"The knife," her mother said in awe. "Do you think that is from the night Lucky tried to hurt Dane near the under under?"

Liam snorted. "And got a leg full of his own knife."

"Exactly," her mother continued. "But was that knife from the under under? Or from the night Seth was—" She closed her eyes and dipped her chin.

Willow asked, "Or did Lucky find the cornerstone that is Home?"

Liam shook his head. "Then, why was he sniffing around the Sun Trips bait dig?"

"Did you see the size of those jewels?" Raine asked.

Her father wasn't looking at Liam. He was looking at her. "We weren't the only ones watching Dane and Lucky tonight."

The room fell silent as all eyes turned to him and waited.

"There were two men. They must have been hiding in the same bushes Harmony and I were."

Her mother craned her head to face him. "Henry?"

"It's okay. You didn't see them." His expression was unreadable. Textbook Henry. "And I don't think they saw us until—" He took a deep, cleansing breath. "Until we left our cover like Chief Osborne told us not to."

The silence was deafening. She wasn't sure how long it lasted.

It was Zoe who broke it. "When will you talk to Matt?"

They looked to her for that now. As if she and Matt were a couple. She guessed they were. She shook her head. "Sometime in the morning, I suppose." Now was as good as time as any to tell them. "We are taking a trip to Vegas. We leave in the morning."

"What?" Liam said, hopefully louder than he meant to.

"I ran into Eli Murphy at the farmer's market. He told me Blake Eaton lost millions in Vegas a few years ago and has been trying to make up for it ever since."

Zoe held up a pointed finger. "There must be dozens of casinos in Vegas."

Raine nodded. "Eli called him one unlucky rodeo craps clown."

"Cowboy Crowne Casino," Zoe said. "How long will you be gone?"

"One night?" Raine shrugged. "Maybe two. Matt picks me up tomorrow afternoon."

"What about the parade?" Willow asked.

The parade. How could she have forgotten about the parade?

"You take over for me. I need to do this. I'll be able to talk to Matt more on the plane. I'll make a text thread and keep you all updated. We're getting close. I can feel it."

The knife was in an evidence bag and currently stuffed in the back of Matt's waistband; so was the one used to murder Seth Clearwater. With Lucky's file beneath his arm, he walked into the interrogation room that also double-tripled as the booking and visitation room.

The table in the middle of the room was aged yet sturdy. Lucky sat with his cuffed hands folded. The tats and dreads didn't match the IIPD-issued gray sweatpants and shirt.

Setting the file at the edge, Matt sat at the opposite side. "You've been busy."

Lucky lifted his hands. "These really necessary?"

"Standard procedure," Matt lied.

Without opening it, Matt set an open hand on the file.

Lifting his brows, Lucky looked around the room and said, "Diving at night isn't against the law."

Matt folded his hands and leaned forward. "Attempted murder is." Patting the file, he added, "I expect you know that's not all we have."

Lucky smiled wide enough that his gold tooth shone in the florescent lights. "You need proof."

Leaning forward, he reached around his back, pulled the knife from his waistband and set it in the middle of the table. Yellow gold, with two enormous emeralds and an even larger ruby set in the handle.

It was like watching a cocaine addict look at a few lines.

Tiny beads of sweat formed on Lucky's upper lip. "A city boy like you might not know that divers wear knives."

Matt reached around and did the same with Seth's murder weapon. He set it next to the first one. Other than the jewels being closer together, it was a match.

Lucky's eyes dropped. His head tilted and he brought his face closer.

"Interesting," Matt said. "The fact that you've obviously never seen the first one shows how very set up you were."

Lucky tried to turn his head away, yet he couldn't get his gaze to move from the treasure that lay between them.

Matt waited a good long while. "You haven't killed anyone, Lucky. You're being used. Who gave you that knife?"

Lucky dropped the lids of his eyes to half-closed, then shook his head slowly.

"What could possibly be worth being an accessory to Man One?"

He still hadn't asked to lawyer up. Matt would give him the night to think about it. Or two.

He stood and pushed in his chair. "I have a plane to catch," he said as he picked up the knives and stuffed them back in his waistband. "The last time someone involved in this mess sat in that seat, he ended up killed in his cell." Matt scratched the back of his head. "We still haven't figured out how."

"You don't get it," Lucky said to Matt as he walked to the door. "And I got nothin' to say."

"It's too bad a small county like this can't afford cameras in each cell," Matt said as he reached for the door handle.

"A key card," Lucky blurted.

Matt paused. He didn't mean to, but there were only three key cards to enter the cellblock. One was in the safe. He held one and the other—

TWENTY-NINE

Matt sat with a hip on the corner of his desk. Zoe offered to take Bella to the vet for boarding, saving Officer Cummings from more exploitation. Officer Galloway was on his way in.

"Morning, Chief," Galloway said. "You wanted to see me? Nice job with Nemo. That was brilliant."

"It was Dane Corbin and Liam Morrison's idea mostly. Come in and have a seat." Matt shut the door behind him and took back the spot on the corner of his desk. He spoke softly. "It's time for me to go. I plan on one night, two max."

Galloway nodded.

"I don't want anything to happen to Lucky Nemo while I'm gone or any other time."

Jerking his chin up, Galloway said, "Ah. Like Chief Roberts."

It was Matt's turn to nod. I'm having four new key cards to county made today. I'm going to leave one for you with Officer Pence. I have one for Cummings, too."

He needed to sink in what he was trying to say without saying too much. "Only the three of you," he said with more emphasis.

The muscles in Galloway's face fell. "Oh," he said. "Yes, sir."

"I'll have the fourth." He stood and paced. "Cummings will give his copy to Lucy Green to use in the day during her shift."

Galloway's eyes looked like a man who just ended red-eye shift. "Why don't you go home and get some sleep? I'll leave my cell on if you need anything."

"Yes, sir, Chief. You can count on me."

It was good to know that this was true. Two down. One to go. He finished up his report on the night before with his door open.

Taking his cell from his pocket, he checked to see if there was a text or a call from Raine. No messages. He would call her as soon as he was done with this.

As eight o'clock neared, he sauntered to refill his coffee. With it steaming beneath his palm, he made his way to county. Not to see Lucky, but to wait for the only other key card holder.

Like clockwork, the back door opened at 7:55 a.m. Lucy Green was followed by her father, the mayor.

"Morning, Miss Green," Matt said and took a sip of his coffee.

"Oh," Lucy jumped. "I didn't see you there, Chief. Good morning to you."

Her father followed close behind. "Beautiful day, Mayor."

"Indeed, indeed, Chief. Indeed, indeed."

"Lucy, I'm going to need to borrow your cell block key card this morning."

Her eyes went right to her father, then dropped to look at the floor.

And Matt had really hoped she wasn't involved.

"I took the emergency copy out of the safe for you and placed it on your desk." He held out his free hand and waited.

While looking at the floor, she nodded and pulled the card from her purse. He took it from her without incident and placed it in his back pocket without checking it over.

Keeping her head down, Lucy went to her station at reception behind the county jail glass and Mayor Green on to his office.

Matt gave him time to get settled, or should he say to stew.

Taking Lucy's key card, he looked it over, and then shook his head.

The mayor's door was open. Matt barely made it to his office when Green said, "Come in, Chief. I'll explain."

Matt walked in and shut the door. He sat in a guest chair and set an ankle on his knee.

Green took a breath so deep, his chin lifted. "It was found in the parking lot."

"Which parking lot? By whom?"

"We don't know."

"How do you know it was found in the parking lot?"

"It was left on my desk in an envelope." He opened his top drawer and pulled one out. On the front in black magic marker, it read, "Found in parking lot."

Classic.

"You made a copy." Matt slapped the key card Lucy had given him onto the mayor's desk.

"It was damaged." Sweat formed around Green's receding hairline. He opened the envelope and pulled out a dirty, bent key card. On it were the words, 'Do Not Copy.'

"Why didn't you report this?"

"I was. We were. But, then it showed up. No harm done."

"Except the murder of former Chief Neil Roberts."

Green's eyes darted to his. He seemed honestly surprised at the connection.

Matt really liked Lucy Green. "I'm going to have to have her escorted out."

Green stood. "This is Ibis Island," he started.

"This is murder."

"Roberts had more enemies than a politician."

Ironic coming from a mayor. "Be glad I'm not putting the both of you in a cell next to Lucky."

Raine drove her four-wheeler from Zoe's place. Willow had already come to get Raine's truck. Everyone should have a cocktail dress in the passenger seat of their four-wheeler on an island. Zoe was making her bring it. At least it wasn't bridesmaid blue with lace straps.

As she rounded the north side of the island, she checked off items on her mental list. Willow would use Raine's truck and be on call for any turtle issues. Zoe would cover for Willow's section. Her mother would care for Chloe.

Tourism was slowing down and wouldn't pick up again until the holidays. The long pier out to the restaurant and fishing spot was nearly empty of the hundreds of tourists of the holiday months.

She passed the only fire station. Firefighters worked on their float for the parade. No fair. They had a garage to store it during the daily rains of September.

Raine refused to allow herself to fall into the abyss of insecurity again. He hadn't called or texted. So what? In an hour, he would be picking her up to fly out to Vegas together.

Of course, that was work, not pleasure.

The lot to the island museum stood empty. Even though the oldest structure on the island, it was hard to fill the lot during busy seasons, let alone slow ones.

She almost didn't recognize Glen Oberweiss. Generally, a peaceful man, he and another were nose to nose, waving their arms like they were ready to go at it. As she passed the museum, she noted it was Mayor Green.

"Sheesh, Mayor," she said. "Did you run over his cat?"

Willow told her to pack a swimsuit. Her mother told her pack lingerie. They were going to be gone for less than twenty-four hours.

Turning off the road, she made her way along the north public access to the beach. There was just enough time to take another sweep of the Gulf side of the island before she left for Vegas.

As she passed Sun Trips Touring, she noted the tarps in the lot flapping in the wind. Dane kept the equipment circled and was determined to keep lookout nights.

Tonight, she and Matt would get enough evidence to arrest Blake Eaton. He could share a cell with his accomplice, Lucky Nemo.

Families arranged themselves in natural socially distanced pods.

It seemed to be some unwritten rule passed down through the ages … no one sets up camp within ten feet of another.

Locals and seasoned tourists knew to keep their food on the down low. Not that food was prohibited on the beaches, but the gulls could spot a novice from miles away. The new arrivals had about five minutes tops before a small colony would circle their heads and dive for their potato chips. It always starts as a fun game, always. Until the divers become too many. The rookie tourists learn to put the food away and the gulls move onto the next.

She drove past beach bags sitting in chairs and covered with beach towels, not so much from other tourists but from the ravens. They were much smarter than the gulls and waited for the beach-goers to leave their things unattended. Eventually, they would find a bag left uncovered and have free reign digging through it until they returned.

Turning the four-wheeler inland, she headed toward a cluster of Beckett rentals. She had time to stack unused furniture before moving on. Three tourists played Spike ball in the sand far from the water. The game was catching on as a more popular pastime every year.

When she arrived at the cluster of rentals, she stopped the four-wheeler but didn't turn it off. She didn't need to. Sitting for a moment, she scanned each of the condos with an extra visual check. Every piece of unused furniture was stacked, and she could swear those were amber-colored bulbs in newly installed cylinder lights.

Matt stared out the tiny window as houses and streets became smaller. Pieces of this investigation were fitting together. Pieces he didn't want to fit together.

Turning his head, he brought his lips to Raine's ear. She smelled like lavender and crystal-clear saltwater. Whispering, he tried to explain. "My folks have connections with several of the casino owners in Vegas, including the Cowboy Crowne. It's a long story, but he listened to our situation and agreed to set us up with chips ... to be returned including any winnings, of course."

Raine set a hand over his. "Why are you doing this?" she asked, not at all whispering.

He laced his fingers with hers. "I don't have the same sense for Eaton as you do," he said as he looked back out the window. The clouds took over his view. "But this is a lead, and I won't leave any stone unturned."

He checked his surroundings. You can't take the cop out of a man, even with a beautiful woman on the way to Vegas. On the other side of her sat an elderly woman preparing what looked like some kind of stitch something. Raine shook her head at him but didn't offer commentary.

"I do have a sense for Oberweiss," he said.

The muscles in her face fell. "Glen? That's wrong."

"Not necessarily as a suspect. There's something else. I'm going to bother him some more. He doesn't like it when I do that, which adds to my sense."

"I saw him and the mayor in a heated argument this afternoon," she confessed. "But what I meant is, why are you bringing me with you?"

THIRTY

Nodding, he thought about it. "There are three parts to that," he answered. "First off, I'm in love with you. Secondly, it's helpful to have a—"

"Wait. Whoa. Wait. You can't just say that. You're going to declare your love to me on an airplane then move to a secondly?"

An eyeball appeared between the seats in front of them.

He ran his free hand across the back of his neck. "You have a point. I suppose whispering the words in your sleep don't count."

There it was. Three shades of red creeping up her neck and over her jaw. It was turning into his favorite.

He explained, "It's helpful to have an islander with me for this, and I want you to meet my parents." Oberweiss and Green in a heated argument. Interesting.

"You lost me at ... wait, your parents?"

He nodded and then glanced back out the window. The sky was clear now, and the land concealed by a thick carpet of white. "They're flying in from Reno and meeting us for lunch tomorrow." He turned and looked into the brown of her eyes. They had turned red as well and were glossy.

He rotated a bit, as much as seats in coach would allow.

"Raine, I'm not the romantic type, and sometimes I do stupid things like declaring my love on an airplane, then move to a secondly." He trailed his fingers over her warm cheek. "You gave up a lucrative future as a hotel manager to live on peanuts saving a species. You always drop to a knee when speaking with children. You shed tears over the death of helpless creatures, and hire the most questionable of humans to serve on your team. You are fiercely loyal and love your family unconditionally. You think public displays of affection are awkward, and you are the one." He shrugged. "As I've said before and have a feeling I might need to say another time or two, I am a patient man, Raine Clearwater. I can wait."

Her mouth seemed to be stuck open. "That's the dumbest thing I've ever heard."

He took a deep breath. "Not the response I was hoping for."

"You say all those nice things to me, but say you're not romantic?"

Both the elderly woman and the head attached to the eyeball between the seats nodded.

"This isn't supposed to be this easy."

"Well." He lifted the corner of his mouth. "You do have that nasty temper."

Raine stood at the bathroom mirror holding her hair straightener. She eyeballed Zoe's cowboy hat and boots, shrugged, and put down the dreaded hair device. She'd put makeup on, hadn't she?

When she came out, Matt was craning his head, peering up the egress window. "They said the room had a window. Not sure if this counts." He turned to face her. "I should have gotten us something more—"

He paused for a moment, and then dropped to his knees on the floor and sat on his heels as if he was at a hatchling release. "You look … wow."

A short, black cocktail dress with cowboy boots and hat? She smiled. "I'll take it. Why don't you have to wear a hat? Zoe said I have to wear a hat."

"I don't have a Zoe, but I do have the boots." And jeans, and button-down white shirt. Yum. What had they come here for again? Eaton, yes.

Her smile was short-lived. "I've never been to a casino before," she confessed. Then added, "Definitely not as a fake wife."

He pulled his chin back, then stood. "I thought you've been to Vegas before."

Nodding, she draped her brown leather cross-body purse over her shoulder. "I have, many times, actually. Those trips were all sea turtle conferences."

He sauntered behind her, wrapping his arms around her waist, and kissed the side of her neck. "And, your turtle people never took time after conferencing about conservation numbers to try their luck at the wheel?"

The others did. She shook her head, but she didn't squirm away. In her mind, it was progress. Instead, she rotated to face him and pressed into him, hugging her knee around his thigh as she kissed him slow and easy.

He crooned around her mouth and ran his strong hands up the length of her spine. Letting his scent fill her lungs, her head fell back.

"Let's not honeymoon here," he whispered as he covered her neck with his lips.

For the second time since she came out of the bathroom, she metaphorically patted herself on the back for not pulling away. It was almost like being a normal girl.

Until he pulled out a small box from his pocket.

"Hold up there," he said. "The color has left your face. Before you faint and I've lost my arm candy for the evening, this is on loan. We can't pose as a married couple without rings."

She did actually feel dizzy and leaned her backside against the hotel room desk.

Flipping it open, he explained that Ibis Island Crown Jewelers let him borrow them for props, but her sense of hearing had all but gone. It was the same with all of her other senses. All but her sight. It was a plain silver band with a single, round diamond in the center next to a matching simple band and were the most beautiful rings she'd ever seen.

A myriad of dreams and possibilities, fear and insecurities rushed through her like waves coming in and covering an exposed and helpless turtle nest. She was Raine Clearwater. Even as the oldest, she hadn't married, not because she'd turned away unworthy suitors, but because there were no suitors.

She was a pariah, unapproachable, and apparently needing to add mood swings to her repertoire.

A gentle finger lifted her chin, making her senses come flooding back. Looking at the ceiling to prevent any damned tears, she said, "Hmm?"

"What did I say wrong?"

She let her lungs fill and forced a smile. "Nothing. Ready? Let's gamble."

He stared at her longer than comfortable before kissing her once and setting the box on the desk behind her.

Rolling her shoulders, she took the things out and shoved them on her finger.

Unlike the most beautiful woman in the casino on his arm, Matt had gambled in Vegas. Plenty.

A waitress slithered by, handing out complimentary drinks. Raine ordered a vodka and orange juice. Again.

He'd never had a distraction while betting before. Between Raine, craps, and talking to gamblers about Blake Eaton, he made sure to nurse his two fingers of whiskey.

A man whispered something in Raine's ear, making Matt's own heat cover his neck and face. She leaned over him, he'd hoped to tell him what the guy said, but instead reached over his shoulder, picking up a $1k chip. He grabbed her wrist. "See that marker? We wait until it reads, '*off*.'"

Skipping the Proposition Bets, he decided on the Pass and Don't Pass lines. A dark man in a black shirt wearing a cowboy tie sat down next to him and set his cash down for chips like he was a regular. Matt had already done this a dozen times around the table, but what the hell? It was why they were here. He leaned over. "Name's Matt. Don't mind my wife. She's had a bit to drink."

"They do that," the man said. "It's all good."

"You a regular here?" Matt added as the dealer took his chips from a Horn Bet on twelve and Matt replaced them with two $1k chips on E. "Our friend, Blake Eaton, told us this was the place."

The man nodded twice. "Name's Blake, but not Eaton. Never heard of him." The guy put $10K on any craps. Matt manned up and put $4k on the Pass Line. The guy rolled a two.

"Way to start the night," Matt said to Blake who wasn't an Eaton.

Raine dipped her lips close to Matt's ear again. This was next to impossible. All around him was the smell of stale cigarettes and alcohol. She smelled like orange juice, lavender, crystal-clear saltwater, and orange juice. Could orange juice be sexy? "Why does two win for him and not us?" she whispered loud enough for Blake to hear.

"That's Any Craps, honey. It's complicated."

Winning that roll, Blake held the dice as all bets were placed.

"That hurts my brain. Waitress?" she called.

Matt agreed to keep a low profile with his loaned chips and put $1k on Don't Pass. Blake rolled a three.

"Sweet!" Matt yelled louder than was comfortable for him. "Thanks, man."

The dealer traded dice with Blake. As Matt and the others around the table waited for bets to be made, Blake gestured on the other side of Matt. "Those two are regulars, too."

Matt lifted his gaze to where the man gestured. He nodded. "Keep going, man. You've got this roll."

He watched the two. Between Matt and them was a man in his sixties smoking a cigar and sitting this one out. The boys wore hats bigger than Zoe's, one with earrings in both ears and the other with one in his nose. Nose Ring threw back a shot and rubbed his hands together before placing $40k on the Pass Line. Blake went for a three Horn Bet.

Matt would be damned if Blake didn't roll a one and a two. Nose Ring lifted his chin in defeat and bellowed, "No!" His friend pointed at him and laughed.

"What's their problem?" Raine slurred in his ear.

Matt regretted allowing her to turn down dinner. "Oh, um, honey. They just lost $40 thousand," he said low.

Raine tipped over her empty glass. "What?" she bellowed louder than Nose Ring. "Forty thousand as in dollars? Who? Where?"

Nose Ring flicked his fingers toward her like she was a fly.

Matt clamped his eyes shut.

She marched up to him and stuck her face inches from his. "Do you know how many sea turtles forty thousand dollars would save?"

"Control your woman, dude."

Matt toyed between waiting this out or scooping her up and heading for the door.

"What did you say to me?" Raine mumbled.

Nose Ring rolled his eyes and put 50k on number nine. "Wasn't talkin' to you."

She grabbed his arm and turned him back to her.

Matt stood and grabbed up his remaining chips.

"Wait. A. Minute." Nose Ring threw back his head and laughed. "Are you from the island with that loser Blake Eaton?"

Matt's ears perked up and, fortunately, seemed to have the same effect on Raine.

"Maybe," she said flatly.

"What a loser. Are you a loser, too?" Nose Ring stepped much too close for Matt's comfort.

THIRTY-ONE

M att struggled between working the man for more information and punching him.

"What if I am?" Raine said and shifted her shoulders. "What's losing a couple hundred thousand dollars? You just dumped half that."

He had the smartest, most beautiful drunk woman on the planet. Matt looked around. Just about everyone was watching. The man in his sixties kept puffing and betting.

"Psht," Nose Ring said. "More like a couple mill. He's been trying for years to win it back. You have GOT to be the turtle freak he talks about. The dude thinks he's some treasure hunter who owns a bar on an island in Florida and that makes him a world renowned celebrity." He changed his voice to sound like a toddler. "He told me all about the widdle turtles," he said, moving his head from side to side. "And, how the customers wuv to play with them."

Matt squinted and watched through a single open eye.

Raine pushed Nose Ring with both hands, knocking him to the ground. "This is my husband," she said, pointing randomly behind her, "and he is going to beat you up."

From behind, Matt grabbed her around the waist. "Come now, sweetheart. I think you may have had too much to drink."

Glaring at Matt, she drew her chin back. "What? I stood here all night long, and you're gonna let this red neck ass-hat talk to me that way?" She drew her arm back, aiming at said recovering red neck ass-hat and clenched a fist.

Matt picked her up like a football. She kicked her legs hard enough to clear out a wide berth as he carried her to the exit.

At the click of the hotel door, Raine opened her eyes. He was back. The clock read 8:58 a.m. Her eyes still stung from a night of crying. What Blake Eaton did was unimaginable. She hadn't checked her phone since yesterday. Behind her, the bed moved. Mustering a grin, she turned.

He held out a to-go cup. "Coffee. Regular, black."

Pushing herself to a sitting position, she took the cup and held it between her hands. "It's perfect."

She took a sip as he toed off his boots and removed the plastic cups and the ice container from the tray on the desk. Curiosity caused her to sit tall and cross her legs on the bed. A brown grocery bag with a handle sat on the corner of the desk.

Setting the tray on the bed in front of her, he opened a paper napkin and used it as a tablecloth. He set out two bagels and a container with four kinds of cream cheese. He could make her smile in the darkest of times. But then, he pulled out a short vase with an array of blue and yellow carnations. As he set it in the middle of the makeshift table, her heart came out of her chest and wrapped around each petal.

Facing him fully, she crisscrossed her legs. "Blake Eaton murdered my brother for a night in Vegas." She regretted the timing of the words even before she finished the statement.

Nodding, he sat on the bed and stretched out his legs as well.

"My parents taught me that when a couple has a significant

201

conversation, that it's important to be close, face-to-face, and touching if possible."

"The beach," he said.

He remembered. "That's right," she said.

He turned and faced her, moved the tray next to them, and crossed his legs, too.

"You brought me breakfast in bed."

Leaning in, he said, "I did."

"With flowers," she said around his lips.

"Mmm hmm," he said through a long, slow kiss.

Taking a deep breath, she pulled away. "Two million is not enough."

He took a deep breath, and then let it out so heavily, his shoulders moved up and down. "No, it's not."

"And, he would have gambled away the rest if he had it."

Matt closed his eyes and nodded. "Yes."

"He's not the only one involved."

"We are getting closer," he said and placed his hands on her knees. "Husband rolled off your tongue. I liked it, even if it was slurred."

She smiled. "Are you trying to distract me?"

"Not at all." He ran a thumb over her thigh and around to the sensitive spot behind her knee. "I've been able to get to know you through your family, your volunteers, and the people of Ibis. You have just me. You know I am—"

"A patient man," she finished for him. "I know, I know." It was difficult not to squirm away. Even though she knew what she must look like at that moment, she stayed strong. "You stop what you're doing to investigate an overnight beach sleeper under a bench, and take her with you even when you discover she's a dog. You take a Saint Bernard into your home, because the other dogs at the animal shelter bark too much. You sacrifice chances of keeping this promotion because you want to do what's right for others. You even removed your reserved parking spot. You're not a boss, you are a leader. Even though your differences were huge, you stayed with someone for eight years."

All he said was, "Oh."

Gathering her composure, she placed her hands under his. "Marriage is forever. Not just forever until one of us feels like it's not. Sickness and health, good and bad."

His back straightened and his brows lowered. "Yes," he said slow and low.

"I am ready," she whispered.

Windows with draped curtains lined the entrance to the restaurant. Stainless steel letters over white painted wood read, The Grandstand. Matt told Raine it was one of his parents' favorites, but she couldn't see how. The inside was bigger than the Ibis Island City Hall. County jail included.

Matt bent down and whispered in her ear, "Do I have to get a tux?"

Oh, the heat. It was going to be their secret. For now, at least. It would definitely not be appropriate to tell her family, and if they weren't going to tell her family, they weren't going to tell anyone.

"I don't think so. They have dresses and suits at the place. Tuxedos even, but I would say only if you want to." His fingers wound around hers and squeezed. Why wasn't she freaking out?

They were inside one of the larger casinos, waiting in what felt like a shopping mall. The restaurant was next to them.

Everything was white. The curtains, the walls, the tables. White and stainless steel. She stood next to him in a cocktail dress, light cardigan and flat sandals, worried that she was overdressed. Or, maybe underdressed.

She spotted them before he did. It had to be them. Both very tall. Matt looked to be a mixture of the two, yet more like his mother.

His mother's face lit when she saw Matt. The emotions of joy for his sake were more than sensible. She picked up her pace, dodging people as she trotted over.

Except, when she reached a few steps away, Raine realized it wasn't Matt she headed for. Carol Osborne opened her arms wide and wrapped them around Raine, squeezing just enough to make Raine's eyes and mouth open wide. It was a good thing Raine's expression was hidden behind his mother's back.

Patting her twice, Raine began to pull away, but it appeared his mother wasn't finished hugging and held on.

When she was finally free, Raine said, "It's so nice to meet you, Mr. and Mrs. Osborne. Matt speaks very highly of you."

"Carol and Bryce, please," his father said. "Likewise."

Carol slid her arm through Raine's and tugged her toward the entrance to The Grandstand. As far as Raine could tell, it was a single, yet large space, and there had to be a hundred tables. Buffet stations scattered about the area with chefs cooking behind most of them.

"I have so many questions," Carol said. "First, let's sit. You are going to love it here. They truly have the best food in town."

The line to get in was several yards deep, but moving fast. It seemed there was some kind of easy pass lane for regulars or members. The four of them stood in the pay-for-your-meal line. And pay, they did. Raine could have taken care of an entire mortgage payment for the cost of the meal. Matt and his father argued over the bill for a moment. Gladly, Raine stayed out of it.

"Have you always lived on Ibis? How extravagant! I can't wait to visit." Carol still had her arm laced in Raine's. Apparently, Matt didn't mention Raine's personal bubble issue to her.

"My whole life," Raine said through her teeth, knowing Carol didn't mean it as a dig.

"It sounds like a dream. Matt says you run the island." Carol rubbed the side of Matt's arm as she spoke.

Raine shook her head. "That would be your son, actually. He's taken over nicely." Oh, that sounded awful. "I mean that in a good way. The chief of police before him struggled in that department."

Placing her free hand over Raine's forearm, Carol stopped and looked Raine in the eye. "I'm very sorry to hear about your brother."

She meant it. Still, Raine looked to the floor. "It was a long time ago." Yet, the pain of last night still felt raw.

It was even a pick-your-own seat place. Raine thought the fee should at least come with a hostess. She had to admit the food smelled incredible. She could smell the roasted vegetables and grilled meat. Bryce chose a table with wooden seats and spindles lined around the booth like a miniature fence.

"You and Matt are working a night patrol?" Bryce asked.

"Oh, yes," Raine said as she slid in. "I'm just doing consult."

"You're going to love the food here," Carol said. "Seafood to any kind of steak, they will cook it for you fresh to order. The desserts are homemade and to die for."

Raine decided to stay away from seafood this far from water and, away from her vegetarian family, chose a thin bacon-wrapped filet with roasted asparagus.

When they came back together at the table, Carol asked, "Were you and Seth close?"

Raine paused mid-bite. Her gaze dropped to her plate. She almost didn't answer, but then said, "We shared a deep love of family and of nature. He was a photographer, mostly underwater."

"Oh! Do you have any pictures?" Carol took a bite of her grilled lobster.

She did. When was the last time she pulled up that album on her phone? Far too long, she admitted, as she pulled her phone from her purse. Scrolling to find a good one, she realized they were all good and tapped one of two baby sea turtles swimming at the surface far from shore.

Carol and Bryce leaned their heads together. Carol covered her mouth with her hand. "He took that? It could be framed or even made into a mural in a nursery."

Raine had hundreds that could. She decided these two were sincere and easy and that she could get used to having them in her life.

THIRTY-TWO

M att stood between the two hired witnesses and in front of the officiant. Although small, the room wasn't too bad for a pay-by-the-half-hour wedding venue.

Raine watched him from the other end of a short line of empty pews. She hadn't chosen a wedding dress or even white. Her tan shoulders framed a light green dress and, in her hands, were the blue and yellow flowers he'd given her that morning.

After thirty plus years, he was marrying the best woman he'd ever known. At that moment, he thought he loved her more than breath.

Music started from speakers in the ceiling. With a smile as big as the sun, she started her slow walk toward him. A tear dropped over her cheek and into the flowers.

As she stepped to him, she handed them to the witness on her side. He reached for her hands and took them between his. The ring he'd picked out sparkled in the lights. Her hands were warm and melted in his like they were meant to be like that forever.

"We gather here today," the officiant started in his baritone voice, but Matt wasn't paying much attention. He winked at her and, unfortunately, there was no red that spread up her neck or crept around her cheeks. She just winked back.

The man cleared his throat.

"Oh," Matt said. "Raine Clearwater. You value everything that means anything. Nature, living creatures, human and not. You're passionate and selfless, unpredictable and completely impatient. I don't believe in fate or things meant to be, but I believe in you. We fit, you and I, and with this ring, I promise to love you forever. For better or for worse, for richer or for poorer."

From his pocket, he took out the simple band that matched the solitaire diamond ring and slid it on her finger. Her eyes were brighter than a Florida sunrise.

"I don't have a ring," she whispered to the officiant as if she didn't want the invisible guests to hear. "I love the comfort and ease that is you. I love the ways we work together and the ways we don't. I love the way you're patient with my impatience and even the times you're not. You listen and more importantly you hear. You are my anchor in the storms. You are as stable as the tide cycles and as committed as a sea turtle finding its way back home. I even love when you're right, and you are right, Matt Osborne. This is meant to be. In sickness and in health, to love and to cherish. Until death do us part, I promise to be yours forever."

The man placed his dark hands over theirs and said in his low voice, "By the powers bestowed upon me, I now pronounce you Mr. and Mrs. Matt Osborne. You may kiss the bride."

"She's um," he said to the officiant, "keeping her name."

"Gotcha. By the powers bestowed upon me, I now pronounce you Mr. Matt Osborne and Mrs. Raine Clearwater."

Matt didn't need to be told twice to kiss his bride. This was their moment, and he would remember it always. Sliding his hand over her wet cheek, he laced his fingers in her hair and wrapped his other hand around her waist. He laid his mouth on hers.

Her arms slipped around his back and squeezed, diving in with lips and tongue, soul and promise. His friend. His wife.

One last peck, and he set his forehead on hers. Her eyes sparkled behind tears and her smile blew through him like the tropical storm.

Raine didn't like keeping things from her family. The black sky was cloudless as the plane descended. Now, she would keep two things from her family. Two very big things.

She wondered if he noticed the way she kept lifting the fingers of her left hand to look at the ring. Or, how she would ever afford to buy one for him.

"It's just for a few days," he said as he closed his laptop and stuck it in his personal item bag. He'd read her mind.

She turned to him and nodded. "I know." He would not mean the wedding. Who knows how long it would be before they shared their news. After Zoe's honeymoon? After Willow's wedding? All she could think about at that moment was Blake Eaton and how to catch him.

Taking her hand, he turned the ring around her finger, then pulled her hand to his lips and kissed it. He lifted his eyes and mouthed the words, 'I love you.'

'Forever,' she mouthed back.

"It might be less than a few days," he added.

Closing her eyes, she nodded again. "I trust you."

"The next few days will be very busy," he said.

Inhaling deeply, she closed her eyes. "For me, too." So much to catch up on. The long list was appreciated.

"We haven't talked about where we're sleeping." His words were awkward. It made her smile.

"Sleeping?"

"Well, yes. Staying," he corrected and pushed his bag beneath the seat in front of him.

"Staying," she said as a statement rather than a question.

"Living." This word was with purpose.

"I have a house," she offered.

"I have an indoor shower." He paused as they touched down.

She much preferred the wide-open spaces, water, and palm trees of Florida, over the neon lights and loud noises of Vegas.

Ignoring the directions, passengers unbuckled their seat belts and collected their carry-ons as if it wouldn't be another twenty minutes before they could begin departure.

"I tell you what. I'll go get Bella, and we'll take turns for now. My place tonight." He pulled out his phone and turned off Airplane Mode. A slew of text and voice mail alerts beeped and vibrated. The plane ride had only been two hours.

Reaching in her back pocket, she pulled out hers and did the same. Crickets.

Pulling the phone closer to his face, he read and then listened.

Matt loved the way Raine's left eye twitched when she was irritated. Bella would appreciate having a backyard, but he wasn't living at her place until he had a chance to add an indoor shower. And, he definitely wasn't living separate from his wife. Compromise.

As with just about everyone else on the plane, he pulled out his cell and turned off Airplane Mode. It was like a chorus of bells, ring tones and whistles.

After a relatively quiet thirty hours, Matt's phone was unusually filled with messages after a three hour plane ride. The first text was from Glen Oberweiss.

i called the station and left a message
need to see you, chief

He pulled his phone closer to his face. The next was from Officer Pence.

oberweiss called
sounds important

The plane trolleyed the runway and the captain made some kind of announcement about weather or time, but Matt wasn't really listening. He switched to voice mail.

"Matt, this is Glen. I know it's after hours. I just left a message at the station. Can we meet? I can come in, or we could meet here. You've got my number."

Looking around, Matt noted Raine sitting with her hands clasped together tight. He kissed her on the side of her head and listened to the next voice mail at the same time he opened the next text.

It was Cummings.

forgot to tell you, chief

the vet called

they found someone to adopt Bella

she was picked up this afternoon

His heart fell into his stomach. He didn't know if it was from losing her or her finding a family.

The next voice mail was Glen again. "It's getting late. I'll keep my phone on just in case and stop by tomorrow during working hours."

The next text was Galloway again.

911 to the Oberweiss house

the missus is hysterical

chief, hes unresponsive

Grabbing the back of his neck, he said, "No. Damn it." Then, louder, "Damn it!"

"Matt," Raine said softly and nudged him.

He darted his eyes around the plane. The passengers were quiet staring at him.

"Bumped my head," he said.

Turning his head to Raine, his eyes stung. He closed them and whispered, "Not Oberweiss."

As his muscles tightened, the sounds around him faded. Ibis was forty minutes away. He had to get off this plane. All he could sense was Raine's warm hand resting on his forearm.

As soon as he exited the plane, he would call the state police and request a black and white escort back to Ibis.

Lights flashed in circles over the neighborhood houses. The ambulances. The Ibis black and whites. Anger ripped through Matt like sand in a desert storm. Throwing his car into park, he waved off the state escort and left it running. "I'll call you," he said to Raine.

She nodded. "I know. It's okay. It's going to be okay."

He sighed and looked her in the eye. She should not be the one saying that.

Closing his eyes, he nodded and headed toward the front door. A maroon sedan was parked in front of the house with exhaust steam trickling from the tail pipe.

Two EMTs stood in front of the Ibis Historical Museum talking with Galloway. Matt knew what that meant. Without giving himself time to process, he marched to the front door.

"Chief," Galloway said.

Matt stuck up his pointer finger.

He could hear her from where he stood. Jan Oberweiss wailed cries of loss. Grabbing the door handle, Matt gathered his composure and stepped inside.

She was in the arms of Timothy Hart. He stroked the back of her hair as her body shook with her sobs in his arms.

Oberweiss lay on the floor behind her, in the doorway between reception and the first viewing room. The coroner stood pecking notes on her iPad as an EMT covered his face.

"No!" Jan wailed. "This can't be, Timothy. It just can't." Wiping her nose with the back of her hand, she dug her forehead into his shoulder.

"Now, now," he crooned as he noted Matt in the room. Blinking twice, Hart stroked her hair a bit faster. "It's okay. I'm here."

Jan craned her head toward the body of her dead husband, then threw her head back. "I can't. I just can't." She fell to her knees on the floor and buried her face in her hands.

"He was so healthy. This isn't," she said between sobs, "supposed to happen. Not like this."

Hart dropped to the floor with her.

Fisting the front of his shirt, she pleaded, "Timothy, you understand. This is what happened to your father. It doesn't make any sense."

Hart's eyes grew larger, but he didn't look to Matt.

"I know. I know," Hart said. "These things are hard to take, yes."

Hart couldn't seem to help himself. He made a sideways glance toward Matt.

It took zero effort and no pretending. Just like what happened to Hart's father? Matt glared at him with untethered rage.

Noticing that Hart was looking at something, Jan craned her head. "You!" she screamed and ran to Matt. She lifted her arms as she ran and pounded the sides of her fists on his chest. "This is your fault. You have him so stressed with all of these pointless accusations." Covering her mouth with both hands, she corrected, "Had him. You had him so stressed out. As long as you live, you'll know this was your doing."

To some degree, she was right. Loud enough for Hart to hear over the sobs, Matt said, "Officer Galloway, take my calls. I'll be leaving ASAP for Circletown, Georgia."

He should have kept his plans to himself. Circletown was Hart's hometown, the place where his father was dead and buried. Matt had checked on it himself. The way it made Hart's eyes grow wide and crazed was worth it.

THIRTY-THREE

The sun would be up soon. Raine hadn't slept. She'd cleaned the dishes. And vacuumed the floors, and detailed the bathroom. She had to admit, the shower was quite nice.

All but Bella's crate. She just couldn't fold it up or even clean it out. She wondered if her new family would want it. Of course they would, and she wasn't giving it to them.

He'd called like he said he would. Glen Oberweiss had died of heart failure on the floor of the Ibis Island Historical Museum. He didn't mention if it had anything to do with the phone and text messages Glen had left him, and she didn't ask.

A key jiggled, and then turned the lock on the door. Draping the damp rag over her shoulder, she stepped into the hallway.

Matt looked like he'd been awake for days.

He tiptoed in, and when he saw her, looked to the clock on the wall.

He made his way to her and wrapped his arms around her, holding her tight. The weight of him pressed down on her shoulders. Without speaking, he stayed this way for a long time.

"Come," she said. "Let's get you to bed."

It was their first night as a married couple. She imagined it was like no other. She had so many questions but wouldn't ask any of them. Not tonight.

Like a zombie, he took off his clothes, leaving them in a heap on the floor. She was already in her t-shirt and pajama shorts.

How many times had he come home to deal with nights like this alone?

Sitting on the edge of the bed, he turned to her. "I have things to check on in the morning, and then I might be taking a day trip to Circletown, Georgia. An overnight at the most. I need you to stay here." He closed his eyes tight, and she thought he might cry. "I need you to do your best to act like nothing is amiss."

She'd never heard of Circletown. Her eyes grew wide. "I'm not a good liar, but I'll try. The parade is tomorrow."

Ignoring mention of the parade, he lifted her left hand and examined her wedding ring set. "You put them back on."

"I know. It's stupid. I just wanted to wear them while I slept. Except, I haven't slept yet."

His eyes lifted to hers. "This is not the wedding night I had planned for you."

She forced a smile. "You had plans? We have time. You are stuck with me for the rest of your life."

"Glen wanted to tell me something. Something that I think got him killed."

She clamped her eyes shut. "Glen was murdered?"

"Maybe."

He pulled her under his arm. He was tense but gentle, sad but attentive.

"He died the same way as Timothy Hart's father."

Raine sat up and faced him. "What are you saying? You think it's Timothy Hart? That Hart killed his father and then Glen?" She looked around the room as if pieces to the puzzle could be found there. "And Chief Roberts and, and, and my brother?"

He didn't speak, nod, nor shake his head.

"They all died in different ways," she barked. "Aren't murderers supposed to kill people all in the same way?" she asked like an idiot.

Still nothing.

"Why Glen? He's the only one who didn't get a piece of the wet uncharted." There. She said it out loud. "He's the only one who didn't become suddenly rich after my brother was murdered."

"This is not a safe time, Raine." His voice was low. "It will help me focus on the next steps if I know you are not alone on the beach or making house calls."

"I promise." It didn't even hurt to say it.

He pulled her beneath him. His hands were slow and tender.

When two become one.

———

Matt sat at his desk with his face in his hands. He hadn't even turned the light on yet. Slowly, he picked up his desk cordless and dialed the number he'd been avoiding.

"Circletown Police Department. This is Nick speaking. How can I direct your call?"

"Chief Miller, please. Tell him this is Chief Osborne of Ibis Island. He'll remember me."

Matt pinched the bridge of his nose with his thumb and forefinger as he waited. It helped keep a headache at bay.

Miller answered fast enough. "Chief Osborne. What can I do you for?"

"About that Hart Will." Couldn't hurt to ask? "I know you can't tell me the amount of the inheritance. I'm just wondering if you can help me out with it."

"Oh. That." There was a pause. "You're right. That information is confidential and would need a warrant to share."

Another pause.

Matt almost gave up when Miller added, "But I suppose I can tell you that I was having coffee this morning with some guys. The funeral director mentioned that old man Hart's funeral still isn't paid in full."

Giving up on the bridge of his nose, he accepted the headache.

"I do appreciate all of your help these past few months, Chief. Yes, that is helpful."

"Hope you catch whatever son of a bitch you're looking to catch."

A light rap on the door was followed by, "Chief? Should I come back later?"

Putting his face in his hands, Matt turned his head to look. It was Cummings. He looked younger today. Too young to be a cop.

"Is there anything I can do before I head out on patrol? Get you some coffee?" Cummings swallowed hard. "Go pick up the dog?"

Closing his eyes again, Matt shook his head. "She was adopted out."

Cummings looked to the corner of the room where the dog dish sat but didn't comment about it. Instead, he sat down in the guest chair closest to the door.

"I, uh." Cummings scratched his whisker-free face. "Knew you would want to know that Lucky made bail last night."

Lifting his head, Matt sighed and nodded. "Of course, he did."

"Um, yes. And, Miriam Roberts was released from the hospital to finish healing at home." He squirmed in his seat.

There was no way Matt was going to get a warrant to open the will of Hart's father or to exhume the body for traces of a poison that would cause cardiac arrest to an otherwise healthy man. He was failing this island. He was failing the Clearwaters. He was failing his wife.

Tapping his fingers on the chair, Cummings offered, "Good news is the float is ready."

The parade.

"And, and, and Mayor Green has his convertible all decked out and ready for you."

Why not? Matt was sure Green had something to do with all of this.

"Sir, can I turn on the light for you?"

Rubbing his hand over his forehead, Matt nodded.

Another knock on the door followed with the lights flipping on.

"What are you sittin' here in the dark for, boss?" Glory stood in the doorway, a bright green short skirt matched impossible green shoes. "We've got a parade to get ready for. Extra help will be here in a couple hours." She stepped to the side.

"This here is Randall Elmhurst. He would like to talk to you about the ad." She winked as she said the last word.

Matt had no idea what ad she was talking about or why she had a sudden aversion to using the intercom system when someone wanted to see him.

Cummings slithered out of the chair and shimmied along the door to the hallway. "I'll be around for a while yet if you need me, Chief. Welcome back."

He'd never asked how the trip went.

Matt stumbled to his feet and held out his hand. The man was very tall, very thin, and held a folded newspaper under his arm.

Taking his hand, Mr. Elmhurst shook and Matt was fairly sure, bowed.

"Thank you, Chief, sir, for seeing me."

"Please come in and have a seat." Everyone else was.

The man opened the newspaper and offered it to him. "This picture, here, it is me."

It was the ad Matt had Glory put in the paper. The one of the tall, thin man standing in the rain, watching the Beachfront roof collapse on Willow. Matt didn't have the energy to ask why he had no umbrella.

"I visit the island sometimes on weekends, sometimes for a week here and there. Lovely place, isn't it?"

Matt just looked at him.

"Well, I love to walk the pier out to the restaurant and fishing dock and was actually just stopping to enjoy some people watching…Is this a bad time?"

Matt shook his head back and forth two times. "No, thank you. Please continue."

"Well, sure enough. That is me standing there, but I'm not sure what I can do to help."

The ad read, 'Person of Interest.'

"Thank you for coming in. A crime was committed that evening. Do you remember seeing anything out of the ordinary?" More out of the ordinary than standing in the rain people watching with no umbrella.

"Oh, yes," he said. "That roof collapsed on that poor woman. Out of the ordinary, yes, but I'm not sure a crime."

Matt questioned him further, but not like he should have. The point was moot. He took his information and told Mr. Elmhurst he would call if he had further questions. "Here's my card." Matt took one from the business card tray and handed it to the man. "Call me anytime if you think of anything new. I do appreciate you coming in."

Escorting him to as far as the breakroom, Matt thanked him again and stepped to the coffee maker. Pence was there. "You're early," Matt said.

"Bad trip?" Pence asked.

"I hadn't thought so," Matt said. "Thank you for coming in."

"It's parade day. Of course, I'm here." He stood to top off his own mug. "Really hard to hear about Glen."

Matt closed his eyes. It was a useless death. He nodded. "I really liked him." He turned and leaned his butt against the counter. "Listen, I'd like you to keep an extra eye out today."

"Cryptic, but okay," Pence said and sat in one of the chairs. "Anything you want to add with that directive?"

"Not yet, no." Matt took a sip. "Only, do I really have to ride in Mayor Green's convertible?"

His intercom buzzed. He could hear it down the hall from where he stood. Now she uses it?

Apparently, Pence heard it too, because he said, "She can see you standing here."

Craning his head down the hall, he spotted the back of Richard Beckett. He set down his coffee so fast, some spilled on the counter. He left it and made his way to reception.

"Richard," he said and waited to see Beckett's reaction, knowing he may very well be looking at an accessory to murder.

When Beckett turned around, he was barely recognizable. He wore old jeans and a white undershirt. His hair was out of place and there were no sunglasses setting on his head. His eyes were so swollen, Matt swore he'd aged ten years since he'd seen him last.

THIRTY-FOUR

Beckett's hands were shaking bad enough that Matt led him to the nearest reception chair. "Can I get you some water?"

Shaking his head fast, Beckett spoke one raspy word. "Glen."

Electricity shot through Matt's entire body. He was wide awake and every piece of him on full alert, but he forced himself to remain still. "Yes," Matt said low. "It's a terrible loss, a terrible loss."

Beckett buried his face in his hands and whimpered.

He could use this. This was his chance. "Richard." He placed a hand on his shoulder. "I'm here for you. Come, walk with me."

Richard looked around. "Oh, the parade. Chief, no." He wiped his tears with the palms of his hands. "This is important, Chief. An emergency."

"Yes, yes. I am right here. We will talk on the way."

As always, the students did a knock up job on the float. Raine stood in front of the giant paper mache loggerhead. Timothy Hart was in the vehicle in front of her, sitting in Matt's spot on the back of Mayor Green's convertible. It bothered her more than she could put

220

a finger on. Balloons and shiny green streamers dangled from the sides and back of the car.

For the fourth time, she looked down at her empty finger. Despite the heat, locals and tourists alike lined the street up ahead. They sat in folding chairs with their children in front of them.

"Where's Matt?" her mother asked as she stood next to the Turtle Watch float, waiting for the signal to start marching. Like the rest of the Turtle Watch float participants, she wore the bright orange Ibis Island Turtle Watch t-shirt that read, 'Turtle Patrol.'

Raine forced a smile, then said honestly, "I wish I knew." It bothered her that Hart was in Matt's spot more than she could put a finger on.

Her sisters walked on the other side of the float, her father with her mother. Dane and Liam had their own float to man. Each year, Sun Trips Touring cheated and pulled one of the pontoons as their float.

Police dotted the scene. She wasn't sure if they always did that for parades, or if Raine was uber aware of them this time.

The drums from the inland high school marching band began. The band teacher blew his whistle and they were on. Raine smiled and waved. Willow, Zoe, her mother and father passed out Turtle Watch coloring books, tattoos, and stickers.

Hart and Mayor Green waved like they were celebrities. Maybe for Ibis, they were.

"You haven't told us about your trip," Zoe called as she walked at a snail's pace and waved to bystanders.

"I just got back last night," Raine qualified.

Taking a handful of stickers from her apron, Zoe yelled, "Excuses," and headed over to a group of children.

As she spotted him, an ease came over her. He looked tired. They both did. But, he was here, coming up a side street on a golf cart of all things. He was with someone. She couldn't tell who, only that he wasn't in a uniform.

This is what her life would be like now. Unforeseen things happening that changed plans and expectations. Her job as PPH was no different.

"Raine," her father said.

Shaking her head, she realized he wasn't calling her but bringing her back to the present. Flipping on a smile, she waved from side-to-side.

It happened all at once. She was sure she missed something. Hart grabbed hold of Mayor Green's arm, and then elbowed him hard. They both turned their heads to Matt.

He was walking toward the convertible now, with two officers and … Richard Beckett wearing jeans and a t-shirt. Hart's head started jerking all around. Police were casually closing in.

Raine stood frozen. Watching. Waiting.

Until Timothy Hart jumped from the top of the car. Her mother was the closest parade walker. He walked right to her. That was odd. What did her mother have to do with anything?

From the back of his pants, he pulled out a gun and twisted his arm around her mother's neck all at the same time.

Time seemed to slow like it was stuck in molasses.

Screams came from everywhere. Bystanders tripped over chairs as they scrambled for safety. Her mother was quiet but shook in Hart's grasp.

Afraid to move her eyes from her mother, Raine forced them to look for Matt.

His arms were sticking out in front of him, palms down, slowly motioning to Hart.

"You think this is over?" Hart yelled in a crazed voice Raine didn't recognize. "Get back. Everyone get back!" He used his gun hand to direct the closing group of police away.

From the corner of her eye, she saw a shape soar through the air and sucker punch Hart in the side of the head. He dropped to the pavement like a rag doll. Raine's body caught up with the scene and started shaking all over as her father tackled her mother and covered her with his body.

Officer Cummings dodged in and picked up the fallen gun as Officer Galloway checked the lifeless Hart's vitals.

Matt bellowed to the crowd, "Everyone, please remain calm. We have the suspect apprehended. You're all safe now." He turned in a slow circle as he led the crowd. "It is best if you exit slowly and calmly to your vehicles."

Her ability to check the surroundings came flooding back. Her sisters ran next to her parents and squatted on the street next to them. Her mother was nodding reassuringly as her father looked over her face, her head, her arms.

Officer Pence was putting handcuffs on Mayor Green. It was like watching a fiction movie too outlandish to view.

The Ibis Island County Jail may have never been so full. Timothy Hart, Richard Beckett, Lucky Nemo, Mayor Green, Blake Eaton. Miriam Brown had been transported to the bigger facility inland that provided a medical wing.

Since he'd arrested the entire board in charge of voting him permanently on or permanently off as Ibis Island chief of police anyway, Matt allowed Henry and Harmony behind the one-way glass next to the interrogation room.

"We knew," Beckett said as he sat on the other side of the small table in the center of the room. "I think we all knew." His hands were cuffed in front of him.

At least he was talking. The others still stuck to their rehearsed stories. 'We all felt really bad about it. One minute he was there, the next he wasn't. The last place we saw him was the Crystal Springs Cavern.'

If it wasn't for the Clearwater sisters, Matt would have never known that to be unlikely if not impossible.

"The treasure. It made us——" Beckett closed his eyes. Matt could hardly believe there were any more tears left in there, but one fell down regardless. "We allowed it to get to us," he amended. "Hart said he found Seth that way. The treasure would be confiscated if we reported it. There was nothing we could do about the death anyway, so why not get the treasure?"

His cheeks were raw and his eyes nearly swollen shut. "We made sure our stories matched. Practiced them as if it was the logical thing to do."

Matt had questions. Dozens of them. Was Glen in on it? Why didn't he come up on sudden money? It was all being tape recorded anyway. Tape recorded and watched by Henry and Harmony Clearwater. So for now, he listened. He thought of his wife, and he listened.

"We let ourselves believe it. When Chief Roberts was killed, we convinced ourselves it wasn't Hart. Who didn't want Roberts dead?"

"But Glen?" The tears started falling, then in buckets. "Oh, Glen. Jan. You didn't deserve this. He wanted to tell. The guilt weighed on him. Hart hounded them like a hawk, pretending to be a concerned friend."

Between them sat a glass of water. Matt pushed it toward him.

Ignoring the water, Beckett continued. "I don't know what happened. Why Hart snapped or how he made it look like a heart attack, but I knew…"

Matt knew. Glen was going to confess. That was why he called. They would find the same drug in Glen's system that Hart used to kill his father. It would be enough to exhume the senior Hart's body. They'd found the bottom of the rabbit hole. The truth always came out.

"We sold the treasure on the black market. I kept some. It's in my gun cabinet in my basement. Take it. Take it all. I don't want it. Not any of it. I think Hart, Green, and Chief Roberts did, too, but not Eaton. He gambled it all away. I'm sure of it."

His shoulders fell, and he took a drink.

"And, Miriam?"

Beckett closed his eyes and shook his head. "She's been involved with Hart since the beginning. Hart suspected Seth had found something. I think she tried to use Seth Clearwater but fell for him." He dug his palms in his eyes. "Or maybe not."

"And Lucky?"

"I don't know. Maybe hired by Hart? Maybe he promised him some treasure? You can't understand, Matt. It's a drug."

So, he'd been told.

"And Glen's portion?"

"He would never tell. Eaton broke into his place once. Searched everywhere."

The door opened. What the hell? It was Henry Clearwater. Matt stood quickly. "Wait a minute, now," Matt said. He didn't see this coming.

He stood at the door, messing up Matt's last chance at keeping his job. "Anyone can be sorry when they're caught, Richard."

Beckett sucked in air and nodded. "I know. You're right." More tears dropped on the table in front of him. He didn't even attempt to wipe them away this time.

Henry's eyes were red as well, but at least he stayed by the door. "You were trying to be a better man before you were caught."

Blinking fast, Beckett looked up. His bottom lip quivered like a child.

"Will he get a plea deal?" Henry asked.

Matt was speechless. Literally. What a cluster.

"I don't want one," Beckett said.

You say that now, Matt thought.

"You changed your priorities and you came to the chief, here, to confess. To give closure to all of us. You deserve one. We want you to know—all of us—that we forgive you." Minus the sobs, tears fell freely down Henry's cheeks. "We can all rest now."

THIRTY-FIVE

No one had answered the front door. Raine guided Matt around to the back of the Ibis Museum where the walking paths framed the mangroves with garden markers describing native plants for visitors.

Jan Oberweiss sat on a stone bench looking out at the bay. "This was his favorite spot, right here. We sat together, watching the boats and planning the next museum exhibit or sailing trip."

Raine sat on one side of her.

"I've been cleared to tell you," Matt said from the other side of Jan. "That Glen tried to contact me several times the night he died, by text and voice mail. I was on a plane and didn't get them in time."

Jan stared at the bay expressionless.

"He was going to tell the truth, Jan." Raine took her hand.

Jan's fingers were cold and bony, but she squeezed Raine's hand back hard.

"He and Seth were the best of friends," she said.

Matt looked around at the place. He'd already dug around the corners in case this was the cornerstone that is Home.

"They loved history and that darn Luciana Bezan's legendary treasure. Only, I suppose it wasn't legendary."

Matt squinted at the back of the building. "Did you have some tuck pointing done to the bricks?"

Taking a deep breath, Jan didn't turn but answered. "Seth did it, yes. About six months before he died."

He looked to Raine. She shrugged. "That was just like Seth," Raine said as Matt strolled to the corners of the building. "I didn't know you sailed," she lied. "I thought you just had the boat you keep in the inland docks."

Tapping the corners, he looked to Raine, and then gave a thumbs up. Bubbles of electricity crept over her skin. They were right. All of them. Seth, too. It was like a drug.

"I have some questions I need to ask, Mrs. Oberweiss." Matt came and squatted in front of her. "But, it can wait. I will do my best to put a rush on the autopsy. We'll get him back to you as soon as possible."

Closing her eyes, she rocked back and forth. Raine thought she saw a nod.

Solemnly, they backed away to Matt's SUV. He opened the door for her, and then sauntered around to the driver's side.

In case anyone was looking, Raine kept expression from her face and body. "Is it there? Matt! Do you think it's there?"

He nodded. "We'll find out. For now, we should keep this between you and me." As he backed out of the drive, he added, "Which means we're on our way to tell your entire family."

Litter from the parade had already been cleared away. Tourists rode their bikes and drove their golf carts like there hadn't been a hostage situation that morning. Ibis birds walked in the grasses, looking for food. Flowers covered the bushes in pinks, red, and purples. Life went on.

"Will you keep your job?" she asked as they drove.

"I'm not sure. It will be up to the new board."

"New board. Everything is so, so mixed up."

He took her hand, lacing their fingers together. "Mixed up, but right." Lifting her hand, his warm lips rested on her fingers.

The nerves returned as soon as they bumped over the hump at the end of her parent's drive. All of the cars were there, of course. A family mourning loss all over again.

There was no sound from the roof. The goats would long be in their pen by then. As he parked the car, he turned to her.

"Ready?" she asked.

"Always."

Sweat formed around Matt's hairline. He hadn't asked Mr. Clearwater for Raine's hand in marriage. He took his daughter to Vegas and returned married. He'd watched the man level a large man with one punch.

Raine had made it all the way around the SUV and stood at the door. "Are you coming?" she asked through the closed window.

No time for a pep talk, Matt opened the door. Too much noise came from inside. This was not the sound of a home in mourning. "What do you suppose is going on in there? Is this really a good time to tell them?"

"Are you chickening out?" she said through an evil grin.

"No." Maybe.

But, when she opened the door, there was a dog. A giant dog. "Bella?"

Her furry body stiffened and her head jerked toward the door. Trampling Zoe, she ran and leapt for him. One hundred pounds of puppy knocked him to the ground and sat on his chest.

"That will teach you to give her up again." Raine stood over him with her arms crossed.

He couldn't hardly speak with the weight of her on his diaphragm. "How?" he croaked.

"The family took her back," Zoe said. "She peed on their floor."

Matt rubbed around her ears, almost forgetting why they had come. "Good girl, Bella. I'm sorry we gave you up. It won't happen again."

Other than the sound of Bella panting, the room became silent. Brows dropped and eyes were all on him. "We?" Harmony asked.

Raine kneeled next to him and sat on the backs of her feet. "We have a few things we need to tell you."

Pushing Bella from his chest was not going to work, so he rolled to his side and toppled her off. He sat on the floor next to Raine. Giving up, he let Bella sit in his lap.

"We found the cornerstone that is Home," Raine blurted.

"We think we found," Matt corrected.

She turned to look at him with her light brown eyes and smiled. "Probably found."

"Oh, Matt. Raine." Harmony grinned and shut her eyes. "We knew we could count on you."

He wasn't sure which, 'you,' she referred to, but he would take it since the next news might not be as well received.

"That's incredible. Fantastic. Where?" Dane asked.

"We went to tell Jan Oberweiss that Glen was trying to come clean about Seth. About the treasure, before Hart poisoned him." He twined his fingers between Raine's. "I've been all over this island digging in corners of homes for buried treasure. Except, it wasn't buried. I noticed some tuckpointing that was newer than the surrounding brick work. Jan said Seth had done it."

"Six months before he died," Raine finished his sentence. "He had found that treasure six months before he was killed."

The expressions were maybe happy. Relieved definitely. But, not what Matt had expected. Grieving effects everyone differently.

"You said news plural," Willow said.

"Forgive me, us. It just happened," Raine stuttered. "Well, of course, it didn't just happen."

Matt tried to help. "We'd been talking about it. Well, not really, it, but us."

He opened his mouth to apologize to Henry as Raine blurted, "We got married in Vegas."

So many eyes, large and wide, followed by a room full of mouths all in the form of little Os. Willow was first. She jumped. "Yes!" she cheered and fist-pumped the air.

Harmony followed with a squeal worthy of a teenage girl. Dane and Liam walked over and punched him in the arm. Grown women were jumping and hugging.

This was certainly not the reaction he had expected.

Henry watched his family from his recliner. Matt stood and walked to him, sitting on the spot on the couch nearest his recliner.

Raine pulled out the rings, put them on and displayed them for each to see. "You're not mad, Zoe? You haven't even had your honeymoon. And, Willow. I didn't mean to budge."

They just hugged and the men slapped backs. He swore he heard Zoe say something about legal sex and Raine whispering back, "I know! Mom was right."

Matt turned to Henry. "I am deeply sorry for not asking for her hand. Your blessing is important to us, to me."

"Apology accepted." His smile didn't reach his eyes. "Today was an important day all around. A good, important day."

White lights affixed to frames of snowmen and Santas hung from light poles along the streets. Palm trees covered in colored lights blinked in the nighttime sky.

Matt took one more drive down Beech Street. It could be his last in this vehicle.

He parked in the spot next to the empty one that used to be the chief of police spot. He never could bring himself to park there.

At sixty degrees, the late afternoon air was chilly. Maybe that made him officially a Floridian. The cars of each of the new board members were there. They would make their decision tonight.

Interviews had taken them weeks. As he walked through the front door, Glory was there, nail file in hand and a magazine on the desk. "Hello, Chief. They're all here."

Officer Cummings stood briefing Officer Pence as they completed their shift change duties. Cummings spoke of a minor traffic accident at the entrance to Pelican Bridge, and Pence razzed him about his cushy shift. Yeah, he'd take just this. Every day.

He stopped in the break room to turn off the coffee maker. The scent of burnt coffee wasn't dissipating anytime soon, but even graveyard shift wouldn't drink that stuff.

Even though it was open, he paused for a moment at the door. Hanging from a high corner was a gold-plated, jewel-encrusted dinner plate with the inscription below that read, 'from the Smithsonian, to Ibis Island.'

They all sat around the table. The new Ibis Island City Board. Clarence Jenkins, the owner of CJs, Jan Oberweiss, the owner of the Ibis Island Historical Museum, Walter Trainor, the city worker, even Oliver Lindenwood, because on an island in Florida, the city can vote onto their board a man who occasionally has PTSD episodes. At the head of the table was Henry Clearwater. And, next to him, the island PPH. Mrs. Raine Clearwater.

"Walter, please take attendance," CJ started, "and go over last month's meeting notes so we can call off on them."

They did and Matt waited.

Like Matt was a child, Oliver shook a finger at him. "We're not having any more golf cart discussions."

"Folks don't like it when you harass them about smoking," CJ added, mostly because he was one of them.

"But, you're the best chief of police," Henry said, "that this island has ever seen."

Matt was pretty sure his opinion was a conflict of interest.

Raine's smile went right through him and left him helpless. "And, the other interviews were meh."

He was positive hers was a conflict of interest.

"Let's get this vote over with, so we can get it in the notes and move on," CJ said.

Oliver interrupted, "All in favor of hiring Osborne, here, as chief full-time, say 'Aye.'"

The table went around and gave their ayes and Matt his agreement.

Next item, a Saint Bernard as a City Hall mascot.

ABOUT THE AUTHOR

R.T. Wolfe is an author of intelligent writing for today's contemporary romantic suspense reader. It is not uncommon to find dark chocolate squares in R.T.'s candy dish, her Saint Bernard rescue at her feet and a few caterpillars spinning their cocoons in their terrariums on her counters. R.T. loves her family, gardening, eagle-watching and can occasionally be found working in third world countries with trafficking survivors or on an island with sea turtle hatchlings.

WWW.RTWOLFE.COM

facebook.com/rtwolfe2012

twitter.com/rt_wolfe

CPSIA information can be obtained
at www.ICGtesting.com
Printed in the USA
BVHW081426030522
635996BV00030B/1776